DESTINATION ANYWHERE

Books by Sara Barnard

Fragile Like Us
A Quiet Kind of Thunder
Goodbye, Perfect

DESTINATION ANYWHERE

SARA BARNARD

Illustrations by Christiane Fürtges

SIMON & SCHUSTER BFYR

New York   London   Toronto   Sydney   New Delhi

An imprint of Simon & Schuster Children's Publishing Division
1230 Avenue of the Americas, New York, New York 10020
This book is a work of fiction. Any references to historical events, real people,
or real places are used fictitiously. Other names, characters, places, and events
are products of the author's imagination, and any resemblance to actual
events or places or persons, living or dead, is entirely coincidental.
Text © 2021 by Sara Barnard
Originally published in Great Britain in 2021 by Macmillan Children's Books
Jacket illustration © 2021 by Maggie Edkins
Interior illustration © 2021 by Christiane Fürtges
All rights reserved, including the right of reproduction in whole or in part in any form.
SIMON & SCHUSTER BOOKS FOR YOUNG READERS
and related marks are trademarks of Simon & Schuster, Inc.
For information about special discounts for bulk purchases, please contact
Simon & Schuster Special Sales at 1-866-506-1949 or business@simonandschuster.com.
The Simon & Schuster Speakers Bureau can bring authors to your live event. For more
information or to book an event, contact the Simon & Schuster Speakers Bureau
at 1-866-248-3049 or visit our website at www.simonspeakers.com.
Interior design by Mike Rosamilia
The text for this book was set in Apollo MT Std.
Manufactured in the United States of America
First Edition
2 4 6 8 10 9 7 5 3 1
Library of Congress Control Number 2020949719
ISBN 9781534483903
ISBN 9781534483927 (ebook)

For Mum and Dad,
who waved me off,
and welcomed me home

NOW

THE PLANE

"Boarding complete."

This is it. I'm out of time. I stare at the send icon on my phone screen, willing myself to press it. My heartbeat—already way faster than usual—thunders harder in anticipation of that one tiny moment, the final step in setting this all in motion.

Despite myself, my thumb swishes downward, my eyes flicking to the start of the email I've been drafting since I walked out of my house, got on a bus, went through departures, boarded, found my seat, and buckled up.

Mum and Dad,

Don't freak out. I know you will anyway, but don't.

(There's no point. By the time you read this, I'll be in the air. You always say how safe flying is, Dad. So you don't need to worry, because when you read this, I'll be the safest I've ever been.)

I'm doing this because I have to go. I just have to go. I tried to tell you about how I have nothing left and I HAVE TO GO, but you weren't listening. Now I think you'll have to, because right now I'm on a plane.

I'm on flight BA037 from Gatwick to Vancouver. You'll be able to look it up, see? I'm not trying to lie or hide anything. You know exactly where I am. I just had to go, so I'm going. If you've been paying any attention, you know why.

I'll call you when I land.

I love you.

P.S. I'm sorry about using your credit card, Dad.
P.P.S. I'll pay you back.

The captain is cheerfully talking about our estimated flight time, how sunny it is in Vancouver, how he expects there may be "a few small bumps" over Greenland. He asks for all electronic equipment to be put into flight mode.

I swallow. Steel myself.

Send.

There. It's done. I put my phone into flight mode and settle back against my seat, watching the terminal slide slowly by as we taxi to the runway. In a few minutes I'll be airborne. England will drop away underneath me, getting smaller and smaller and farther away, and all my problems and heartaches and regrets and mistakes will shrink along with it. The next time I set foot on this soil—who knows when that will be— I'll be someone different; someone changed. Not someone new, exactly, but maybe the person I was always meant to be.

We're on the runway. The engines roar, the plane pushes forward. Beside me, a woman in a green jumpsuit whispers, "Off we go."

I close my eyes. I finally smile.

Off I go.

BEFORE

aka
Why I gave up everything
and ran away
from my life even though
I'm only seventeen and my parents
are going to kill me
aka
When I still thought things could be good

Day one of sixth form college. Day one of my new life! New me in new clothes. (Skinny jeans and a white T-shirt with a daisy necklace—a classic look, but not constrained to a particular personality, not until I found out what that personality needed to be.) And, most important, a new attitude. The attitude? Positivity. Me—aka Peyton King, sixth form student, new girl—a friend in waiting. I was ready.

I was so ready. Never mind that I didn't particularly want to be at sixth form college, especially not studying what my parents had dictated instead of what I actually wanted, which began and ended with the word "art." No, I was still ready. All of that was irrelevant, anyway, because I had one goal and one goal only: I was going to make friends. Actual, honest-to-God, know-all-your-secrets, WhatsApp-group-having, drinks-in-the-park-with friends.

What had happened at my old school was just a blip. A five-year-stint-in-hell blip. Yes, it was soul-sucking, not having any friends. Yes, it almost destroyed me. And yes, the relentless bullying will probably cause me residual trauma that will haunt me into my adult years.

But! That's done now. All in the past. Fresh start, new me.

"Welcome!" a smiley-faced woman said from one of the info desks that had been set up in the main entrance corridor to the college.

"Hi!" I said. *That's it, Peyton. Enthusiasm.* "I'm Peyton King!"

The woman nodded, scanning down a list of names and crossing off mine when she reached it. "Here's your welcome pack," she said, handing it over. "You'll find a campus map in there, the dining hall timetable, that kind of thing. Orientation is in the common room at nine. Do you have any questions?"

How do I make friends? Will people like me? Why didn't they like me before? Do I look okay? How's my hair? Am I doing the right thing? Will people like me?!

I shook my head. "Thanks!"

(Is it possible to be a little bit drunk on your own hope and expectation? If yes, then I was. You can see it in all those exclamation marks.)

I headed toward the common room for the orientation, both hoping and not hoping that it would involve those awful breaking-the-ice games that are excruciating but also work. I wasn't sure if they'd think they were necessary, because though it was mostly on its own campus, the sixth form college was officially connected to Eastridge High School, and most of the students came from there. It also made up one part of a three-school consortium, so there were lots of students from those feeder schools as well as entirely new students, like me. This was my new life—finally. I was out of the hellhole that was Claridge Academy, away from everyone who had bullied me, everyone who had let it happen. I was free, and now I could start again somewhere new.

The day before, I'd had my hair done by my mum's hairdresser. I'd told the woman exactly what I wanted— something approachable, low-key, nothing try-hard, nothing too look-at-me—and she'd taken my thick, mousy waves and turned them into a mid-length, rich brown cascade with coppery lowlights, falling easily to my shoulders in straight, unwavy lines. Perfect. I'd been practicing how to straighten my hair all summer in preparation, and now I had the hairstyle to match.

See how ready I was? So ready.

The orientation was awkward. We were all gathered in the common room to listen to a welcome speech—more like a lecture—from the head of sixth form, Mr. Kirby, who barely smiled, before we were broken off into smaller groups at random to get taken on tours around the campus. I was put with two other girls who spoke exclusively to each other, barely glancing at me, and three boys who didn't say a word. Not a great start.

"What school do you come from?" I asked one of the girls when we got dropped off back at the common room after the tour, determined not to let this first opportunity pass without even trying.

"Eastridge," one of the girls said. She said it possessively, her head gesturing unconsciously to her friend, answering for both of them. "What about you?"

"Claridge," I said. "The academy."

The girl made a face. "Why'd you come here?"

I did not say, *Because I have no friends and if I don't make friends I will die.* I said, "Because that place is a shithole." Which, as far as I was concerned, was absolutely true.

It came out wrong; too loud and too vehement. To my ears, I sounded try-hard, the worst thing to be. I smiled, but that felt wrong, too. I could feel a flush working its way up the back of my neck. One conversation and I'd already failed.

"Well, Eastridge is okay," the girl said, shrugging.

"This isn't Eastridge anymore," her friend reminded her. "This is college. Totally different."

"I'm trying to be nice," the girl replied, frowning. "Like, encouraging."

The other girl rolled her eyes, which didn't seem very friendly. But it was her who said to me, "What registration group are you in?"

I looked hopefully at my registration sheet. "S6."

"We're both in S2," she said, shrugging. The shrug said, *Sorry*. It said, *We're not going to be your friends*. It said, *Bye*.

"Okay," I said.

"We have to go there now," the first girl said. "Registration."

"Okay," I said again. What else could I say?

I hoped they might invite me to go for lunch with them later, but they didn't. They just smiled awkwardly at me before heading off together.

This is fine. It's fine. I'd had my first social interaction and it hadn't ended in shame or tears. That could be my practice run; I couldn't expect every conversation to lead to friendship. *Stay positive.*

I ate the packed lunch I'd brought by myself, sitting on a bench in the sun. I sketched one-handed as I ate, imagining myself in some distant future, graduation cap on my head, friends all around me, big smiles. That was all I wanted in life. Not the graduation cap—I could take or leave that—but a friend. A best friend, the kind I read about in books. Everyone had best friends in the books I loved, the ones about ordinary girls like me. They had multiple best friends, sometimes. Whole squads of them. A lot of the time they made me feel lonely in my own friendless reality, but I kept reading them. I devoured them, learning how to be a good best friend, so one day—*one day*—I'd be ready.

Let's get this out of the way. I know what you want to know. You want to know why I was so obsessed with making friends at sixth form college; how I could have gotten to that point in my life without having friends. You're thinking, *You must have friends. Everyone has friends.* You're thinking, *How could you go through all those years at school and not have friends?* Or maybe you're thinking that I must have had friends when I was at school, and I lost them because I did something awful. Now you're wondering what I did.

So let me say first, that it is true; I didn't have friends then, and I'd never had friends. Not real, actual friends. People who I'd chosen and liked, people who'd chosen and liked me. People I hung out with on Saturdays and planned days out with and talked to on WhatsApp. People I was tagged with in photos on Instagram. People who made me friendship bracelets.

The second thing to say is that it wasn't some big incident that made me friendless for all my years at secondary school. I'm not even going to say something dramatic like everyone hated me, because they didn't. In a weird kind of way, I think it might all have been easier if they did. I wasn't hated; I was hounded. (Fox hunters don't hate the fox; it's just sport to them.) Teased, laughed at, ignored. Occasionally tolerated, more often noticed only to be used as the butt of a joke.

(Now you are thinking, *Okay, but why? What was wrong with you?* You are imagining what was so disagreeable about me that I was the bullied kid. Maybe you're thinking about bullied kids you know or knew, and you're judging me alongside them. Stop that—leave them alone. Haven't they suffered enough without being your life benchmark for who deserves to be a target?)

So the third thing is to try to explain why I spent five years at my school, Claridge Academy, friendless and alone. Trust me, this is something I've thought about a lot. (A *lot*.) I've tried to put some kind of narrative over it to make it make sense. Because I get it—it does sound weird and unlikely. One friend, surely, at least once? No friends? Ever?

Yes, I had a handful of transitory, temporary almost-friends over the years. Let's call them Occasionals. There was Soph in year seven, who in another life would have been and remained my best friend, but who abandoned me very early on, somewhere around the bake sale incident—more on that later—and spent the next five years steadfastly ignoring me. I can't really blame her. If it had been the other way around, I probably would have saved myself, too.

I was on the school netball team with girls from other forms and year groups, and most of them were friendly to me. Even the handful of girls from my form left me alone when we were in netball mode, like it was an accepted safe space. Sometimes Imi, the wing defense from my year, invited me to come with her and her mum for McDonald's after away games. She never spoke to me during actual school time, but still.

There were other people along the way who made it just

about bearable. Tiny little tethers to goodness, or at least *ordinary*, that kept me from giving up completely. In the library, a quiet and safe escape during lunchtimes, there was the librarian, Ms. Randall, who knew me by name and talked to me about what I was reading like she cared what I thought. The art block, all white walls and the smell of linseed oil, and Mr. Clayton from year nine onward, who always smiled at me like he understood, quietly taking me aside after a lesson to tell me that the small studio was open at lunchtimes for students to use if they wanted. The small gang of misfits that gathered there to draw and create, every one so different and from across year groups, rarely talking to each other—and never outside that lunchtime respite—but glad, all the same, that they weren't alone.

And that was it for me, all the years I was at Claridge. You might ask, *How do you get through school without a friend?* And the answer is, the same way you walk through a downpour when you don't have an umbrella. Head down, shoulders hunched, as quickly as you can.

I still haven't told you why, though. And that's what you want to know. Like I said, it wasn't one big event; it was several small incidents. A kind of snowball effect of no-one-likes-Peyton-King. Here are a few of them, just so you can get the gist. I'll start at the beginning.

My school, Claridge Academy, had a uniform that featured a blazer that they claimed was unisex. On my first day in year seven I, along with a bunch of other girls in my newly assigned form, wore that blazer. One by one, the other girls realized that wearing the "unisex" blazer as a girl was deeply, deeply uncool and discarded it. I had the misfortune to be the last to catch on. The last girl to wear the blazer, and the one who earned the "*Why* are you wearing *that*?" from Amber Monroe. (She features heavily in these anecdotes. That same day, she asked me what my name was, and when I told her it was Peyton, she screwed up her face and said, "*Why?*" with such disdain I almost wanted to apologize for existing.)

Year seven. A bake sale; the kind of thing that seemed bizarrely important at the time, even though all we were doing was selling fairy cakes in the school cafeteria. We all had to bring in cakes and biscuits to sell, and I brought a tin full of homemade salted caramel butterfly cakes, which were fat and creamy and delicious. A group of us were all arranging the cakes on the table when Amber Monroe said—I remember how casually she said it, even mischievously, like it was a joke we were going to share—"Heard you poisoned yours, King."

What I *should* have done, if I'd had a seventeen-year-old's wit and confidence, was laugh and say, "Yeah, with cocaine." That would have been great. The kind of joke that was funny *and* cool. But I didn't. I stuttered, I went red, and I said, my voice a nasal whine (or at least, it is in my memory), "No! No, I didn't!" And then Mo Jafari's voice, coming from behind me. A lazy drawl. "Sounds like you did."

Word got around, obviously. No one bought, let alone ate, my beautiful cakes. They all seemed to think it was so funny. Especially when I cried.

Year eight. Health class under the control of a guest speaker who'd come to talk to us all about healthy relationships. She, cheerful and oblivious, suggested we all move from our usual assigned seating to sit with our friends. As my heart plummeted down into my stomach, I watched as everyone else happily, thoughtlessly moved around the room, pairing up, separating off into clearly defined mini groups and trios. I was left, face flaming, eyes tearing, staring at the floor, not having moved from my seat, hoping no one would notice. I think the guest speaker would have graciously let me be invisible, as I clearly wanted, but Amber Monroe's loud, confident voice sounded across the entire room. "Oh my God, Peyton, do you actually have *no friends*?" She sounded so horrified. Loudly, affectedly horrified, but still horrified. Like the fact of my friendlessness was so horrible, even she was almost sympathetic at having to be faced with it. "Oh my God," she said again, so loudly. So loudly. "Peyton King has no friends!" (You might think that's the kind of thing people forget and get over. Let me tell you, it is not. That phrase may as well have been carved in stone. It never left me.)

Year eight. I decided I should find out why people didn't like me so I could work on the problem and fix it. I sent a message to one of the nice girls, Kerry Bridges, in my form, one of the ones who got her work done and had her hair brushed nicely and never made trouble. She'd never tried to be my friend, but she'd never been mean to me, either. The message said: **Kerry, sorry to message out of the blue, but I hope you can help me. As you may have noticed, I don't really have many friends and people don't seem to like me, and I wondered if maybe you knew why and you could tell me so I can make things better! If you can't help, no worries! But thanks for reading :) Peyton.**

(Are you cringing for my twelve-year-old self? Yeah, me too.)

Kerry Bridges screenshotted that message and sent it to

one of her friends. Who sent it to two of her friends. Who posted it on Snapchat. Everyone in my form saw that message. Everyone in my year saw that message. It's possible the entire school saw it. It turns out that being friendless is bad, but *trying not to be* friendless is worse. I may as well have gotten up on the stage during assembly and stripped naked. In the long run, it probably would have been better for my reputation.

For what it's worth, Kerry wrote me a letter after that incident, apologizing for sharing the message, insisting she didn't know what would happen and saying that she was sorry. She stuck a smiley-face sticker on it and slipped it through the slats of my locker. But she didn't try to be my friend, or tell people to stop when they laughed at me, and she never did tell me why no one liked me. I guess by that point she thought it was obvious.

Year nine. Mo Jafari figured out that P. King sounded like *Peking*, as in Peking duck. Suddenly, and for the rest of my time at Claridge, I was "Duck," and any number of variants that included, but were not limited to: Duckie, Quack, Quackers, Goose (as in *Duck, duck, goose*), and Fucka (as in Fuck a duck). These may sound like affectionate nicknames, just a fun little joke we were all in on. Nope.

Year ten. By then I'd mostly rode the bullying storm and was just a loner no one talked to. It wasn't a good life, but it was better than being hounded. And then the head of art, Mr. Clayton, chose a painting of mine to be framed and hung on the wall of the school cafeteria. This was a big deal; only year elevens usually got selected for that kind of honor, and it was mostly for their final art projects. Mine was a painting I'd been working on in the studio during my lunch breaks, which was my newer place of refuge from the rest of the school. It was sort of my own version of *The Starry Night* in that it was a painting of my town at night with the skyline rendered tiny (and gray and muted) under a huge, vibrant night sky. Mr. Clayton said it was "fantastic," a word I'd never heard him use before. It got announced in assembly and the whole school clapped dutifully, and I was so proud and happy, even when Amber Monroe and her friends were way too enthusiastic, whistling between their teeth, waving at me and doing mock little bows.

It had been hanging for three and a half days when I got called into the head teacher's office, where I found Mr. Clayton waiting, a deep frown on his face. My painting had been desecrated—that's the word he used. That morning before registration someone had Sharpied KING TWAT across the entire surface, complete with a crude attempt at a cock and balls beside it. (Even at the time, I thought that a vagina would have made far more sense, and it said so much about who'd done it that they were unable to draw one.) There was no saving the painting. My work was destroyed, and it broke my heart.

My whole form got bollocked for it. Everyone knew I was a social pariah, even the teachers, and so it was obvious what had happened and why. Our head of year, Mr. Karousi, kept us all in at break time to find out who did it. It was Joe Hedge; we all knew that. Literally everyone knew, but no one said a word. And I sat there in that room, listening to the silence of everyone protecting him as if he was worth protecting, rage burning in my chest and my hands and my eyes. He was just going to get away with it. He'd done something so cruel—not just mean, but *cruel*—and they still didn't care.

So I said, just when Mr. Karousi was winding down, talking about how disappointed he was that no one was going to take responsibility, "Everyone knows it was Joe."

A tiny collective gasp swept across the room. Joe turned to me in shock. Amber's eyes smoldered with fury. Mr. Karousi frowned at me, like I'd confessed to the crime myself. Mo Jafari muttered, "Shitting hell, King."

"Why won't anyone say it?" I asked. I was full-on crying, my voice a choked shriek. "It was Joe."

Joe, who didn't bother denying it, was suspended for four days and lost his place on the football team for two months. It was the first time anyone actually faced consequences for what they'd done to me, and I was glad, despite everything.

Glad until the following week when we were long-distance running in PE. I was jogging along on my own, as per usual, lost in my own comfy thoughts, when someone knocked into me from behind. When I stumbled and fell, too startled to even cry out, hands grabbed at my arms, pulling me off the side of the track. The playing field must have been freshly mowed because there were small piles of grass dotted around the perimeter of the track, and it was into one of them that I was pushed down, face-first. Grass in my mouth and nose and eyes. My head held down. A male voice in my ear. "Eat the grass, grass. Fucking eat it."

They left me there, and I cried and coughed out grass and wished hell and herpes on all of them. When I finally got to my feet and staggered to the finish line, Mr. McGee told me off for "taking so long"—ignoring the grass stains on my PE kit, the grass in my hair, the grassy tears streaked across my dirty face—and sent me into the snake pit that was the changing rooms. There, I was completely ignored by Amber and her friends, which was merciful, but also all the other girls, who probably thought of themselves as good people and always hugged their friends when they cried. Which was agony.

I think that whole incident was when I started to get angry. Really angry. The kind of angry that gets called "rage" instead. The burning rage that settles in and stokes the fire of every emotion. I was angry at being shoved into a pile of grass, yes. But the rage came from the absolute fundamental unfairness of it. It wasn't fair; it wasn't right. Joe had done something wrong. Not questionable or on the line, but actually *wrong*. Destroying someone's work is wrong; destroying someone's art is wrong; hurting someone is wrong. Wrong, wrong, wrong. And yet he was protected by everyone I was meant to call a peer. And in their eyes, *I* was the one in the wrong for being a "grass," essentially for simply *pointing out* that he was in the wrong. I was the one who was truly punished for the whole incident. He was even more of a hero; I was even more of an outcast. It made no sense at all.

In school, cool is currency, and cool, apparently, is letting shitheads get away with being shitheads. It's praising them for their shitheadery.

Anyone who believes that the world operates on a basis of right and wrong has never been to secondary school.

Anyway, I endured five years' worth of the kind of thing I've just described. Five long, horrible years where the best I could hope for was being ignored. I hadn't ever done anything wrong, not even anything particularly embarrassing; I was just the unlucky one.

That was what I told myself when I was trying to be positive, anyway. Way back then, when I was first starting college, and I allowed myself to hope. There wasn't something fundamental about me that my bullies had seen; it wasn't going to be the pattern the rest of my life would follow. I could make friends just like anyone else, and then everything would be better.

I was so sure of that second part, that's the thing. That everything would be better. Did it even occur to me, then, that friends might not be the answer? That I might make friends and it could go *wrong*? (And I mean really wrong. Like, *really* wrong.) No. I just had all that stupid hope.

So that was me, first day of sixth form college, hoping. For friends—*any* friends—to make everything better.

Well, I got the friends. I even believed things really were better. For a while.

NOW

VANCOUVER

But they weren't better. Obviously.

I look out the tiny window of the plane, trying to make out the solid ground so far below me it may as well be just a drawing. Greenland, apparently. A whole country full of people with their own full lives and problems. If I'd been born there, would I have had the same problems? Or is it all pure chance, the people you're surrounded with, the school you go to, the friends you make or don't make?

Above my head, there's a distinct but gentle ping and the seat belt sign turns red, just as the plane gives a lurch.

"Oh no," the woman in the green jumpsuit next to me murmurs, quiet but emphatic.

I settle my head back against my seat, trying to ignore my sinking heart. Turbulence doesn't much bother me, but still. As far as omens go when you've just left your entire life behind, it isn't a great one, is it? My stomach twists and the plane jolts. Let's be honest, I'd take this physical turbulence instead of life turbulence if it was a choice. At least I know this bumping around thirty thousand feet in the air will end soon.

My seatmate clearly doesn't have this perspective, though. She has her eyes closed, fingers gripping the armrest. Every now and then, an involuntary whimper escapes her gritted teeth. I watch her for a while, wondering whether I should say something to reassure her.

"It's okay," I say.

She doesn't move her head when she responds, as if she thinks extra movement will send the airplane into a tailspin. "What?"

"It's okay," I say again. "Look." I pick up my cup of water and move it to her tray table. "See how the water barely moves?"

She frowns, her eyes traveling to watch the ripples on the water.

"Something to focus on can help if you're scared," I say. The plane judders and I point at the cup. "See, it doesn't even spill."

She looks at me, this time actually turning her head. "You're very brave."

"Not really," I say. "Turbulence isn't dangerous. It just feels that way."

The plane gives another bone-shaking rattle and the woman lets out a tiny shriek, then closes her eyes again, breathing in slowly. She says, "What's the difference?"

I'm not sure she actually wants an answer, because it's clear what the difference is. Instead, I say, "What are you going to Canada for?"

"I live there," she says, eyes still closed.

"Oh, cool," I say. "Are you Canadian?"

"Yes," she says. "Well, no." She opens her eyes. "I'm actually American, but I've lived in Canada for nearly twenty years. It's taken good care of me."

As off-the-cuff descriptions of countries you're escaping to go, this is a nice one to hear. I pocket it for later, imagine myself saying it to someone in the future. *I went to Canada. It took good care of me.*

"How about you?" she asks, loud, like she's trying to distract herself from whatever spiraling thoughts are happening in her head. "What's in Canada for you?"

"I don't know yet," I say. "I'm going to find out."

She looks at me again, startled. "What do you mean?"

"I don't have a plan," I say. "I'm going on, like, an adventure."

"To Canada?"

"Yeah."

There's a pause. "Why?"

"I just . . ." How to explain? "I had to get away. From my life. And Canada just seemed like . . . a good place to maybe do that. Does that make sense?"

"Not really," she says. "But also, yes." The seat belt sign above us both pings off and she lets out a sigh of relief, closing her eyes again briefly, smiling. "God, I really hate flying."

"My dad says being on a plane at cruising altitude is the safest place you can be," I say.

"Really?" She looks hopefully at me. "Is that true? Is your dad a pilot?"

"No," I say. "He's a banker."

She laughs, spontaneous and loud. "Well then, I'm convinced. Why did you have to get away from your life?"

"Long story," I say. It's not really, is it? But I'm not going to try to explain it now. I'm not even sure I could.

"Are you running away?" she asks, eyeing me with what might be concern or suspicion.

"No," I say. But maybe I am. Am I? Is escaping your life the same as running away? Probably. "It's kind of . . . more complicated than that."

It's not like I just *left*, anyway. I gave myself almost a whole day after I decided I was going to leave. I did some research, got my travel documents together, booked myself into a hostel in Vancouver. That's not impulsive, is it? Almost twenty-four whole hours to change my mind, and I didn't.

This morning I went to college—making sure to time my arrival so it was in the middle of lessons and I wouldn't run into anyone I didn't want to see—and had a meeting with my head of year, telling him I'd decided to drop out. He said my parents would need to be involved, that they could all give me time to make a decision, that I shouldn't do anything rash, let's all meet again in a week. I nodded along.

"Why do you want to leave?" Mr. Kirby asked.

"This just isn't the life I want," I said.

All the while, I waited anxiously to see if Dad would get sent some kind of alert that I'd bought my plane tickets using his credit card. Luckily, no alert came. I went home, packed my rucksack with my sketch pad and my most Canada-friendly travel clothes—dungarees, long-sleeved T-shirts, and a hoodie— and left the empty house as calmly as if I was just popping to the supermarket, my big winter coat slung carelessly over my arm.

The whole time, it had seemed impossible that I would actually be able to do it, that I'd really make it onto the plane and up into the air without someone stopping me. But I did.

Since then, I've been trying to figure it all out. How I got here, what I did wrong. And here's what I'm thinking— maybe all these years I've been too fixated on other people. I'd thought that was what I needed to do, but it clearly hasn't worked, has it? After putting everything I had into making friends, I'd ended up with nothing. Worse than before, even, because now I know that having no friends is better than having bad friends. And who wants to learn a lesson like that? If I've been chasing other people to find myself, maybe

I need to stop and just . . . well, be. Get to know who I am without worrying about whether it's good enough.

That's what I'll do in Canada. I won't be lonely; I'll be independent. I'm going to travel across the entire country by myself, one end to the other. It's going to be incredible; it's going to be life-changing.

And when I come back I'll . . . well, maybe I won't come back. I'll be a nomad. Me, a pair of walking boots, my backpack, and my sketch pad. I'll become one of those life coaches who gives inspirational talks about the power of being alone.

This is my chance to be someone else, like I tried in college, but better. In a whole other country, I could be a whole different person. But . . . no, I don't want to just be anyone. I want to try being Peyton, really Peyton, the Peyton I never got to be. What have I got to lose at this point? Nothing. It's all already gone.

Considering so much can go wrong, I'm very calm going through border control. I think it's because I know all the possible outcomes, and the worst scenario is that they just put me on the next plane home. If that happens, it would be gut-wrenchingly disappointing, but not exactly life-ruining. I'd have to go home and face the consequences a little earlier than I'd hoped, but I'd still have *done* it. My parents would have to listen to me. Things would have to change.

So I answer the questions about why I've come to Canada with the bold-faced lie I'd prepared, explaining that my beloved grandad, who lives in Alberta, is due to have surgery, so I've come to take care of him. My grandad does exist, and he does live in Alberta, but as for beloved . . . well, let's just say I've literally never met him. For all I know, the surgery thing could actually be true. I don't feel guilty about using his existence for my own benefit, though; serves him right for walking out on my actually beloved grandma all those years ago and abandoning my dad. But anyway, his citizenship is a handy backup excuse for everything whenever I see a snag in my plan coming. *Why have you come to Vancouver if he lives in Alberta?* "We're going to spend a few days in Vancouver because I've never been, then have a road trip." *What about the surgery?* "That's not until next week. It doesn't affect his driving." I have an answer for everything, which I would once have said was unlike me. I even make a joke about maple syrup, then apologize, saying he—Barry—must have heard it a hundred times already. He rolls his eyes, shaking his head, but there's a small smile on his face when he stamps my passport. A huge smile on mine.

I'd told Barry that Grandad was picking me up at the airport so we could spend a few days in Vancouver before a road trip to his place in Alberta, but of course there's no one waiting in the arrivals hall, though I still do that senseless thing people do when they come through arrivals, looking at everyone's face as if somebody might have surprised me.

Luckily, they haven't. I've made it. I am in Canada. I find a row of seats in an information area and sit down, letting out a long breath. Now seems like a good enough time to take stock. It's just after eight p.m. here, which means it's . . . what time at home? I look up and see a display of clocks showing the times all over the world. *London, 04:09.* I promised my parents I'd phone them when I landed, but maybe they'll be asleep? I connect to the airport Wi-Fi and watch as my phone all but explodes.

There were replies to my email from both my parents, and WhatsApp messages saying, essentially, the same thing:

Dad

WHAT????

Mum

PEYTON!!!!

The messages got gradually more articulate after that. I scroll through them, watching my parents realize in real time that I really am on the plane, that it's taken off. They tell me that I have to come straight home. They remind me that I'm seventeen, that I've got college, that I can't just run away. Reading the messages should probably panic me, but I'm weirdly calm. They finally ebb and then stop with a final instruction to call them **THE MOMENT YOU ARE THROUGH SECURITY**, regardless of **WHAT BLOODY TIME IT IS**, because they **WILL BE AWAKE WAITING**, and also that they'll be **WATCHING YOUR FLIGHT** so they'll **KNOW EXACTLY WHAT TIME** my plane will land, and if I don't call them they will **SEND THE MOUNTIES AFTER YOU**.

Mounties? I look up "mounties." Canadian police. I roll my eyes, relaxing a little, because I know things are okay really, underneath the all caps, because they haven't done what I was really worried they'd do, which is call the airport ahead of my arrival to tell them to put me on the first plane home. I have a chance here. Something in them, even subconsciously, has given me this chance.

I take a deep breath and call home.

"Peyton!" Mum's gasp of a voice, answering after barely one ring.

"Hi," I say.

"You—" she begins, then stops. "We . . . I can't believe you—"

"I'm sorry," I say.

"How could you do this?" she asks. "*Why* have you done this?"

"I told you," I say. "I explained, in the email."

"But you can't just leave, Peyton," she says. "I know you think you can, but you can't. You have to come home. You've got college."

"I dropped out of college," I say.

"You . . . you what?" She sounds a bit faint.

"I dropped out," I repeat.

"You can't drop out," she says. "You have to be in education, Peyton. It's a legal requirement."

"Or have a job or an apprenticeship," I say. "I told them I've got a job."

"Peyton!" She's somehow both faint *and* shrill now. "You can't . . . This isn't . . . "

There's a brief, muffled conversation on the other end, a protest, something that sounds like a whimper, and then my dad's voice is coming through the phone, so sharp it's like it cuts right into me.

"Peyton!" he barks. "This is ludicrous. You cannot drop out of college. We're not even going to have this discussion."

"It's already done," I say. For so long, Dad using that voice on me would have sent me into a panic, but right now I'm calm. What can he do from so far away?

"It very much is *not* already done," he says. "I'm going to call your college and straighten this out."

"You could," I say. "But I'm not coming home even if you do, so you'll just have more aggro to deal with. Plus, the legal-requirement thing Mum mentioned is on the parents, not the students. So if you want to get a fine or whatever, then go ahead. Not my problem."

"*Peyton!*"

"I'm seventeen," I say. "And that college isn't what I want. It's never been what I wanted. And I'm so unhappy. I'm *so* unhappy." I hear the crack in my voice, feel the tears spring into my eyes. "And you've known that for years and you haven't done anything. And you *made* me go to that college even though you know it's not what I want. I don't want to be a lawyer. I want to be an illustrator."

"That's what this is about?" he says, his voice a mix of incredulity and frustration. "We've never stopped your art. You draw all the time. You're throwing this ridiculous— *dangerous*—tantrum because we helped you make the right choice about your education?"

"*No*, Dad!" And finally my voice has risen to match his, emotion getting the better of me. "I'm doing this because I *have* to. Where have you been the last six years? Can't you see what's happened to me? I don't have any friends. I don't have anything. I'm just *nothing*. And I don't want to be nothing, Daddy." The "Daddy" slips out, betraying me. But I need him to see me as I am, my life as it is. It matters too much.

Quietly, he says, "You're not nothing."

"I feel like I am."

"Peyton," Dad says. "If this is some kind of breakdown—"

"It's not," I say. (Is it? Maybe it is.) "It's what I have to do."

"Regardless," he says, as if a breakdown is the kind of

thing you can "regardless" away. "You can't just . . . fly away like this. We have to know where you are."

"You do know where I am," I say. "I'm right here."

"With my credit card, I assume."

I swallow. "Just for emergencies. I've got money saved." All those years of having no friends to have experiences with and spend money on have finally paid off. I've got a decent chunk of savings accumulated. It won't last forever, or maybe even very long, but it's enough for now. For this.

"I'll cancel the card," he says. "I'll book you a flight home and then cancel the card so you can't use it."

"Okay," I say. "I won't get on the flight, but okay."

There's another silence, longer this time. I can hear Dad's breathing, the regular bursts of exhalation through his nose. What I'm learning is that if you do something so extreme, so beyond the boundaries of what is acceptable, so out of character, there's actually nothing that can be said. I have blindsided my parents so completely, they're left floundering in my absence.

"Peyton," Dad says eventually, like repeating my name is a way of getting some kind of a grip on me, all these thousands of miles away. "Get on a plane and come home. Right now."

Is that the best you can do? I think, and I'm surprised and maybe even a little disappointed. *That's your final card to play?* My whole life I've carried this basic daughter assumption that my parents really do have the ultimate power over me, that I could never *really* defy them in any lasting, meaningful way. But now I'm standing here, my feet on the steady ground of a different country on the other side of the world, and what can they do? Nothing. They can't will me back home any more than they can magic themselves beside me and physically drag me to an airport. Even the threat of Dad canceling his credit card is—I realize it in this exact moment—empty. If he does that and I really don't come home, I'll be stranded and unsafe. However furious my dad is, and however I've hurt his pride, I know that nothing is more important to him than my safety. He would just never take a risk like that.

And so I'm free.

"I love you," I say. "Both of you. I'll email you, like, every day, if you want. But I'm not coming home, not for a while."

Our conversation circles for a while—Dad gets angrier; I stay calm—until Mum takes over again. Her shrillness has gone and now she's in practical mode, asking me exactly where I'll be staying, the address, phone number, any and all plans I've made.

"I can look after myself," I say, once Mum has run out of questions. "You can trust me."

"No, I can't," she says. "Clearly."

When we hang up, I cry. It's more a physical cry than an emotional one; all the stress of the last twenty-four hours—maybe even longer—pouring out of me. In England, if I had done this, everyone would have politely ignored me, but this is Canada, and four different people quietly and kindly ask me if I'm okay, if there's anything they can do. To each, I stutter that, yes, I am; no, I don't need anything; no, there's no need to call anyone; yes, I'm really fine, thank you. I think a big part of me had assumed that the "Canadian people are really kind" thing was just a stereotype, but it turns out it's actually true. At least here, in Vancouver airport.

I should leave, find an Uber, make my way to the hostel, but every time I think about standing up and moving, my knees go all wobbly. All my confidence has faded and I am suddenly very, very aware of how far from home I am, how un-England this country is, and I haven't even left the airport yet. I think I'd been imagining Canada as England, just farther away, but already I'm overwhelmed by how very not the case that is. Oh God, I'm in *Canada*. I'm sitting on a bench on the other side of the world. The *wrong* side of the world. *What the fuck have I done.*

I try to breathe. *This is fine. I can do this.* I unlock my phone and stare at the time, the wrong time—English time. I open my settings and change my timezone so I am officially on Pacific Standard Time. *See,* I say to myself. *I'm here. I can do this.* I stand up, lifting my rucksack onto my shoulders. One thing at a time.

I'd chosen the hostel mainly because it was one of the only ones that had a bed in a dorm room available at such short notice that also looked nice and, most crucially, accommodated seventeen-year-olds. It's part of a North American chain of hostels called the Sunshine Hostels, or Sun-Ho. The Vancouver one I'm staying in is called Sun-Ho-Van and it's bright and cheerful when I arrive, even in the dark.

The girl behind the reception desk has a part-shaved head and multiple piercings in her ears and nose. Her badge says AMELIA—NEW ZEALAND. She greets me cheerfully and talks through the hostel facilities and rules too quickly for me to really keep up as she checks me in and goes through my documentation. I hear something about "group activities," but she's already sped on to breakfast, which seems more important, so I don't ask for more details.

There's a photo of a tortoiseshell cat in a big frame resting on the reception desk, with a cardboard speech bubble pronouncing, *MY NAME IS TEAPOT! WELCOME TO VANCOUVER! YES, I HAVE BEEN FED!* I smile.

"Our hostel cat," Amelia says, nodding at the picture as she slides my travel documents back over to me along with my room key. "She's usually in the common room or hanging out here. Wherever she gets more attention. She's good for a cuddle if you feel homesick. Or, like, just like cats. The only thing we ask is that you don't feed her. She's well fed, trust me."

The dorm room is bigger than I'd expected, with two bunk beds on either side of the room and four lockers along one wall. No one else is in the room when I get there, though I can tell by the three other beds that they're all taken. The top-left bunk is free, so I climb up onto it and take off my rucksack, looking around. I think, for probably the fiftieth time since I landed at Vancouver airport, *I made it*. It still doesn't feel real.

I sit there for a while, just staring into space. It's after ten on a Monday night, so I probably won't be on my own in the dorm room for very long. I can't face the idea of even talking to anyone else tonight, so I should get ready for bed quickly, but I can't quite bring myself to move. *How is it still Monday?* This might be the literal longest day of my life. This morning I woke up in my own bed. Now I'm on the other side of the world, sitting on the top bunk of a bed in a youth hostel in Canada.

I pull out my phone and message Mum on WhatsApp.

Me:

Got to the hostel and I am fine. Just going to go to sleep. I love you xx

She replies immediately, even though it's—I quickly calculate the time in my head—about six a.m. at home.

Mum:

I love you too. Please check in when you wake up xx

Me:

I will. Don't worry xx

Mum:

Might as well tell me "don't be a mother" xx

Me:

😆 Please don't send the police after me?

Mum:

So long as you check in regularly and send me your itineraries and I can be sure that you're safe.

Me:

Is Dad OK?

Mum:

He'll be fine. Get some sleep, my little bird xx

Me:

xxx

I can pretend that I don't cry again, but I do. I'm so tired and overwhelmed. And then, when I finally get myself together and unpack what I need for the bathroom, I realize I've forgotten to pack pajamas. Basic error, Peyton. Really basic. I'll have to sleep in my clothes tonight. Also, no towel. I have to go back down to reception to rent one for one Canadian dollar.

Amelia, still behind the desk, eyes me. Specifically, my wet, red eyes. "Everything okay?" she asks as she hands me a worn orange towel.

I nod, taking it. "Thanks." I turn and leave before she can ask anything else in her knowing-but-gentle Kiwi voice.

"The desk is manned twenty-four seven," she says. "Always someone here if you need anything."

I glance behind me to nod at her, because I think I'll cry if I have to speak. I jog back up the stairs and find the bathrooms, locking myself into one of the private cubicles, which turns out to contain a shower, toilet, and sink in one space hardly bigger than a wardrobe.

When I'm under the water—hot but dribbly—I repeat to myself my mini mantras. *Independence, not loneliness. I have chosen to be here. I want to be here.* I remind myself that I can go home at any moment, if I want. I am in control of myself and my life.

By the time I finally crawl under the covers, I'm too tired to really feel anything. I curl myself up, tucking my face into the crook of my arm, ready to let sleep take me. But it doesn't. I just lie there in the dark, heart pounding, feeling the *Canada*ness of Canada all around me. It still seems so unreal, even as the sheets rustle beneath me and the mattress sinks under my weight. I am here; this is happening. Tomorrow, I will start my adventure for real. I'll go out into the city and explore, like the intrepid adventurer I am choosing to be. Tomorrow will be the start of finding what I'm looking for.

That's what you thought last time.

No. Stop. Don't. This isn't like that. I can learn from the mistakes I made then and not make them again. Or maybe it's just one mistake I need to learn from. Namely, *make friends at all costs.* Such an obviously wrong thing to think, but I didn't just think it—I believed it. Didn't I put everything I had into achieving it?

I want to reach into the past and grab hold of my own shoulders. I want to say, *Not that way. You're doing this all wrong. Not him. Not them.* That road I'm already on, spread out before me. A road that has somehow led me here, to this bunk bed and the dark, half a world away.

BEFORE

aka
Last time I was
planning for
tomorrow
aka
That day I met
my friends
(Or thought I did)

Day two of college, day two of my new life. Not quite exclamation-mark levels of enthusiasm; my optimism faded somewhat by the previous day's lack of friend-making and the fact that I had math first thing, which I was dreading. Why had I let Dad talk me into taking math? *Why?* I told myself that I could live through one week of it, tell Dad I couldn't bear it and then switch it for something else.

There wasn't assigned seating, but everyone who knew each other—presumably the Eastridge students—had gravitated into pairs and toward desks. I dithered, glancing around at the other stragglers, like me, wondering whether to offer a smile to a stranger and hope we could grab a desk together.

This would have been the best thing to do, and I should have done it, but before I could the teacher, Mrs. Landon, sighed with impatience and started pointing us toward different seats. "You," she said, pointing at me. "There."

The seat was beside a lanky boy whose attention was on

the boy and girl sitting behind him, all three of them mid-conversation. I slid myself awkwardly onto the stool, wishing I'd acted more quickly. Now I was stuck here. A couple of desks over, two of the stragglers from before were sitting together, smiling nervously at each other but already chatting away. *That could have been me! Goddammit.*

But then. "You all right?"

I glanced over automatically and the boy, my deskmate, was smiling at me, all casual. Friendly, even. He had shaggy brown hair, messy in an unstyled way, and eyes almost the same color.

A greeting! A normal, friendly greeting from a normal, friendly person. Like I was normal, too. *Don't fuck this up, Peyton. Do not fuck this up. Smile.* I smiled. *Say hi.* "Hey."

Yes!

"Consider this a very easy intro session," Mrs. Landon was saying. "I'm going to go over what you can expect to cover this term and this year, when I'm going to be scheduling in tests and practice exam papers, that sort of thing, so I'd suggest you take notes. If you're unsure about anything, ask now. If you ask me something later that you could have asked now, I *will* remember and assume you weren't listening."

Intense. I thought wistfully of the art studio, where I would be right now if I had any say in my own life. The wide-open spaces, the peaceful hum of everyone at work. I pulled out my notepad and pen, trying not to sigh.

"I'm Travis," the boy whispered.

"Mr. Fuller," Mrs. Landon said. "Let's not get off on the wrong foot."

Travis smirked at her, tapping his pencil to his head in a mock salute, which earned him an eye roll. He didn't say anything else to me for the next half an hour, but I basked in the casualness of our exchange. I listened as he carried on a patchwork whispered conversation with the pair behind us—a girl that I gathered was called Flick and a boy whose name never came up—and made mental notes of the way they talked to each other, how often they insulted each other but in a way that was met with laughs, so it was obviously okay.

"Damn," Travis said when Mrs. Landon had started going from desk to desk, handing out textbooks, and I realized with a shock of joy that he was talking to me. "Your handwriting is crazy neat."

I felt instantly, instinctively, hot with shame and embarrassment, tensing against whatever else was to come. But the determined part of me reared up, trying to shake it off. *No. No. Things are going to be different here.*

"Yeah, it's an old trick," I said. I almost didn't recognize my own voice. "Look neat, hide the messy truth."

Travis laughed. "Sneaky." He glanced behind us. "You hear that, Flick? You got to at least pretend to be neat."

"Pretend to be neat?" Flick said, which made me realize that when my voice had come out slightly different it was because I'd accidentally mimicked hers. "If you're pretending to be neat, doesn't that mean you *are* neat? Like if you pretend to be confident, that *looks* like confidence, therefore you *are* confident?"

Should I turn slightly in my chair like Travis and join in? Is that how people make friends? But what should I say? *I pretend, therefore I am.* Yes! Wait, no. *What if they don't get the reference? What if they do and they think it's pretentious?*

"No amount of confidence can hide the mess that is you,"

the boy next to Flick said. I heard her shriek and smack him, his laugh in return that was more like a cackle.

Travis didn't speak to me again for the rest of the lesson, and neither did they. As I watched the three of them walk off together toward the dining hall, I cursed myself for missing my chance, though I still wasn't sure if it would have been okay for me to have joined their conversation.

Later, after a lunch spent walking in a slow loop around the college rather than braving the common room alone, I went in to drop my things into my locker and saw them again, part of a larger group sprawled over the sofas. As well as Travis, Flick, and the boy, there were two other boys and one girl, all talking animatedly, probably multiple conversations at once. Flick was in the lap of the boy she'd been sitting with earlier. Judging by the way he had his hand curled around her upper thigh, I guessed he was her boyfriend. Which surprised me, because they hadn't seemed to really like each other much earlier, in between all the insults. But what did I know?

I imagined myself walking over to them, smiling and saying . . . what? What would Amber Monroe do? *No, I don't want to be like Amber Monroe. If she's the price of having friends, friends aren't worth it.* I opened my locker and started offloading the day's accumulation of papers and books into it. I should concentrate on finding one friend first, not expect a group to open itself out to me. The next class I went to, I would speak to whoever my deskmate was. I would find something to compliment—their phone case, their shoes, their handwriting, even. And then at some point, a little later, I'd pretend I hadn't heard something the teacher had said and ask my potential friend if they'd heard, and they'd reply because people like being helpful. *Yes, solid plan. Chin up, Peyton.*

I shut my locker door and there was Flick, standing beside me, smiling. "Hi!" she said.

Oh my God, it's happening. I forgot all about my helpful potential friend with the nice phone case.

"Hi," I said, very casually. It sounded too much like *her* "hi," but whatever.

"You were in math this morning, right?" she said. "You were next to Travis?" She pointed over her shoulder. "That guy?"

I nodded.

"And you've got neat handwriting," she said.

Weird thing to remember, but okay. I nodded again.

"Amazing!" she said. "So you were taking notes?"

"Yeah?" *Damn, that sounded too suspicious.* I tried again. "Yeah! Why, do you need them?"

She lit up. "Oh my God! Yes! Well, not me, my boyfriend. Eric. He's an idiot. I'd give him mine, but he says I take shit notes." She laughed a little bit too hard. "You seem like you probably take great notes, though. With your neat handwriting and everything." She smiled hopefully at me. It was the kind of smile that reassured me, somehow, that she wasn't being mean, even though this whole setup was the kind of thing that, at Claridge Academy, would have led to my notes ending up in the toilet or something. But Flick's smile had a touch of need in it, a desperation I couldn't understand but still recognized.

"If you want, you and me could compare our notes and go over them together," I said. "And then you can give him yours."

Mistake. Her brow furrowed. "I don't actually take shit notes. He just said I did. They're fine."

There was something in her face, the start of a judgment forming, and it terrified me. Her face said, *Why are you making this weird?*

"Oh, I know," I said, and my brain was working so fast to fix the mistake I'd made that I ended up saying the thing I had definitely not intended to say. "I just don't know anyone here, so I'm trying to make friends."

Instant, nauseating mortification exploded in my chest, filling my blood with a disorientating mix of heat and ice. I felt sick. *Why did you say that? Why, why, why?*

But Flick's brow unfurrowed, her smile returned. "Aw!" she said. "With me?! That's so sweet."

I blinked, trying to smile around the horrified grimace that was threatening to creep across my face.

"I mean, run while you still can, but sure, okay," Flick was saying, laughing. "Want to come over and meet the gang, then? If you actually don't mind sharing your notes with Eric, I mean."

I opened my mouth, and the bell rang. Loud and obnoxious, destroying my first potential friendship in literal years.

"Or tomorrow," Flick said easily, shrugging. "What's your next class?"

"Psychology."

"Me too!"

Oh my God. God who actually exists and is smiling down on me. God who has finally, finally, sent me a friend. "Yeah?"

"Yeah!" She laughed, possibly at me, but I wasn't sure. "Come on. Maybe we can sit together; none of my friends are taking psych, but I thought it sounded cool. I like your bag." She didn't even bother going back to her friends or her boyfriend, just waved at them as we headed out of the common room together, side by side, like friends. "So where've you come from? Are you a consortium kid?"

"Nope, I was at Claridge," I said. "The academy."

"Cool," she said. I didn't correct her. "I didn't even think about leaving—is that weird? I know this place isn't technically Eastridge, but it kind of is, you know?"

"You're from Eastridge?"

"Yup. Most of us are, I think. Some of us have known each other since we were literally babies." I wasn't sure how literally to take that "literally."

"Is it weird having to share with all the newbies now?" I asked, proud of myself for saying something so normal.

She grinned. "Nah, it's about time we got some new blood."

In psychology, she sat beside me like it wasn't a big deal, and I tried very hard not to beam like a child. The teacher talked nonstop from the beginning of the lesson to the end, breaking down the course structure and what we could expect to learn over the year, so Flick and I didn't get a chance to chat, but sitting together was enough.

At the end of the lesson, when we headed out of the classroom, Eric was waiting by the doorway to the building and off they went. I'd hoped they might invite me somewhere, but I told myself it was fine that they didn't; we weren't friends yet. The important thing was that Flick threw a wave over her shoulder as she went, that I hadn't said anything stupid, that we'd had a normal conversation.

Hope fluttered in my chest, a caged bird. My head went, *Maybe. Maybe, maybe, maybe.*

NOW

VANCOUVER

I wake up groggy. The dorm room is empty—I'd been vaguely roused out of sleep a few times in the night and then again in the morning by my roommates coming and then going again—and I'm jet-lagged and disorientated, unsure what country I'm in, what day it is. I'd dreamed about Flick.

I reach for my phone to find it's full of messages, mostly from Mum, plus one from my brother, Dillon. Mum's are mainly logistical, clearly based off research she's been doing since I left, asking me about currency exchange, telling me where the hospitals and police stations are, what the emergency number is in Canada. She's also sent me the full names, addresses, and phone numbers of four different people she "sort of" knows in British Columbia—three former colleagues and a second cousin—and even Grandad in Alberta, which surprises me. She must really be worried. Finally, she's screenshotted all the flights leaving Vancouver airport for the UK over the next forty-eight hours, "just in case."

I reply, **Good morning. I love you.**

Dillon's message is less logistical.

HOLY SHIT, PEYTON!

I feel the grin break across my face as I send the Canadian flag emoji in response. I don't think I've ever elicited a "Holy shit, Peyton" from Dillon, who has always treated me with an affectionate and protective older-brotherly indulgence rather than the respect of an equal. Now the ellipsis flashes onscreen.

Dillon:

YOU BAD. ASS. BITCH. Can't freaking believe it.

Me:

You proud?

Dillon:

PROUD AS FUCK. Mum and Dad are losing it. They don't know what to do.

Me:

They can't do anything.

Dillon:

Dad CANNOT deal with that. Listen, seriously, are you safe? You need anything?

Me:

They can't do anything.

Dillon:

OK. You need money or help or anything, call me, OK? I'm serious.

Me:

OK!

Dillon:

Damn, P. I mean this in a good way,
but I never knew you were so cool.

When I'm washed and dressed, I go into the breakfast
room, where a small group of guys are clustered around
one table, talking in Australian accents with the kind of
animated excitement I can't bring myself to pierce with my
awkward English hello. I hover by the bagel table, staring
at the range of food, more aware of myself than I've ever
been in my whole life. Eventually, I grab two granola bars
and leave. So much for appreciating the hostel's amazing
free breakfast.

I head out into the Vancouver morning, trying to muster
the boldness I'd felt when I first arrived. It's a beautiful day,
crisp and bright, with only the occasional wisp of cloud
showing against the blue sky. Here I am, in one of the most
beautiful cities in the world, ready to explore. This is why
I'm here, isn't it? I'm ready for adventures, transformative
experiences.

I'd intended to walk confidently in whatever direction
made sense, but I falter when I've only walked about five
feet. Vancouver looked incredible from the air and in all the
pictures I'd seen, but I tell you what it looks like now, from
the ground: it looks like a city. I'm just standing on the side of
a city street, which looks as urban and unfriendly as any city
street, except the road signs and traffic lights are different.
There are people everywhere, some harried, some calm, alone
or with friends, all with a plan and a purpose. They all belong

here, and I am a visitor. A visitor with no friends and no plan and no purpose.

Anxiety rises in my throat. I almost turn and run back to the hostel.

No, Peyton. You can do this. I take a deep breath and head toward a familiar sight: a Starbucks. I'll get a drink, have a little sit-down and take stock. I know big chains are peak capitalism and that's bad and everything, but right now the green-and-brown interior, the logo on the cups—it's all so comforting.

I order a tea, and the barista laughs at me, which makes me feel more British than I've ever felt in my life. But when I tell him my name, he spells it right on my cup, which has never happened before, and he smiles and says, "First time in Vancouver?" When I nod, he says, "Awesome! Welcome!" and it's really nice.

Sitting on one of the cozy armchairs with my hands around my tea makes me feel calmer. I pull out the map I'd taken from the pile at the reception desk at the hostel and see that it's actually one from a sightseeing bus company. Helpfully, the tourist attractions are all marked on it. Maybe that's what I should do today: a hop-on, hop-off tour of the city. That's a good way to get to know it, right? Straightforward, manageable.

Then I see the price. Seventy dollars.

"Okay, no," I mutter to myself. I have savings, but I don't have limitless savings. I'm going to have to be careful if I want the money to last long enough to get as far across Canada as possible. And I'm an intelligent person, aren't I? I can figure this out myself. If I use the map, I can find my way around on the transit buses to get to the same destinations. I can be self-sufficient. And that will be better, because I can space it all out and not have to do everything in one day.

I stay in the Starbucks for an hour, reading through the map and using the Wi-Fi, trying to make some kind of a plan for my first day. By the time I leave, I'm feeling better. I can definitely do this. I can. Independent, that's what I am.

I decide I'll get a bus to Granville Island, which is one of the places highlighted on the tour map, taking my time to very carefully figure out which bus I need and when it will be arriving by trying to connect to a random bank's Wi-Fi as I walk past. I finally think I've figured it out, wait thirteen minutes for a bus, and then realize when I've been sitting on said bus for ten minutes that I'm going in the wrong direction. First, I panic. Then, I dither. Finally, I get off the bus.

I'm pretty defeated, I'm not going to lie. This city is overwhelming and I was an idiot to think I could handle any of this on my own. How am I going to even begin to try to make my way across this gigantic country if I can't even get a bus across downtown Vancouver?

I take a breath and decide on a change of plan. Seeking solace, I follow signs that lead me to an entrance to Stanley Park, which I discover is like a huge version of Hyde Park, so huge it contains an actual forest. I head inside and wander around for a while, just letting the parkness of the park soothe me after the stress of the city. At the outer rim there's a seawall surrounding the entire park that is—according to the information board I diligently read in its entirety—nine kilometers long. I sit down, looking out across the harbor.

Finally—this is what I was expecting. The sky is so wide and so blue; the mountains look like they've jumped right out of a picture book about mountains; the sea stretches out and on before me. I stay there for a while, telling myself to appreciate this moment, where I am. I want to bookmark this moment in the map of my memories. Find myself in it whenever I start to feel lost again.

On my way back to the hostel, I stop off at a gift shop and buy a postcard of the Vancouver skyline at sunset and address it to my parents. Rather than write a message, I draw a quick sketch of myself sitting on the front steps of the youth hostel, smiling. I give myself an explorer hat and exaggerate the size of my rucksack, turning my Converse into walking boots. I title it *PEYTON THE EXPLORER* and add a tiny subtitle, so small Dad will have to put his glasses on to read it: *who loves you very much.*

I spend extra on postage to make sure it gets to them as fast as possible. I hope it will be enough.

When I get back to the hostel it's late afternoon. I head straight to the kitchen area to make myself some tea. A woman in full hiking gear is sitting in the corner, reading a magazine with her headphones on. Two guys are having what looks like an intense conversation. I take my tea into the games room and find the group of Australians from this morning playing pool together. I hover uncertainly, then decide to hedge my bets and go to the common room, which is empty. There are a few tables and a couple of sofas to sit on, one of which is currently occupied by the tortoiseshell cat from the photo on the front desk.

"Hello, Teapot," I say. The cat rolls onto her back with a deep, contented yowl and I smile. Animals are so much easier than people.

I have a look at the bookshelves but nothing appeals, so I settle myself carefully beside Teapot, pull out my sketch pad, and draw her instead, taking my time, relaxing into the quiet, the motion of my hand, the sweep of my pencil.

I stay there for a while, even after Teapot has gotten bored and sauntered out, sketching freely. As the afternoon wears on, people start to filter in and out of the room, some on their own like me, but others talking and laughing together. I assume at first that the latter group are already friends, booked into the hostel together, but I realize as I eavesdrop shamelessly on their conversations that I'm wrong. Most have only just met and are getting to know each other. Maybe this should have been obvious the whole time, but I swear it doesn't occur to me until I'm sitting in that common room that this hostel could be full of people like me; travelers, their lives on hold, everything temporary, ready to make friends.

The thought sears me with a jolt of pure hope. I've been so caught up in how independent I'm going to be and how traveling is a solitary thing that I haven't even thought about what a youth hostel actually *is*, what it means: people. So many people, all in one place, looking for other people to hang out and have experiences with. It's not like school or college, where we were all stuck with no escape whether we liked each other or not.

This realization is why, ten minutes later, when a group of guys all with different accents come into the room and scatter around one of the tables, I put aside my sketch pad, silently will my heart to stop racing, and smile. The tall, well-built guy, the oldest-looking among them, notices me and smiles back, wide and friendly.

"Hello!" he says. He has a Russian accent and a loud, confident voice. "You are new."

I nod. *Don't be shy. Do not be shy. What's the point?* I stand up, squeezing my sketch pad to my side for comfort as I do. "I'm Peyton."

"Hello, Peyton," he says. "I'm Seva. We are about to play cards—would you like to join us?"

Is it really that easy? Could it actually be so easy? I nod again, sliding into one of the free seats. Apparently, yes.

"When did you get here?" Seva asks me, tapping a pack of cards out from its box and beginning to shuffle them.

"Last night," I say. "Late. Um." I hate the "um" as soon as it's left my mouth. "How about you?"

"A week," Seva says. "I finished a work contract and now I am here until I find another one. Lars and Stefan"—he points to two of the guys, who smile at me—"have been here since Saturday. And Beasey and Khalil"—he points to the other two—"since Sunday."

"Do you all know each other?" I ask.

"We do now," Khalil says, and his accent is Scottish. Scottish! I'm so excited to hear a British accent that I beam at him, probably too wide, but I think he understands because his laugh, though dry, is warm rather than mean. I know mean laughs.

"Maja," Seva calls, and I look over to the doorway to see a woman around his age, ginger-haired with glasses, coming into the room. "Hello. Come and play cards." He turns to me. "Maja arrived the same day as me. We have bonded."

"Have we?" Maja says with a laugh. To me, she says, "Hello," as she pulls out the free chair beside me and sits down. "What are we playing?" she asks the group. She has a German accent and a small, calm smile.

Seva suggests we play blackjack, which reminds me of long-ago camping holidays with my family; Dillon and I dealing endless hands inside the tent to pass the time while it rained outside.

I manage to keep up a hopefully natural smile as we play, nodding along and laughing at other people's jokes, allowing myself to relax slightly. Seva has kept up a running commentary the whole time, and I envy him for how comfortable he clearly is in this environment of small talk with strangers from all over the world. Maybe I'll be like him in a few years' time, talking to everyone I meet like they're already my friends, and making them so in the process.

"Peyton," Seva says. "Have you ever met a Russian before?" When I shake my head, he says, "Am I what you expected?"

What's the best answer? I go with, "No."

To my relief, everyone laughs, including Seva.

"I am not surprised," he says. "I do not fit the stereotype. I can live with that." He looks around the table as he cuts the deck. "What do you think of when you think of Russia?"

"Bots," one of the Scottish guys, the one with glasses, says almost apologetically. What did Seva say his name was? Beasey?

Seva does a tiny robot with his gigantic hands, a mournful expression on his face. "Meep morp," he chirps. It's adorable.

"Spying," Khalil says.

"Vodka," Lars says, and Seva grins.

"Best vodka in the world, yes, that is extremely true. But bots? Spying?" He *tsks* for effect, a smile still on his face, shaking his head. "People, when you travel, they don't see you as a person—they see you as the country you represent. They forget they are thinking of stereotypes." He clears his throat and starts dealing out cards again. "I love meeting people from all over the world," he says. "Getting to know them beyond the stereotypes by staying somewhere like this. Stay here long enough and you'd meet the whole world."

"A youth hostel?" I ask.

He nods. "The interaction, the atmosphere. It draws a particular kind of person. Even though we are from all over the world, we have this in common. We're all trying to find something."

I can see in everyone's faces that they are thinking the same thing I am, which is, *What am I trying to find?*

"Adventure," Seva continues. "Inspiration. Escape."

"Freedom," Maja puts in, nodding. "Ourselves."

All of the above, I think. And then, *Why am I just thinking that and not saying it?* "All of the above," I say out loud.

"And some good quality poutine," one of the Scottish guys says, and I don't know what this means but I laugh when everyone else does.

Seva grins as he deals out the final few cards. "We're all travelers, explorers, runaways."

"I wouldn't say *runaway*," Maja says mildly.

"Everyone who travels is running," Seva says. "In some way."

I wonder if this is really true.

"I like *explorer* better," Beasey says. "It's much cooler."

Lars and Stefan are talking about skiing, asking each other and all of us if that counts as traveling, or if it's a holiday.

"What about you, Peyton?" Seva asks me. "Why are you here?"

What a question. "I'm not sure yet," I say.

They all look at me, waiting for more. The cards that Seva dealt are all waiting for us, but nobody moves to pick theirs up.

"I'm just going to explore Vancouver for a bit," I say. "Then move on. I'm going to try to get as far across Canada as I can. That's really as far as my planning went." They all look so baffled that I feel the need to add, as if they're border control and I'm trying to explain myself again, "My grandad lives in Edmonton, so there's that, too."

"You're going to see him?" Maja asks.

Definitely not. "Uh," I say. "Yes."

I guess this technically means I'm lying to her and all of them, but this is all temporary, so it doesn't feel like it matters. I'll probably have forgotten all about them by the time I get even close to Alberta.

"Do you drive?" Khalil asks. He's holding one of his cards between his forefinger and thumb, spinning it against the table.

"No," I say. "And even if I did, I couldn't hire a car here."

"So how are you going to travel?"

"Bus, probably," I say. "The Greyhound, maybe. I thought I could figure it out as I go."

They all look dubious. Maja and Seva glance at each other.

"The Greyhound doesn't really run in Western Canada anymore," Lars says. He gestures to Stefan. "We looked into it when we were planning our trip."

"Oh," I say.

"And anyway, do you know how long it takes on a bus between, say, here and Edmonton?" Khalil presses.

"No," I say, feeling a flush start to work its way up my neck toward my face. Why is he pushing this? What's it to him?

"A long time," he says. "Probably a whole day. Canada is *big*. Like, really big."

"That's why I came," I say, trying not to get defensive. "Because it's so big."

"You're a runaway?" Maja asks.

"No," I say. "My parents know where I am."

Everyone seems to be full-on gawping at me now, and I try to smile, willing my face not to burn too brightly. This is my punishment for deciding to interact with other humans instead of shutting myself away in a safe hole of solitude. This is what I get for forgetting what a failure I am at normal social interaction.

"But you don't have a plan at all?" Beasey asks, his cheeks lifting in a confused smile.

"I want to figure it out as I go," I say again.

"Shit," he says. "That's brave."

"And by brave," I say. "You mean stupid."

"No!" he says. "Brave! I mean, yeah, it's . . . well, unusual. To go traveling without a plan. But people do stupid brave things all the time."

I can't help laughing. "Thank you?"

"We can help you make a plan," he says, looking around the group. "Right?" Everyone nods. I open my mouth to say that I don't want anyone else making a plan for me, that the whole point of this is that I do it by myself and learn how to turn loneliness into independence or whatever it was I'd decided on the plane, but he's already bulldozing on. "You won't find better travel planners than a random bunch in a hostel at any given time." He smiles with such confidence. I wonder if he's ever said anything he doesn't mean with his entire heart. "You could hitchhike," he suggests.

"I could!" I say. "What a fun game. See how long it takes for Peyton to get murdered."

He laughs, a kind of bark laugh, like it had taken him by surprise.

"It's different for men," Maja says.

"Exactly," I say, glad for an ally.

"I'm traveling on my own, too," she says to me. "I can give you tips, if you need any."

"That would be great," I say. "Thanks."

"Isn't the hostel running a day trip tomorrow?" she says, turning to Seva for confirmation, who shrugs back.

"Yeah," Beasey says. "To north Vancouver. We're going." He gestures to Khalil, who nods. "Should be good."

"Like a guided tour?" I ask, as if it matters.

"Yeah, with subsidized entry and travel," Khalil says.

"Good way to see a lot of stuff, save a bit of money."

Are they inviting me? Or just telling me? Is there a difference? "Cool," I say. "I'll go, too."

"There we go," Seva says, laughing. "That's one day's plan, at least. Now"—he picks up his cards—"shall we play?"

BEFORE

aka

MAKE FRIENDS

MAKE FRIENDS

MAKE FRIENDS

My third afternoon at college, and a free period in the middle of the day. I went to the library, intending to get a head start on my homework (translation: sketch) and found, to my pure joy, Flick, already sitting at one of the desks, scribbling away. She was sitting beside another girl, one I recognized from the sofas in the common room.

(A brief snapshot of my brain in the fifteen seconds it took me to cross the library floor and sit down opposite her: *It's Flick! I should go and sit with her! Will it be weird if I sit with her? Maybe. Wait, will it be weirder if I don't sit with her? Shall I say something when I do? How quiet is the library meant to be? Don't look too excited to see her. Be cool. Shit, what if she thinks I followed her here? Shit, you're too close to leave now. She's looking up. She's seen you. Be—*)

"*Hi!*" she mouthed, face lighting up. She gestured animatedly to the seat opposite her, then down at her textbook, rolling her eyes. I figured this meant, *Sit down! But I have to work, ugh.*

I sat, glancing at the other girl, who was intently studying the textbook in front of her. I waited for her to look up and acknowledge me, but she didn't. I looked back at Flick, who rolled her eyes again and shrugged. *Okay, clearly this is a thing.* I pulled out *Othello* from my bag—I wasn't about to start sketching in front of them, because what if they thought it was weird?—and tried to relax into what I hoped was a companionable silence. Flick's friend still hadn't looked up. After a couple of minutes, there was a swish across the table, and then Flick's notepad in front of me.

Hi!

I looked up. She wrinkled her nose at me, like a rabbit. I wrote, *Hi!* and swished the notepad back.

Omg. Can you believe I have homework ALREADY

Crazy!

I want to die. And Casey won't let me talk when we're "STUDYING." BOOO. How are you?

Fine! You?

Meeeeehhhhhhhhh.

Let me tell you what a moment like this feels like to someone who was bullied and friendless for five years. It felt like the sun had risen inside my chest. And yes, I know how ridiculous and cheesy that sounds, but it's true. Sitting there with Flick, swishing that notepad back and forth, how she smiled when she put pencil to paper, how it was so incredibly ordinary. The simplest happiness.

When the bell rang, I'd read about a page of *Othello* and it couldn't have mattered less. Flick's friend—Casey—rolled her eyes indulgently at Flick and then raised her eyebrows in a kind of *hello* at me. I smiled awkwardly back, taking my time packing up my bag so that it would look natural for me to walk out with them, hoping they'd invite me for lunch.

And then, when we were outside the library doors, joy of joys—"Want to come to lunch with us?" Flick asked.

Yes! Yes, I do want to go to lunch with you! A million times, yes! "Sure," I said.

"Case, this is Peyton," Flick said, gesturing at me.

"Hi," Casey said. She had none of Flick's effusive friendliness, and the contrast made me anxious, immediately convinced she'd hated me on sight.

"Hi!" I said, overcompensating. I could *hear* myself overcompensating, and yet I still couldn't stop myself. "I'm new. I'm from Claridge. The Academy."

Casey nodded, but she didn't say anything. Later, when I'd gotten to know Casey, I'd understand that this was normal for her. At that moment, I felt panicky, seeing disdain in her gaze, imagining her shaking her head at Flick, leading her away from me.

Luckily, Flick was Flick. "Come on," she chirped. "I'm so hungry."

In the dining hall, we met up with Eric and Travis, who barely acknowledged my presence, and the other two guys in the group, Callum and Nico, who seemed so interchangeable to me at first that I kept getting them confused. They were all Eastridge students and had more or less grown up together, though there were some vague references to an ex-girlfriend of Travis's who'd been part of the group for a while, then dumped. (I wasn't sure if the dumping was Travis-specific, or if the whole group had turned their backs on her. I didn't ask.)

That was the first time I hung out with the group as a whole, and though it's hard now to remember a time before I knew them, I remember how, from the outside, they seemed so cohesive. A group of friends with their own history, all but impenetrable. It made me anxious, worried there was no room for me. I thought my way in was Flick, because she was a girl and there seemed to be room in her life—like there was in mine—for a girl best friend. She couldn't be happy being surrounded by guys all the time, surely, and though Casey was part of the group too, she barely spoke and seemed to be in a constant state of eye rolling, usually *at* Flick. (Casey, distant and aloof, never felt like an option for me.)

What I learned though, quite quickly, was that latching on to Flick wasn't really possible. She was way too bound up in Eric, for one thing, and for all her friendliness, she could be incredibly flighty. Her attention span was short, for people as much as anything else. Sometimes we'd be in the middle of a conversation and she'd blink at me like I'd just appeared out of nowhere. I was paranoid that her interest in me was linked entirely to my shiny newness, and that once that had faded, she'd forget me and, in consequence, so would everyone else.

As the first few days of that school year—my new life— went by, I felt like any progress I was making wasn't enough. I was convinced that if I didn't cement myself in with them—or with anyone—soon, I'd lose my chance, and I'd be relegated to the outskirts once more.

That couldn't happen. So I dropped business studies and replaced it with economics, which meant Flick and I had three classes together instead of two. (If this sounds extreme, it really wasn't; I didn't care about any of the subjects I was taking, and I had no more of an objection to economics than I did business.) She was pleased—so pleased it surprised me— telling me how much she hated economics, how she didn't have any friends in the class, but now she had me. It was the first time she'd actually called me a friend, and I basked in it. We sat together in the classroom, side by side, and I doodled a tiny Flick comic in the margins of her notepad. *Oh my God!* she wrote. *You're so good?!!!*

It was progress, but it still didn't feel like enough. Her attention was so fickle, and Eric seemed more confused by my presence than anything else. I was convinced that just one word from him would change her mind about me. A couple of weeks in, she wrote, *I don't understand any of this :(* in pencil on my sketch pad, and I wrote back, *I could help?* even though no one was ever allowed to draw in my sketch pad, let alone write actual words. *Yes please!* she wrote, and it was worth it. That's how I became Flick's tutor in a subject I barely understood myself.

But it worked. It worked because, that following week, she invited me round to her house on Saturday. Her friends were all coming over that night, she said, but if I came round earlier we could study together and then I could stay and hang out, if I wanted?

I wanted. I wanted so badly that when I got home, I ran upstairs, flung myself into my room and sang.

NOW

VANCOUVER

In the morning, I wake up early, still feeling the residual effects of jet lag, to find an email from Dad waiting in my inbox.

Peyton,

I have spoken to your head of year at your college and explained the situation, that you are having a difficult time and are not best placed to be making such important life decisions right now. He understands that you need some time. (In fact, he seems to be more understanding of this than I am.)

Your place at college is being held for the time being, provided you are not gone so long that you won't be able to catch up on what you have missed. I told him you are a bright, sensible, and intelligent girl. Please prove me right by coming home and returning to college, where you belong.

I am ready to book you on the first flight home. We can sort out any problems you are having when you are back on British soil.

Your mother and I miss and love you very much. We are very worried. Please come home.

Dad

I feel the weirdest combination of rage and sadness reading his email. I hate that he's tried to steamroll over everything I want and need by talking to my head of year and trying to undo the decision I've made. What does he mean by "explained the situation"? It seems very unlikely that he would actually have said, out loud, what happened before I left, not to mention where I'd gone. Not if he was simultaneously trying to paint me as "bright, sensible, and intelligent." Maybe he said I'd been in hospital, but not why. Maybe he used a word like "accident."

I can see his worry underlying every sentence, though. I can read how helpless his frustration is, not just because he can't force me to do what he wants, but because he doesn't understand my unhappiness. He's my dad. I know he wants me to be happy; he just can't grasp that my idea of happiness doesn't match his. Knowing this is why I can't bring myself to be angry when I reply to his email, telling him I won't be going back to college and I won't be coming home for a while, but that I love him too and am sorry to disappoint him.

When I get down to the breakfast room, I make sure to actually get proper food instead of just granola bars. I'm not quite brave enough to try using the waffle machine, even though I want to, so I stick to toast and cereal instead. I turn around, tray in hand, to see the two Scottish guys waving from their table. I head over, trying not to beam too wide.

"Hi," I say.

"Morning," Khalil says.

"Morning," I say.

"Toast and cereal?" the second guy says instead, incredulous. "Seriously? You came to Canada, literal home of maple syrup, to eat toast and cereal?"

"Okay, judgy," I say, amazing myself. "No one's asking you to eat it."

He grins. "I'm full up on waffles anyway. *As it should be.*"

"Don't mind Beasey," Khalil says. "He can't help being himself."

"Beasey?" I repeat, hoping my tone of voice isn't rude. "Is that really your name?"

Beasey nods, clearly used to the question. "It's my surname," he says. "First name William, but there were a bunch of Williams in my class at school. Five, to be exact. Beasey caught on pretty quick, and now everyone calls me it, even my sister. Though I'm not sure if she just does it as a joke."

"I had the opposite problem," I say.

"Yeah?"

I nod, pointing at myself with what I hope is a rueful smile. "Peyton."

"Ah," he says. "There weren't five Peytons in your class?"

"I don't think there are even five Peytons in the country," I say, even though I know this isn't true. There were six other Peytons born in the UK the same year as me, which I know because I looked it up years ago to answer this exact question, so that means there must be at least a few more than that by now.

"In *this* country there will be," Khalil says. "Peyton is a very Canada-friendly name. You'll find your people."

I know he's joking, but I can't help the jolt of longing in my chest. *My people.*

"I should look them up," I say. "Go on a mission to find all the Peytons."

"Great idea," Khalil says. "*That* can be your plan for this trip instead of—what was it you're going to do? "Figure it out as you go? In the second-largest country in the world?"

I know he's teasing me, but I tell myself it's friendly, not mean. "Speaking of plans. If they're so great, what's yours? How come you're both here?"

"We're traveling the world," Beasey says.

"Seriously?" I say.

He nods. "Seriously."

"Oh my God," I say. "That's so cool."

They both grin immodestly. Clearly, they've had this conversation a lot, and they love it. "We've done Southeast Asia," Khalil says. "Thailand, Singapore, Malaysia. We just spent six months in Australia, working as well as traveling."

"Where did you work?" I ask.

"Just a couple of bars," Khalil says. "We spent some time in New Zealand, too."

"Not enough," Beasey puts in.

"Not enough," Khalil agrees.

"And now you're in Canada?"

"Are we?" Khalil says, looking stunned for effect, and I roll my eyes at him. He grins. "Why not, eh?"

"That's so cool," I say again.

Khalil smirks. "Says the girl who hopped on a plane to Canada, of all places, on, what . . . a whim?"

"Hey, I had my reasons," I say, pleased with how cool and mysterious I sound. (Or think I sound.) "So what brings you here?" I ask. "To Vancouver?"

"One," Khalil says, holding up a finger. "Very cool city."

I nod. "Of course."

"Two," he continues. "A friend of mine is at uni over on Vancouver Island. I said I'd swing by this way so we could go and say hi."

"Friend," Beasey says, meaningfully.

"Friend," Khalil confirms, straight-faced.

"And three," Beasey says, rolling his eyes, "is that we wanted to work a ski season in Banff, which is in the Rockies, over in Alberta, but we couldn't find a way to stay and work there without actually losing money."

"The whole point was we'd earn enough to move on with," Khalil says. "Like we did in Australia. But it didn't work out."

"So we're just going to go hang out there for a couple of weeks," Beasey says. "Stay in a hostel, like we are here, maybe ski a bit, do a few hikes—weather permitting—and then move on."

"Where's next?" I ask.

"The US," Beasey says. "Well, through there, anyway. We're going to go down the West Coast, then into Mexico."

"Sounds amazing," I say wistfully. "I'm so jealous." Jealous of the plan, of them being intrepid explorers and seeing so much of the world, but mostly jealous of how they have each other. They're so easy together. It's clear they've been friends for years.

"Well, before all that, we're heading to Vancouver Island in a couple of days," Khalil says. "Seeing my friend Heather"— Beasey coughs, then laughs when Khalil throws a sugar packet at him—"and spending a few days in Victoria, then heading up to Tofino. A couple of the guys are coming too so we can all save money on an Airbnb. They played cards with us last night? Lars and Stefan? They're cool."

"Did you know them before?" I ask.

"Not before meeting here, no, but that's what traveling's all about, right?" He says this so easily. "Meeting people, going on adventures. It's not just what you see—it's who you see it with."

Is that true? I hope it's true. I want it to be true so badly.

Beasey's laughing. "*Nice.* Deep."

"It's true," Khalil says, grinning, unruffled. "That's how we met Heather," he adds to me. "Last summer, when we were working near Sydney. She's Australian. She's at the university over in Victoria for a semester."

I smile. "You detoured all the way here for a girl? That's so romantic."

He frowns. "We were coming this way anyway."

Beasey meets my eye and shakes his head, smiling drily.

"She's just a friend," Khalil adds.

Beasey mouths, *"Just."*

"Anyway," Khalil says. "Peyton, if you don't have a plan, you can come too, if you want. There'll be room in the Airbnb—it's pretty big."

I somehow manage to stop myself saying, *"Really?!"* with the kind of breathless excitement of a literal child. Instead, I nod thoughtfully. "Yeah, maybe—that could be good."

"Cool. And why not, right? It's not like you already have plans," Khalil says, raising his eyebrows teasingly.

"See, this is *why* I don't have plans," I say. "So I get to be *spontaneous* and get invited along on other people's cool-sounding trips."

They both laugh. I made them laugh. These cool, older Scottish guys who've been traveling all over the world. I made them laugh.

We head together to reception to meet up with everyone else going on the group tour and Spencer, our guide for the day. He's Canadian, with shaggy blond hair, perfect white teeth, and a lazy smile. Khalil, Beasey, and I spend the journey to our first stop—Capilano Suspension Bridge Park—chatting about the UK and the lives they've left behind. (I am, obviously, less talkative about that side of things.) They've been away for a lot longer than me and they miss it more, reminiscing about things it hasn't even occurred to me to miss, like Marmite, pubs, Greggs, and British TV.

"And haggis?" I ask, teasing.

Beasey lets out a huff and points at me. "Haggis," he says, with emphasis, "is a *lie*. A big Scottish lie."

Khalil gasps, very loudly. "You traitor," he says. "Surrender your thistle and kilt."

At the Capilano Suspension Bridge Park, we start with the bridge itself, seventy meters above the Capilano River, very wobbly and very cool. Khalil and I challenge each other to walk across without touching the sides, but neither of us makes it more than a few steps without instinctively steadying ourselves. Beasey has gone very quiet, his face rigid, clutching the side with both hands.

"Not a fan of heights?" I say.

"Or vertigo," he mutters, as if he thinks talking at a normal volume will disrupt his balance.

"It's completely safe," I say. "Spencer said it could take the weight of two 787s."

"That sounds like bullshit," he says.

"It's not!" I say, shocked. "He's the tour guide. He knows."

"And anyway," Beasey says, teeth still gritted. "Boeing 787s can't trip up and fall over the side."

"You're not going to trip," I say. "Come on. Most of the group's already across."

A small child comes running past us, shrieking with joy as the bridge judders and sways, and Beasey looks at him with such horror you'd think the kid was on fire.

"I'm going to go back," he says, beginning to claw his way in the opposite direction. "I hate this—oh my God."

"Come on!" I say. "It's fine, honestly. Look, am I scared? No. And I'm a tiny little girl."

"I'm a feminist," he says. "That's not going to work on me. Shame on you for"—the kid starts jumping and Beasey groans—"trying to masculinity-shame me."

I try not to laugh, because he really does look scared. Instead I take my place beside him, resting my elbows on the steel cable. "Isn't this view amazing, though?" I say. "It's just incredible. I've never been anywhere like it. Have you?"

Beasey looks at me like he knows what I'm doing, but he answers. "I grew up in the Scottish Highlands. But yeah, it's amazing."

"Totally worth it, right?" I smile at him and he rolls his eyes but smiles reluctantly back. "Come on." I hold out my hand. "I'll guide you across. I'll be your Support Peyton."

"Then if I trip, I'll drag you with me," he says.

"I promise I won't let you drag me to my death," I say. "Come on. Buck up." I tap his hand and he releases his claw-like grip on the side of the bridge to let me take it. His hand is sweaty. "Try closing your eyes."

"Is that a joke?!"

"Okay, fine, don't then. Just put one foot in front of the other. What's the best thing you've seen since you've been traveling?"

He thinks about it, carefully following my footsteps. "Kuang Si Falls."

"Favorite place?"

"New Zealand."

"Do you miss home?"

"Yeah, but less than I thought I would. Do you?"

"No," I say. I'm not sure if this is really true, but I don't

want to think about it too hard to find the real answer. We've reached the end of the bridge and I carefully, casually, let go of his hand. "Look! We made it."

Beasey lets out a huff of a sigh, a smile lighting back on his face. "Never again."

"It wasn't that bad, right?"

"It was worse," he says. "But thanks for being my Support Peyton."

It makes me feel funny when he says it. "Anytime," I say. "I'm here for all your high-bridge needs. Or at least, for as long as we're both in the same country."

He laughs. "I'm not going anywhere near any more high bridges. But isn't there a cable car up to Grouse Mountain later?" He makes a face. "I hate cable cars."

"You really don't like heights. Haven't you been traveling the world? How can you do that and be scared of heights?"

"There's no halfway liking heights or not," he says. "They're horrible either way. If I'm high up, I don't like it. And I've always been scared of heights, whether I'm in Scotland or Vietnam. You must be scared of stuff, too. What are you scared of?"

Being alone again. "Snakes," I say. "Climate change."

"Ah yes," he says. "Those equally scary things." His eyes suddenly go wide, his smile disappearing.

"What?" I ask, but it's obvious what. We've reached the Cliffwalk, which is a series of bridges, stairs and glass-bottomed platforms across the granite precipice of a cliff. "Oh."

"Nope," Beasey says.

"Face your fears?" I ask hopefully.

"Nope," he says again. "I can accept my limits. This is my limit. You go—I'll meet you all after."

I give him a wave as I hurry on to catch up with Khalil and

the rest of the group. Khalil laughs when he sees me appear without Beasey beside me, shaking his head. "You couldn't convince him?"

"Nope," I say. "That was beyond even me." I love how this sounds when the words leave my mouth; like I have a history of convincing people to face their fears or something, that there's more to me than the loneliness that's the actual truth.

"Well, you got him across a suspension bridge," Khalil says. "That's more than I've ever managed."

After the Cliffwalk, which makes my heart swoop inside me in the best way, we take on the Treetops Adventure, which is a series of small suspension bridges over the forest. There's not enough time to do what I really want to do, which is sit down on one of the canopies and just draw what I see, so I take as many pictures as I can from as many different angles, hoping it will be enough to re-create it in pencil later.

When we finally all meet up with Beasey again, he's sitting on a bench near the entrance to the park, playing on his phone.

"Mate," Khalil says. "You missed out!"

"Devastating," Beasey says, deadpan.

In the afternoon, we get the cable car up Grouse Mountain. Beasey closes his eyes for the whole trip, even when Khalil and I both tell him he's missing the incredible views sweeping right across Vancouver. "I don't care," he says, through gritted teeth. "I cannot tell you how much I don't care."

When we get to the top, our feet on solid ground, he's smiling again, back to the chill person I'd met in the hostel. "Holy shit!" he says. "Look at that view!"

The group splits off and scatters to spend some free time exploring, and I find myself torn between going on the zip line with Khalil and most of the group, or saving money and staying with Beasey. Doing the zip line would be out-of-this-world amazing, and I'm so tempted, but it costs about the same as four nights in the hostel. I can't justify it to myself, not when I'm so aware of the money I've already spent since I arrived. It won't last forever.

"Ah, well," Beasey says, smiling. "The view up here is free. And solid ground is so much safer."

We spend some time together exploring the museum and the shop, trying on a display of hats together. Beasey has just let me take a photo of him wearing a bright red toque when he says, "So what brought you to Canada, anyway?"

I feel myself tense instinctively and hope he hasn't noticed, trying to smile to cover the unease. "Didn't we talk about that last night?"

"Not really," he says. "Logistics more than anything, which isn't really the answer, right?"

"Why not?"

My voice hasn't come out friendly, but he smiles anyway, like he understands, even though that's impossible. "Want to talk about it?"

Obviously, I know exactly what he means. "Talk about what?"

He half laughs. "Okay, then." He buys one of the toques and a postcard—Grouse Mountain covered in snow—and we head back out into the cool air together. "Sorry," he says. "I didn't mean to make you uncomfortable."

I shrug inside my coat, and that's when our eyes meet. There's something physical about eye contact, I realize in that moment. A tug of connection. I *see* him see me.

"You've got some walls," he says. "High ones. All built up."

He mimes layering bricks, one on top of the other. His smile is knowing, but warm. His eyes are kind.

I put my two hands in front of my face in response, peeking out at him from over the top, which makes him laugh.

"Okay, I won't pry," he says. I drop my hands, trying to keep the relief out of my smile. "I am intrigued, though," he adds. "You are intriguing."

"I'm really not," I say. But I want it to be true.

"Okay," he says, clearly unconvinced, still smiling. "Well, if you want to talk, I can listen. Sometimes it can help, talking to someone you don't know very well. Less pressure."

For a moment, I wonder if he's right. I try to imagine telling the story from start to finish. Claridge to college to that last night at Flick's. My sadness turned to hope turned to desperation. I dismiss it. Better he imagines me intriguing than knows I'm pathetic.

"Or you could draw it," he adds when I don't say anything. "You're an artist, right?"

"How do you know that?" I ask, startled.

He laughs. "You've been sketching all day."

Yeah, but I hadn't realized he'd *noticed*. "Drawing the present," I say. "Not so much the past." As I speak, I imagine doing it. Maybe it would help, turning those moments into pencil lines I can control. Re-creating Flick and Travis as characters on a page instead of the people in my memories.

"Just an idea," Beasey says. "We should head to the end of the zip line to meet everyone. They'll probably be done by now."

When we get back to downtown Vancouver, most of the group stays together to get dinner at a burger place called White Spot, and I go along too because I'm feeling cozy and warm in the comfort of the day, emboldened by how well it's gone. I haven't embarrassed myself with these new people; maybe I've even, possibly, maybe . . . made friends.

I go to bed early that night, the residual jet lag I'd been keeping at bay catching up with me. The dorm room is empty and so I sit for a while on my mattress before I turn the light off, playing with my phone. I create an Instagram account—peytontheadventurer—and spend a calming half hour going through the photos I took earlier in the day, adjusting and filtering, adding them to the account to get it going. It's not my first Instagram account, but it's the first for a long time. When I was at school, Amber Monroe and her minions had found my account and harassed me constantly on it, replying to everything I posted with jibes or joke praise or—worse—effusive "sympathy" for the fact that I had the misfortune to be Peyton King, regramming my posts with me replaced by a duck. I tried to withstand it for a while, desperate to hold my head high and ignore it like all the adults said I should, but I gave in and deleted my account eventually. I could have started a new one when I was at college, but I couldn't bring myself to do it, too afraid of what could happen.

But now, I'm here. I'm brave and I'm free. I am living a life where I can have an Instagram account if I want to, and no one can stop me.

In the morning, I find a flurry of messages from my grandma on my phone, ending with a plea that I tell her when she can call me. When I message her to say I'm free, she calls me immediately.

"Peyton!" she gasps, without even saying hello. "It's not true, is it? You're not in Canada?"

"I am kind of in Canada, yeah," I say.

"Oh, Peyton," she says. *"Why?* Please don't tell me you've gone to see your grandfather."

"Obviously not," I say. "I'm not anywhere near him; Canada's huge. I just wanted to get away."

"Hmmm," she says, clearly unconvinced. "To Canada, of all places. Why didn't you come here? What does Canada have that Cornwall doesn't have?"

I smile into the phone. "Good point."

It's true that I usually go to Cornwall when I need a place of refuge. It's always been a place I've felt safe, which is a lot to do with Grandma herself. She raised her son—my dad—as a single parent after her husband—my grandfather—walked out on them both. When my dad was good and grown, she moved to Cornwall with three other divorced friends, and they've lived there ever since, within walking distance of each other's homes. I mean, talk about squad goals. "That twat leaving me was the best thing that could have happened," she told me once, when I asked about my estranged grandfather. "He said he wanted his freedom. Well—who's free now? Me!" She laughed her cackle-laugh. "And I *earned* it, unlike him, the lonely, bitter old man. To think, I could have wasted my life on him. I tell you, Peyton. Women are far superior to men, in every way." She raised her glasses to look down at me. "In *every* way." (It took me a few years to understand what she meant.)

According to her—and my parents, who barely talk about grandad—it's no great loss that I never met him, and I believe her, even though he's an actual artist, and it would be very cool (and useful) to know a real artist. The only contact he has with any of us is the cards he sends on birthdays and at Christmas, like clockwork, and the cards we send in return.

For years, it was me who got to write the cards and address the envelope, because I loved the novelty of the airmail stamps. Grandad had only ever been abstract to me, but those cards were real, flying across the sea, and Grandma was real, and present, and loving.

One of the things I love most about her is how happy she's allowed herself to be, even though she went through a period of the most desperate, lonely sadness. She came through it, and it made her who she was: one of the best people I know. It gave me hope, and spending time with her always made me happy. Long days on the beach, cliff walks with the dogs, barbecues in her garden with her friends and our extended family. She lives in a house on a ridge overlooking the sea, and her living room has the most amazing floor-to-ceiling window. Years ago, she set up an easel there, and when I visited her I'd paint for hours, standing there in the sunshine, looking out to sea. I captured that view in watercolor, charcoal, pencil, acrylics, over and over. Every year I got better. Cornwall and Grandma was my escape, my happiness. And now—

"Peyton," she says through the phone, and I jump.

"I'm fine," I say automatically.

"Are you sure?" she asks. "Your father told me what happened. I was quite alarmed. I had no idea you—"

"I'm fine," I interrupt. I don't know what exactly my dad would have told her—surely not the truth, or at least not the whole truth—but I don't want to hear or talk about it either way.

"Should I be worried about you?"

"No," I say, shifting out of the way so a couple walking up the stairs can pass. "I'll send you a postcard, okay? I'll send you five postcards. But I should go."

"Okay, darling," she says. "Keep safe, and have fun. We

all love you." This is how Grandma always frames this; her love is never something she keeps in isolation. She reminds me at every opportunity how they all love me. The words, so familiar, from so far away, make me ache.

"I love you all, too," I say. "Bye."

I spend the day playing tourist, properly, with Lars, Stefan, Beasey, and Khalil, the five of us exploring everything the consumer side of Vancouver has to offer. We wander around a shopping mall and spend most of our time at the food court, creating a smorgasbord that centers around poutine. "Canada's greatest invention," Beasey says confidently. "Like chips and gravy, but better."

In the afternoon, we get a bus to one of the beaches and hang out there for a while, even though it's cold. I sketch as they play Frisbee, trying to capture the way I feel on the page, the way my happiness lifts and sparks like firelight in the wind. No one makes me feel weird for sketching instead of playing, or makes a grab for my sketchbook, or demands that I draw them.

When we get back to the hostel in the early evening, we find Seva and Maja playing pool with some of the Australians. Bottles of beers get passed around but I shake my head, pointing out I'm underage to avoid any questions about why I don't want to drink. If I'm going to learn from any of the mistakes I made before, the most obvious one is alcohol. I'd really like to at least try to have fun without it.

We team up to play pool—somehow I end up on a team with Beasey—and we lose by loads but still have fun. So much so that I actually feel a little bit drunk. I take photos of all of us, the pool table, Teapot the cat, and imagine sending them to Flick. *Look where I am!* I'd say. *Do you miss me?*

I swallow down thoughts of Flick, try to shake her from my head. She wouldn't believe any of this. *You?* she'd say, frowning and smiling at the same time. *You sure, Pey-Pey?*

I bite down on my lip. *Stop.* I am here. This is now.

"Hey," a Scottish voice sounds from beside me and I turn, already smiling. Beasey is holding out a can of Coke. "Thirsty?"

"Thanks," I say, taking it.

What I haven't been letting myself think all day: Beasey has a nice face. A really, really nice face. The kind of face you see in a crowd and think, *That's a nice face.* His hair is a soft brown tumble, not scruffy but not tidy, either. His glasses have red frames, like a cartoon character or a child, but somehow they suit him and he pulls it off. His front teeth are a little crooked under lips that I want to . . .

Okay, stop it. I take a long sip of Coke and it fizzes in my throat, so familiar, the same on both sides of the Atlantic. It's weirdly comforting.

Stefan lets out a roar of triumph, leaping backward and almost crashing into me as he waves the pool cue in the air, whooping.

Beasey laughs, taking ahold of my arm to pull me out of the way. "Want to sit?" he asks.

I nod, following him to one of the sofas. When we sit, we're facing each other, knees almost touching. He's telling me about how loads of stuff gets filmed in Vancouver; how it's stood in for LA, New York, Boston. The chameleon city, he calls it. His eyes are bright and animated as he talks, gesturing with one hand, fingers flicking unconsciously as he lists films. I'm nodding, asking questions not just because I want him to like me but because I'm actually interested. It all feels so impossibly natural, even normal. And really, really nice.

Someone turns the music up from the other side of the room, and Beasey smiles as he leans forward so I can still hear him, his face angling slightly toward me, his hand coming to rest lightly on my knee. There's a flicker somewhere inside me, a motion sensor going off, the trip before an alarm. A breach in my walls. I look at him and our eyes lock, and I see it. Right there in his eyes. He likes me. He wants to kiss me. He's *going* to kiss me. That warm softness in his smile, the caramel in his eyes. No, *like* isn't the word. He *fancies* me. That juvenile word, something I once wanted so badly I gave myself away for it, for what I thought it would give me.

In front of my eyes, smiling Beasey disappears and there's Travis. Not even Travis from that first night at Flick's, when he was still sweet and hopeful, but Travis on the last night. That awful last night I just want to forget, and all of it had started with one stupid kiss.

I jerk away, almost shoving Beasey in my haste. "No," I say, too sharply, way too loudly.

"What's wrong?" Beasey starts to say, alarm in his voice.

"No," I repeat. I'm almost shouting. "I can't do this again."

"Do what again?" he asks, bewildered.

I'm already gone. Pushing past everyone, finding the door and tumbling out into the corridor. Too wired to wait for the lift, taking the steps two, three at a time. I get to my dorm and it's empty. I take my shoes off and climb into bed, not even bothering to undress, burrowing myself under the sheets and squeezing my eyes tight, tight shut. I can't do this again. I won't.

BEFORE

aka

First Times: Weed, Alcohol, and

DON'T KISS THAT BOY

FOR GOD'S SAKE PEYTON

YOU DON'T EVEN LIKE HIM

That very first time I went to Flick's house, I spent two hours in front of my mirror, trying different hair and makeup styles. Flick didn't wear a lot of makeup, and Casey barely wore any at all, so I didn't want to overdo it by looking like I was making too much of an effort, eventually settling on the bare minimum for my face—with a lip gloss in my pocket for later, just in case—and my hair hanging in carefully loose waves to my shoulders. I wore the black jeans I'd bought not long after I'd started college and a boat-necked black top along with the heart necklace Mum had given me for my birthday. I examined myself from every angle, searching for errors. I couldn't be too much or not enough.

I hadn't been in an actual friend's house since the earliest days of year seven, before my friendlessness became a contagious disease that wasn't worth the risk for anyone. Getting this right was beyond vital. It was the key to my actual future.

Flick was still wearing what looked like pajama bottoms and

a hoodie when I got to her house, which was the kind of relaxed I aspired to be but couldn't imagine ever actually achieving.

"I'd show you around," she said, waving a lazy hand toward the living room. "But there's, like, nothing to see. Want a drink or anything?"

Did she mean water? Tea? *Alcohol?* "No, I'm all right, thanks." I was thirsty, but asking for nothing felt safer.

We worked at her kitchen table, where she'd piled up her textbooks and notes ready for us. She was quiet at first while I started talking her through some of the problems she was having—I'd done my own pre-studying that morning in preparation—careful not to sound too patronizing, but after a while she warmed up, asking me to draw a cartoon version of her who understood economics. I obliged, drawing a mini Flick in a business suit, giving a lecture under a sign that said *OXFORD UNIVERSITY*. She laughed, pleased.

"That's so cute," she said. "Draw Eric, too."

I'd never sketched Eric before, so the likeness wasn't as good, but I obeyed, adding an Eric gazing adoringly at her, eyes wide and enraptured. Her smile grew, her eyes flitting between their cartoon faces, like she was drinking it in.

"You'll have to draw everyone later," she said. "They'll love it."

I had a sudden vision of myself standing at a whiteboard while they all watched me, like I was the evening entertainment instead of a new friend. My stomach dropped. "What do you guys usually do when you hang out?" I asked, hoping for an alternative.

She looked at me blankly. "Er . . . just hang out?"

"I mean, like, what do you . . . do . . ." I trailed off at the look on her face. Was I being weird?

"Normal stuff," she said, shrugging. "Usually we smoke a

bit. Sometimes Eric gets some better stuff, but that depends on his brother, Tyler."

"Smoke?" I repeated, surprised. I hadn't noticed any of them smoking at college.

"Yeah," Flick said. She'd shoved her pencil into her hair and was twirling it lazily. "Like, weed."

"Oh!" I said. "Right. Okay."

"That a problem?"

"No," I said. She could have told me they were building up a supply of uranium and it wouldn't have been a problem with me.

"Mostly we just watch stuff or Travis brings his Xbox, or . . . I don't know." She shrugged again, then laughed. "I've never really thought about it. What do you do, with your friends?"

I swallowed past the sudden blockage in my throat. She still assumed I had friends somewhere. Was that a good thing, that she didn't suspect? Or should I be honest, so she'd know why my access into her friendship group mattered so much? No. That was unthinkable.

"We're mostly art nerds," I said, conjuring into my mind the friends I'd imagined for myself once. "So we, like . . . draw together."

"Cool!" she said. "Well, we can maybe try that, too. I've got Pictionary."

That was a long time ago now, and so much has happened since, and I can't see Flick in the same hopeful, earnest light I did then, but I still haven't lost my affection for her in that moment, so innocently, sweetly, generous with her new friend.

"Ugh," she said, turning back to the textbook. "This stuff is so boring." She tapped her pencil against the page for emphasis. "Why am I doing this to myself, Peyton?" She widened her eyes for effect. "It's been, like, two weeks and I already want to die."

"One day this will seem like such a long time ago," I said. In my head this had sounded like a flippant comment, but out loud it seemed heavy—self-consciously profound. I added, "When you're collecting your exam results and you've got an A in Economics."

She grinned. "God, can you imagine? My mum would lose her mind. She'd be *so* proud." She looked, for a second, wistful. "I bet you get As all the time."

"I do, yeah," I said, and I knew I'd got the tone right because she laughed. "Loads. I'll share them with you."

"Oh my God, best friend for life," she said, and I half basked in the moment and half wondered what it must be like to be so secure that you could joke about something as gigantic as being best friends. "Okay, seriously, the guys will be here in, like, an hour, and I still need to properly get dressed. Help, help. I want to get this chapter done before then."

When they all arrived, almost an hour later in one big group, I was sitting on Flick's sofa with a mug of white wine as if I belonged there, and my feigned nonchalance worked because they barely reacted when they saw me, just smiled and nodded, lifting hands in waves hello. Travis dropped himself onto the sofa beside me—"Hey, math friend"—and produced a packet of Polos from his pocket, holding it out. I took one—I would have taken literally anything offered to me by any one of them—and, looking back, it was all there in that interaction, wasn't it? There was probably a part of me that had already decided what was going to happen.

Flick and Eric were already kissing a sloppy hello, Casey

was rolling her eyes, Callum and Nico were uncapping beer bottles. And there I was, beside Travis, sucking on a Polo and trying not to beam too wide because *I had done it*. I was in a social situation with potential friends. I was at someone's *house*, all casual, like it was normal for me.

"You good?" Travis asked.

I am exceptional. "Yeah," I said. "You?"

He nodded slowly. "Not bad."

"Mum says we can Deliveroo food on her account," Flick announced. "Don't get too excited—it's just a one-off to celebrate starting sixth form, and we've got, like, a limit of about thirty quid for all of us. And it has to involve fries, because I want fries."

I felt an instant jolt of nerves for being the extra person that Flick's mum probably hadn't factored into this offer. Should I offer extra money? No, not in front of everyone. I'd see if I could get Flick on her own later and ask.

We ordered from Flick's preferred burger place and shared out the food when it arrived. The conversation had moved to how everyone felt about sixth form, how it compared to Eastridge, what their plans were for their futures. I kept quiet, listening, trying to decide if I should say "lawyer" or "artist" if they asked me what I was going to be. Which answer was cooler?

"Mum wants me to be a nurse, like her," Flick said, mouth full of fries. "But I'm like, no way. She works crazy hours. Like, crazy. And the job's nonstop, I swear. I don't think she even sits down. I want a job where I get free time, too. Maybe something to do with money, because money jobs make the most money. Right?" She looked expectantly at Eric, who nodded knowledgeably. "See?" she said to me, as if I'd contradicted her. "That's why I'm taking math," she added. "Even though I don't like math. It's a really good A Level to have for lots of good jobs." She tapped her forehead with one finger. "Smart."

"Aren't you failing?" Callum asked.

"Fuck off, no I'm not," she snapped, her annoyance genuine. "Why do you all think I'm so stupid?"

"It's, like, the third week of term," Eric said, almost lazily. "No one's failing yet."

In a lot of ways, Eric reminded me of my brother. He had that patronizing, almost smug, laid-back manner that came with being a middle-class white boy, especially one who had risk-free access—Eric through his own brother; Dillon through his friends—to drugs. He also treated me with the same brotherly condescension as Dillon did, though it felt less affectionate, being that he wasn't related to me and therefore hadn't earned the right to mock me. Dillon would never hurt me; would, in fact, throw himself in front of a bus for me, if I needed him to. Eric's protective streak was for Flick alone.

When the first joint came out that night, small in Eric's bearlike hand, and started making its way around the room, I didn't think twice about taking it when it got to me. "You sure?" Eric asked, affectedly amused.

I rolled my eyes at him, closing my lips around the joint. I was proud of myself for this oh-so-cool response. I'd already figured out, even then, how to handle Eric. He'd clearly assumed I was a good girl, and I was, but that was by circumstance, not choice. I didn't have any particular moral objection to things like weed or alcohol. I'd never gotten properly drunk because I had no one to get properly drunk with. (Bellinis with my grandmother in her garden in Cornwall didn't count, however fun it was.) I'd never tried weed because no one had ever offered it to me. (Dillon was too protective—and too cheap—to share any of whatever he took with his baby sister.) If anyone ever had offered, I would have said yes.

I'd made sure to watch everyone carefully as they inhaled so I had the best chance of doing it properly when it was my turn—I was determined not to cough—but I still made a mess of it, spluttering out smoke in a choked wheeze.

"Aw, a first-timer!" Callum said. "Cute."

"Peyton's *new*," Flick said, and her voice was almost possessive, which I loved. "Be nice."

Everything got a lot easier after that. The weed loosened us all up and then there was more alcohol, a games console wheeled out and connected to have something to focus on. I spoke to Travis for a while on the sofa, though I can't really remember what we talked about. It may have been Polos. Something to do with why exactly there was a hole in the middle, and if it was some capitalist trick to provide less product. Is that the kind of thing Travis and I would have talked about? It seems unlikely, but that whole night, that whole period of my life, seems unlikely now.

We ended up in the kitchen together, him and me. He was showing me where the glasses were so I could have some water. I made some kind of joke about high-ball glasses and being high that must have been terrible but nevertheless made him laugh like he thought I was actually funny. And then he said, "You're funny," like he hadn't thought I would be. I took my time pouring water into my glass, taking a few sips, trying out responses in my mind.

I could feel him looking at me, and when I glanced at him his lips twitched into a smile. Somewhere inside me, some instinct that had been dulled by years without use flickered into life. If I flirted with Travis, acted like I really liked him, made him feel like I wanted him, he'd flirt and like and want me back. And if all of that happened, he could be my boyfriend. And if he was my boyfriend, his friends would be my friends. No more worrying about keeping Flick's attention, or that she or all of them would get tired or bored of me. If I belonged to Travis, I would belong to the group.

I smiled. I let myself lean back a little against the counter so he'd seem taller.

"Hey, there's more to me than neat handwriting."

He laughed again. His eyes kept traveling to my lips—probably because I kept licking them so they'd be wet and glistening. "Seems like it."

"Are you surprised?"

He nodded.

"I like surprising you," I said.

"Yeah?"

I felt so powerful in that moment. I had him so entirely, that's how it felt. The way he was looking at me, the electricity between us. All of that potential and power, crackling under our words. We were going to kiss and it was inevitable and I was standing in the doorway of everything I'd ever wanted. He could take my hand and walk me through.

I was giddy, reckless. I could say I didn't feel like myself, but that wasn't it at all. I felt more like myself than I had for years and years. I said, "Kiss me, then."

It wasn't exactly epic, that first kiss. Not just *our* first kiss, but *my* first kiss. Our lips collided more than anything else. His tongue slid immediately into my mouth—no soft, close-lipped kisses first, no building to The Tongue—and began darting around like it was looking for something. It was all I could do to keep up. I had a vague idea I was meant to kiss *back,* but in the moment I wasn't sure exactly what that meant, not when my mouth seemed full of his tongue and mine could barely move. I moved my body a little closer to his, pressing myself up against him, and that must have been the right thing to do because his arm curled around the back of my neck, mashing our faces even closer together.

I'm not sure how long we stayed there, kissing, but it was probably a while. At one point, someone stumbled into the kitchen, let out a loud "Whoops! Sorry!" and left again. I think it was Flick. Eventually we went back to the living room and Travis squeezed my hand before letting it go—he'd held it all the way from the kitchen—and sat on the floor beside Nico, who slapped him on the back and handed him a controller. Flick and Eric were nowhere to be seen. When I asked Casey where they were, everyone laughed.

It got later; I got sleepier. Between games, Travis sat on the sofa and tugged me onto his lap, where I curled against him like I belonged. Flick and Eric returned, arguing lightly about what time it was, a wide smile on her face. Travis got up to hand Eric a beer, and Flick sat beside me on the sofa, slouching herself down with a loud, contented sigh, lifting her feet to lean against my legs. It was so cozy it made me want to cry. I never, ever wanted to move. The whole world was fuzzy and warm. My friends—*my friends*—were all clustered around me, their conversations a low, easy hum. A voice—I wasn't sure who it belonged to—called, "You out, Pey-Pey?" I waved a vague hand in response, and everyone laughed. Flick's voice, indulgent: "Shh, let her sleep."

I was there. I'd made it.

NOW

VANCOUVER

By the morning, the adrenaline that had propelled me out of the hostel games room and into my dorm room bed has long faded, leaving me in the cold sink of reality. And that is me, fully dressed under thin hostel covers in a hostel bed on the wrong side of the world, the same me I was before, the same me I'll always be. The me that completely freaked out in front of the best people I'd ever met, the ones who'd probably thought I was normal, maybe even a bit cool. Impulsive, maybe, but in a good way.

But no, I've revealed myself. I'm just a teenager who can't handle literally anything. I can't handle not having friends, or having friends, or making friends or keeping friends. Because did Beasey *actually* try and kiss me, or did I jump to the most extreme, unlikely conclusion when he thought we were just having a normal conversation?

Oh my God, I literally pushed him away, didn't I? And basically screamed in his face. And then ran out of the room. And hid.

Why did I leave home? To escape. But I brought the biggest problem with me: *myself.*

I burrow myself down deeper, my face burning hot against the sheets. I'm an unsalvageable disaster. I don't deserve to have friends.

After a few minutes of self-pity/loathing, I find my phone where it's wedged between the mattress and the bunk frame, lighting the screen to see messages waiting for me. Even though I know that none of the Vancouver crew have my number, I still feel a burst of hope that it's one of them. But the messages are from Dillon, asking me how I am, whether I've seen a whale yet, if I've learned to speak French.

Me:

**Was this a crazy thing to do?
Should I just come home?**

Dillon:

Yes. No.

Me:

Which way round?

Dillon:

**You know which way round.
Everything OK, P?**

I consider how to respond to this. No, everything's not okay, but I can't really remember the last time it was, at least not before I got to Canada, and I thought that was going to be okay, but now it isn't, and it's my fault, and maybe this is going to be the pattern of my life, and that is so scary I don't know what to do with it.

Me:

I don't know what I'm doing.

Dillon:

Then figure it out. Make a plan. If I was in Canada right now, I'd go to Tim Hortons for breakfast. And then I'd go and see an ice hockey game.

Me:

On your own?

Dillon:

No, with you, you idiot.

Me:

Talking with Dillon like this, it's so familiar. There was a time when he was my only friend—which didn't really count because he was also my brother—and it was always him I'd talk to when I was feeling anxious or low, worrying about my lack of friends, how much I hated what I was studying at college, how lost I felt. And now I've flown across the world, and our dynamic is just the same. Him offering advice; me flailing around in my own life.

But he's right; I should make a plan. A small plan for today, and then a proper one for this whole mess of a trip I'm trying to take. I'll figure out where to go after Vancouver and how to get there, and that'll be a start. No more friend-shaped distractions. Especially not the adorable, Scottish-accented type, who probably kisses as sweetly as he smiles—

No. Stop. For God's sake, Peyton.

I skip breakfast rather than face anyone, instead taking my phone and sketch pad across the road to the Starbucks where I research public transport to Calgary for ten minutes and then sketch my cartoon-self riding a moose across the Rockies for the rest of the hour. Maybe it's not all that productive, but it's much nicer than the heart palpitations brought on by finding out the cost of getting to Calgary. And that's not even halfway across the country. It's barely a *third* of the way.

I'm feeling more lost than I did when I started, trying to remember what the point of all this was. So far, this trip hasn't looked like I'd imagined it would. Wide-open spaces, minimal people, mountains to climb—that's what I'd expected. But Vancouver is a huge, sprawling urban city, and Calgary will probably be that too, so why exactly do I want to go there? Maybe I should go . . . north? Am I already north? How north do you have to get before you're properly *north*?

"Excuse me." A voice comes from above me and I jump, dropping my phone onto the table. I look up, dazed, to see a woman trying to squeeze past my chair.

"Oh," I say, flustered. "Sorry."

When she's gone—"I love your accent!"—I blink myself back to reality. Of course I can't randomly go *north*, whatever that even means. Get a grip, Peyton. All I need to do is make a plan, just a small one, like Dillon said, to get myself back on track. I think about the guys talking about Vancouver Island, telling me that I should go. Obviously, I can't go with them, but I can go on my own, can't I? Yes. That's the answer. I will plan a mini trip-within-a-trip. Vancouver is huge and urban and overwhelming, but Vancouver *Island* will be smaller, more manageable. It will have all of the good bits—beautiful scenery, wildlife, beaches, places to explore—and none of the stress. Or less of the stress, anyway. There, I will learn how to travel independently, like I'd planned. And then, once I've learned that, I'll put it into practice and start making my way across Canada.

It's a great plan. I feel calmer just thinking about it, marking off places I want to visit and planning an itinerary. I'm actually quite proud of myself, and it's a good distraction from thinking about everyone else, who I studiously avoid when I get back to the hostel in the early evening. I tell myself that they probably haven't even noticed my absence, because we're just traveling friends, aren't we? We're not obligated to spend time with each other. I'm just another random girl in a youth hostel.

"Hey, Peyton!"

I freeze, still facing the vending machine, where I've been trying to choose between a Wunderbar and a Mr. Big—both sound amazing—and force a smile on my face before I turn and see Khalil approaching.

"Oh," I say. "Um. Hi."

"Hey," he says again. He's smiling a small, quizzical smile. "Where have you been? You disappeared."

"Just around," I say, wanting to sound casual, failing hard. "Exploring, you know . . ."

His eyebrow raises, his smile quirks, and I flush with embarrassment. He saw me run out of the room that night, probably heard me shriek at Beasey. And no doubt Beasey would have told him how I reacted at the maybe-probably-not kiss attempt. They've probably been laughing about it.

"But you're okay?" he asks. "You're doing all right? Beasey was—"

"I'm fine," I interrupt, a little too loudly. "I've been planning my trip. Figuring it out, like you all said I should."

He nods. "Okay, cool. We can help with that, though. Seva knows Canada really well, and Lars and Stefan are also figuring out how to get to Banff—"

"I'm fine," I say again, barely listening, because it's hard to concentrate when the residual mortification I'd tried to forget is screaming through my head. "I'm going to Vancouver Island, actually. Tomorrow."

I've surprised him. "Oh," he says. "Really?"

"Yeah, you guys all made it sound so great."

"You don't want to wait one more day and come with us?" he asks.

"I kind of want to do this on my own," I say. "I mean, that's why I'm here."

Khalil doesn't reply for a moment, like he's thinking about what to say. When he speaks, his voice is a little flat, but somehow gentle. "To be on your own."

I swallow, then nod. "Well, yeah."

"Okay, well, at least take my number, and I'll take yours, so you'll know there's someone nearby you can call if you need to. And I'll check in to make sure you're okay, otherwise I'll worry. We all will." He pulls out his phone and looks at me expectantly.

"Why?" I ask.

This time, he rolls his eyes. "God, because we're decent human beings? I don't know, Peyton."

I'm acting stupid, and now I'm annoying him. But no one's ever said they'd worry about me before, at least not someone who didn't share my surname. It's not my fault I don't know how to react; I never learned how.

Of course I don't say this. I take out my phone and we exchange numbers, he tells me to have a good trip and I say the same. There's an awkward pause, and so I say, "Which chocolate bar should I get?" and gesture at the vending machine. "Mr. Big or Wunderbar?"

"Both," he says. "Life's too short to pick just one."

In the morning, before I check out of the hostel, I decide to stop into the reading room to see if they have any tourist leaflets for Vancouver Island. I've already walked all the way in before I see Seva, sitting at one of the desks with his laptop. He smiles at me and says hello as if everything is normal, like I haven't been avoiding him like a little weirdo for the last couple of days.

"Hi," I say. "Can I ask about the clothes?"

He glances down at himself and laughs. He's wearing a suit jacket and tie, as smart as if he were going for a job interview, but his bottom half is a pair of jeans. "I have a Skype interview in twenty minutes," he says. "A company in Toronto. They will only see me from the chest upward."

"Oh, cool," I say. "What's the job?"

"It is not interesting," Seva says with another laugh. "Web design; a short contract, just a few months."

"Is that what you do?" I ask. "Web design?"

He nods. "Among other things."

"I thought you were traveling," I say. "Like the guys."

"I am," he says. "I work and travel. If I do not do one, I cannot do the other." He smiles at the look that must be on my face. "Adulthood, it comes for everyone. What have you been doing?"

"Exploring," I say, wondering if he's spoken to Beasey and

Khalil, imagining them all hanging out like normal people while I've been shutting myself away for what must seem like no good reason. I feel a pang I try to ignore. "I'm going to Vancouver Island later."

"With Beasey and Khalil?"

I shake my head, willing my cheeks not to redden. "Just me."

His forehead crinkles, like he's confused, but he doesn't question me further. He just says, "That will be fun. I wish I was also going."

"Why can't you?"

"Money, time," he says, lifting his hands in a shrug. "If I get this Toronto job, I can know I will have income soon, so I will be able to relax. But if not, I will need to find another job, apply, have an interview. It all takes time."

It all sounds so grown-up. It makes me feel stupid and young, floundering around trying to figure out what I'm doing. He must think I'm such a child.

"Well, good luck," I say a little awkwardly. "With the interview."

He smiles. "Thank you, Peyton. And have a good time on the Island."

It occurs to me when I'm back in my room, packing up my bag and making sure I haven't left anything behind, that I might never see Seva again. Or Khalil, or any of them. It's weird to think how transitory all of this is, that even if I had made more of an effort to make friends, we would still have separated eventually. It seems like even more of a reason to keep myself at a distance, because what's the point of making friendships when they can't last?

Later, when I'm waiting for a bus, Mum calls. Her voice

is so familiar. She wants to know everything about the trip, where I'm staying, where I'll go. She's calmed down a little since I've been here, but she still doesn't believe I really can do this on my own. I listen patiently while she lists all her worries, telling me again that I should just come home.

"Is Dad there?" I ask, when we've talked for a while.

There's a pause. "He doesn't want to talk right now," she says.

"Oh," I say.

"He's very frustrated," she says. "I don't think it's a good idea for you to talk to him while he's in this mood."

"Because I'm going to Vancouver Island?"

"Because of everything," she says. "We had another email from your college today. They're still expecting that you'll be going back imminently."

"Why?" I ask, trying not to get frustrated myself. "Why are they thinking that? I've said that I'm not going to go back at all, let alone imminently. I'm not even coming home imminently."

"Okay, Peyton," she says, very tiredly. "Please don't use that tone with me."

"Can you just please try to explain to him that I mean it about dropping out of college?"

"No," she says. "Because I don't want you to drop out of college, either. There's no harm in you taking a bit of extra time to think about it."

I close my eyes, grinding down on my teeth, then letting out a low sigh. "Fine."

"I know that you're thinking of this as some kind of . . . break," she says. "But that's just not how life works, Peyton. You can't just take breaks from your life. This is your future. You can't risk it all for a holiday in Canada."

"That's not what this is."

"It looks an awful lot like it from this side of the world," she says, and I roll my eyes so hard it almost hurts. "Your father and I have been more than fair. We've been incredibly understanding. But you can't expect us to support you doing something as drastic as dropping out of college and derailing your future. We're your parents. It's our job to think long term."

"I am thinking long term," I say. "And it'll be a long-term life of misery if I finish these A Levels and go to uni to study something I don't want for a career I don't want. Why won't you listen to me? It's not derailing—it's switching tracks." I'm so impressed with myself for coming up with such a great analogy right on the spot that I almost want to write it down. "If I have to stay away long enough for you to finally realize that, then I will."

"Don't you do that, Peyton. Don't you put that on us."

"I'm not putting anything on you," I say. "I'm just asking you to listen to me. You're still not doing that."

She doesn't speak for a long time, and when she does, her voice is defeated. "Okay. We're not getting anywhere here. I hope you have a nice time on Vancouver Island."

I swallow. My eyes are stinging. "I'll send you another postcard."

"Another one?"

"Yeah, I sent one on my first day," I say. "Hasn't it arrived yet?"

"The post hasn't come yet today," she says. "I'll look forward to getting it."

There's a silence. "Okay," I say. "I love you."

"I love you too," she says.

NOW

VANCOUVER ISLAND

Vancouver Island, I discover, is beautiful. It rains almost constantly the first couple of days I'm there, but even that can't dampen how beautiful it is, which says a lot. As I explore, the scenery unfolds before me under the frame of my umbrella, where I'm often hunched, trying to sketch what I see and protect the paper from raindrops at the same time. Victoria, the capital of British Columbia, is a big city, but in comparison to Vancouver's urban sprawl, it's almost homey. I don't get lost on the buses once, and I manage to make my way around the south of the island, ticking off visiting spots on my list, pretty easily. On paper, it's perfect: I'm doing exactly what I'd planned to do when I was sitting on the plane. I'm an independent traveler; bold and brave.

But here's the thing. You know what traveling alone actually is? Lonely. Really, really lonely. And honestly, kind of boring, too. After three days of just me and my own head and no one to talk to, even as everything around me is so amazing, the idea of going across the whole of this giant country on my own is starting to seem less and less of a good idea. I'd hoped I'd settle into it by now, but I haven't, not really. Sometimes I wonder if I want to go home, but that seems more and more impossible, too. What would I do when I got back? Apologize to my parents, let them force me back into college because I have no other choice, fall back into the same misery I was trying to escape? And I'd have nothing to show for it.

So I carry on, doggedly exploring Victoria and its surroundings. Every day I get a message from Khalil, **Still alive?** and I smile every time as I reply, **Yes, Khalil.** If I'm totally honest with myself, I know I'm letting my pride stop me from doing what I deep-down-honestly-really want to do, which is tell Khalil that he was right and I'm lonely and can we please be friends.

After a few days, the restless, lost feeling that had taken over me in Vancouver is back, maybe even stronger than it was before. I want to step out of my skin, parachute out of my life, be someone else. Going somewhere else wasn't enough, clearly. It's me that's the problem. Me I can't escape.

So I decide to go on a day trip to Salt Spring Island, which is one of the smaller islands off the coast. I have to get a bus to the harbor, and it occurs to me on the journey that the reasoning I'd used for this trip is almost exactly the same as the reasoning I used to get me to Vancouver Island in the first place. A smaller island will be more manageable, I'd thought. It will make it clearer why I'm here. And now that's exactly why I'm going to Salt Spring Island. What am I going to do— keep finding smaller islands until I stop feeling overwhelmed in my own life?

I shake the thoughts out of my head. This is just a day trip to a pretty place. It's a totally normal thing to do as a visitor to Vancouver Island. In fact, it would be weirder if I came here and *didn't* visit Salt Spring Island. There—that's solid logic. Well done, Peyton.

I've got time to kill at the harbor before my boat leaves,

so I explore the terminal, where I end up buying a gigantic bag of kettle corn because the seller lets me try some when he hears my accent, and I love it so much I can't leave without taking some with me. It seems like a quirky, fun thing to do until I'm sitting on the boat, by myself, with a huge plastic bag of popcorn on my lap and no one to share it with. If I had a friend, we could talk between fistfuls of corn, chucking pieces at each other, trying to catch them in our mouths. We'd take pictures posing with the bag and post them on Instagram with captions like, **Hand included for scale! #CORNY**

Instead, I'm just on my own, and it doesn't taste as good as it did when I was talking to the friendly kettle-corn guy. Now I've got to carry the whole damn thing around with me for the entire day. Why didn't I get it on the way back? Why can't I get anything right?

Near the front of the boat, I see the sloping back of a tall guy with black curls out of the corner of my eye, and my heart leaps with an excitement that surprises me. *Khalil?* If it's Khalil, I can go up to him, grinning, all cool and confident. "Fancy seeing you here," I'll say. If he's here, Beasey will be, too. They'll help me eat the popcorn. When they laugh at me for buying such a big bag for one person, I'll laugh, too. We can all spend the day together on the island and *what a relief I don't have to spend another day alone—*

The owner of the black curls turns slightly and it's not him. Of course it isn't. I deflate with disappointment, the hope of the day fading in an instant. Khalil had messaged me this morning, right on schedule, as he had each day I'd been here. **Still alive?** I'd replied, **Yeeees.** He'd said, **Beasey says hi!**

A stab of loneliness guts into me and I cram a handful of popcorn into my mouth. There's a couple on the boat near me who seem around my age, having the kind of hushed, gritted-teeth conversation you have in public when what you really want is a private argument. When she turns away from him to look out to sea, he rolls his eyes at her back. Not for anyone's benefit—he doesn't know I'm watching—but because whatever he's feeling inside has spilled out, uncontrollable.

Of course I think about Travis and me. We must have had a hundred interactions like that over our year together as a couple. God, a year. An entire *year.* How did that *happen?*

I know how it happened. I know exactly how it happened, because it was all me. I was the one desperate to be in a relationship with Travis because I was convinced that being his girlfriend was some kind of shortcut to having friends. That is, Flick, Eric, Casey, Callum, and Nico. That group of diamonds.

Now it's me rolling my eyes, except I'm on my own and I'm doing it into thin air. Or maybe at myself. Had I really believed it was that simple? Did I not give myself a second, not once, to think, *Are these really the friends I actually want?*

No. No, I did not.

BEFORE

aka

Peyton and Travis: The Love(ish) Story

aka

Peyton, what the hell were you thinking??

I threw myself at Travis, that's the truth. Wholeheartedly. After those first kisses in Flick's kitchen, we entered that in-between period that seems short in retrospect but felt endless at the time. We chatted over WhatsApp—who knows what we had to talk about then, but I still remember that buzz of hope every time I looked at my phone, hoping for a new message from him—and shared secret, flirty smiles at college. He'd bump my elbow and wink at me in math. A couple of times after our last class of the day, we "took a walk" together, which meant going to the nearest park and kissing on the grass. Those were good kisses, long and slow, the kind that made my heart race. It was all good, actually, but I was still nervous, desperate to have the solidity of a relationship.

Travis really likes you! Flick messaged me, about a week after that night at her house.

I like him sooo much! I replied. Did I mean it then? I can't quite believe that I could have, but maybe I did. Maybe I'd been able to focus on how sweet his smile could be, how good those kisses were, how my whole body warmed up when he took my hand and held it as we walked.

She sent me heart-eyes back. Emboldened, I messaged Travis.

Me:

Thinking about you :)

Travis:

Oh yeh? Thinking what? ;)

Me:

Wouldn't you like to know.

I surprised myself with how good I was at playing the game. I'd learned so much from the books I'd read and the films I'd seen, and it paid off with Travis. Too well, really. I think I got so into following the script I knew so well that I forgot that both Travis and I were real people. I remember how, in those early days, I'd look up and see him next to me, and the reality of him would almost make me jump. I preferred him on the other end of a WhatsApp conversation, just words and emojis and potential.

After a couple of weeks of the in-between, Travis asked me round to his on a Saturday afternoon. (His parents would be out, he assured me.) When I arrived he poured me a glass of lemonade and took me into the living room, which was a sweeter alternative to the beer-and-bedroom scenario I'd been half expecting. He put something on Netflix and started to kiss me and that's how we spent the next hour, the TV and lemonade ignored, buried in each other.

I'm not going to say it didn't feel good. It felt *really* good. He still kissed with too much tongue, but I'd learned how to move my own gently enough to slow his down. We kissed with our eyes closed, so I almost forgot it was Travis I was kissing and went off into my own vague daydream. It didn't matter who I was kissing; it mattered that I was kissing. When his hands went wandering, I liked that too.

We took a break to come up for air. I gulped down some lemonade and smiled at him when he smiled at me. I think we may have talked for a little bit, but if we did, I don't remember what we said. I put the glass down, he reached for me again, and then his hand was working at the zip on my jeans as he kissed me, his tongue wild in my mouth. Wilder than usual, just by the prospect of touching me. It was strangely gratifying, being wanted like that. Even as my heart thundered with a mix of excitement and dread, even as I wished this was all happening with someone else, I still wanted him to touch me. I wanted to feel in his touch how touching me affected him. It was intoxicating. Is that what people mean by being turned on? In that moment, the first time Travis pawed at me, I thought I understood it.

His hand had found its way inside my jeans, and he was rubbing at me through my underwear, and the biggest surprise was that it did feel good. It felt really good. But then he was wrenching my underwear aside, fingers scrabbling, and he was almost grunting into my mouth. His fingers seemed so much bigger than they did when he held my hand, so . . . fingery. Weird and uncomfortable. Poking, jabbing and—*ouch!*—pushing inside me. It didn't feel really good anymore. I wanted the rubbing back.

He'd leaned back slightly to look at me, and I gathered by his face that this was the bit that was meant to be good, that he was expecting something from me. Jab, jab, jab. "You love it," he said.

I really didn't, but it was confusing, that's the thing. I'd never done anything like this before, and he had, so he'd know, right? This was clearly meant to feel good, and if it didn't, that must be my fault.

"Mmmm," I said.

He was looking at me so intensely, waiting for something, but all the intoxicating want I'd had in me before had gone. It was just the physical—very weird—reality of his fingers moving inside me. He was clearly still into it, and what if he realized I wasn't?

Distraction. That was the solution. I put my hand on him, on his jeans between his legs, and he let out a noise, nodding hard. I unzipped, pushed my hand in, found his erection. I wanted him to tell me what to do, but he didn't—he just looked at me expectantly. I moved my hand, almost like a question, and he groaned quietly, biting his lip. Everything about it felt strange and weird, but I carried on, encouraged by the way his breathing changed, how he dropped his head between my shoulder and my neck, like he was surrendering himself to me and my touch.

It didn't take long. I felt his body spasm, heard his groan, felt something hot and wet on my hand. He turned his head to kiss me, sloppy and wet. "You're amazing," he said. I'd never been amazing before. I kissed him back, and it felt good again.

Another two weeks after that, weeks that included a couple of nights spent at Flick's and further experimentation in the locked bathroom with the light off, he invited me to his house again. This time we graduated to his bedroom— his parents somewhere else, which is how he always timed my visits—and his bed. First on top of the covers, lying underneath him with the mattress below me and my body on fire with nerves and anticipation, and then under the covers, layers slowly removed, him with an impatience I knew he was trying to hide, and then sex, brief and painful, the ultimate anticlimax. He held me after and stroked my hair and said he was sorry it had hurt, that it would get better. He said, "Will you be my girlfriend?"

And I smiled so wide and said yes, and he kissed me, and it was all so, *so* worth it.

If this all sounds like it was very fast, then yes, it was—barely a month from never been kissed to devirginized in my boyfriend's bed—but it really didn't feel it at the time. It felt like exactly the right thing to do, not just because it was inevitable but because it was what I wanted. A way to secure the deal, you know? Like putting a deposit down on a house. I know how terrible that sounds, maybe even ridiculous, but I have to be honest about how I was then, how my mind worked when it came to Travis and the group. I think I would have done just about anything to get what I thought I wanted.

And I had it, didn't I? Everything I'd ever wanted. It had gone even better than I'd dreamed it would. I had a boyfriend and a group of friends, people who smiled when they saw me and made room for me to sit down beside them and added me to their group WhatsApp chat. No one was bullying me or even giving me a hard time. Victim Peyton was a thing of the past; a Claridge Academy relic. I'd made it.

But here's the thing: I didn't *feel* happy. Not really. I was surface-happy, sure. But it was a desperate kind of happiness; there was something almost frantic about it. It made me think of a toddler chasing butterflies. I couldn't depend on it, and there was nothing I could do to control it or be sure it was safe.

If I'm going to talk in "should haves," this would be the

moment I'd start. I should have been able to talk about my feelings with my boyfriend, to begin with. And I definitely should have been able to talk about them with my friends— isn't that why people *have* friends? Maybe not the group as a whole, but definitely Flick, who I already thought of—though nervously, silently, like I wasn't really allowed—as my closest friend. I don't know what Flick would have done if I *had* tried that level of honesty with her, but I never did. For one thing, it would have involved telling her where I'd come from, who I'd been, and that was unthinkable. How do you tell someone you want so desperately to like you that you haven't been liked in the past? How can you put that thought into their head, that maybe you aren't likable, and maybe they shouldn't like you either?

They all knew I'd come from Claridge Academy, and even that I'd left because I hated it there, but they didn't know I'd been bullied so relentlessly, and no one ever asked why I didn't talk about former friends. Maybe they were sensitive, or maybe they just didn't care. Only Casey ever came close to knowing, but she never pushed me for more, and as far as I know she never told any of the others. That's another one of my "should haves," actually. Casey. Why did I pin so much of my friend hope on Flick? Casey was right there.

Anyway, that flighty happiness, it was like trying to catch a flame in your hand. It was beautiful, and it was there, but it was fleeting, too dangerous to look at too closely, let alone touch. The only way to hold on to it was to let it burn into me, scarring some part of me I couldn't see but would feel forever, a tender point I would never be able to forget even after it had gone.

Which, of course, is what I did.

NOW

SALT SPRING ISLAND

Salt Spring Island is beautiful. So beautiful it calms my frazzled head, soothing the heat from my face and my hands. If anything is going to make it all worth it, it's places like this. This is why I came here.

It's hours until the last boat back to Vancouver Island, so I can take my time. I explore a few of the shops and stalls near the harbor before I get a bus to Ganges, the largest village on the island. I spend a calm couple of hours meandering around the streets, finding a postcard for my parents and sketching myself happier than I am for them, eating alone at a cafe, staring out at the street.

I leave myself plenty of time to return to the harbor before the boat is due to leave, getting off the bus several stops early so I can head toward the coast and see the beach. I have to walk through forest to get there, and I try to appreciate it as I go, anchoring myself in the moment like mindfulness tells you to, breathing in the cleanest air I've probably ever breathed, listening to the birds.

When I get to the beach, I explore the rock pools for a while before settling myself on a rock overlooking the sea and taking out my sketch pad. I touch my pencil to the paper and let my mind clear, sweeping across the page. I draw what I see in quick, bold strokes, then turn the page, draw myself on the boat, popcorn in lap, my face glum, chewing. Me on this rock, the island a backdrop behind me. I look back over the last few days' worth of sketches, filling them in with extra details. I'll make a map, I decide, of Vancouver Island, and add my sketches from place to place. And then, depending on how far across Canada I actually get, I'll sketch a map of the whole of Canada, like Joni Mitchell did in that song my mum loves.

I sketch Mum and me in her car. She's driving, I'm in the passenger seat, both of us singing. It makes me homesick. I turn the page.

It's a long time before I gather myself up and head back toward the main path I'd been following before. So long that my legs feel stiff. I hug my sketch pad to me as I walk, my one true faithful companion. Wherever I am, alone or not, my hand still draws the same, my sketches are still me and mine. That's something, isn't it? I can be lonely, but at least I have art. What was it Amber Monroe used to say? *"Maybe you should draw yourself some friends."* Well, maybe that was good advice.

I've been mindlessly wandering through the trees, waiting for the path to appear, for quite a long time before I realize that I should have found it by now. I hesitate, glancing around me. Have I been here before? These trees look familiar. But then again, trees are trees. They probably all look familiar.

"Don't panic," I say out loud. My voice is too loud against the quiet, and it startles me, and then I'm embarrassed.

I turn in a slow circle, trying to think rational thoughts. This is an island. There's only so much lost I can be. I decide to walk in one direction, back toward where I think the water's edge is, and then reorientate myself from there.

Except I don't. I walk for ages and the water's edge doesn't appear. Finally, finally, I give in and turn on data while roaming, which I've had off the entire time I've been in Canada because I've got no idea how much data would cost, and I can only imagine how my dad would react if he saw the fees come up on the family data plan. But this is an emergency now. My breaths are coming out all scratchy and my neck feels hot. WhatsApp messages and emails start coming through but I swipe them all away, opening Google Maps and loading up the directions from where I am to where I need to be.

Forty-minute walk. It's a forty-minute walk. Oh my God. I look at the time again, even though I know what it is: 4:28 p.m. I have thirty-two minutes to get to the boat. The last boat of the day. If it goes without me, I'll be stuck here, knowing no one, with nowhere to stay.

I squeak out a panicked "What?" at my phone, as if that will change the time or the distance to the harbor. And then I start to run. My rucksack bangs heavily against my back, the sketch pad I've been hugging to myself for the last hour slippery in my sweaty hands. After a few minutes I have to stop, gasping and crying, to shove the sketch pad safe into my bag and take out the popcorn instead.

It's 5:04 p.m. when I come tearing down the road toward the terminal, sweat covering every inch of me, the popcorn bag bouncing in my hand. I've lost all sense of pride and decorum and am yelling, "Wait! *Wait!*" at the boat, which hasn't left but is fully loaded up and clearly about to depart. Every head in view turns toward me. Smirks. Winces of sympathy. Judgment.

"Don't worry," the boat guy says cheerfully as he holds out a hand to me. "You made it."

I burst into tears as I stumble onto the boat and he recoils, alarmed. "Thank you," I manage. "Thank you so much."

I collapse into a seat, fully wheezing, pulling the hood of my coat up over my face to protect myself from the stares even though I've never been so hot and sweaty in my life. That and mortified. And tired. And so *sick* of being lonely in Canada. No one to laugh with in the good moments, no one to yell at when things go wrong, no one to build stories and memories with.

Remember when you almost missed the boat on Salt Spring Island? I'll say to . . . myself. Quality anecdote. Truly a keeper.

I want to laugh, but instead I just continue to cry. There on the boat under my hood, the popcorn bag sweating in my tightly clenched fist. I've come all this way, and for what? What have I got to show for it? *Nothing.*

I was meant to be seeing how far east across Canada I could go, and instead I'm more west than I was when I started. Recoiling from the hugeness of the country into the relative safety of the islands at its edges. What have I learned? What have I gained? All these things I've seen, the photos I've taken . . . what's the point? I'm alone in all of them. No one to show them to or share the screen with. I'm creating memories, but they're just *my* memories. There'll be no reminiscing, no anecdotes shared and treasured.

I could have done all of this with Khalil and Beasey, like they'd suggested. The only reason I haven't is me. Now I'm alone on the boat, sweating and miserable, the wasted opportunity seems huge, and the embarrassment that drove me away seems tiny. It *is* tiny. Okay, I probably looked a bit stupid, shrieking and running away like that, but is that a reason to exclude myself completely from what could have been something great? No, obviously. One event doesn't have to define a friendship. Maybe if I'd figured that out in school instead of freaking out publicly every time something went wrong, things might have been easier.

It's not too late to finally learn this lesson, is it? *Come on, Peyton. Learn and grow, or whatever. You don't have to do this alone.*

I pull out my phone and open WhatsApp, looking at the cheerful messages from Khalil. **You alive? Beasey says hi!** I bite down on my lip. *Come on, Peyton. At least ask.* **Hey**, I write. **How's Victoria for you guys?**

I watch one tick transform into two, then turn blue.

Hey! *Khalil is typing* . . . I wait, hopeful. **We're in Tofino now!**

My heart sinks. I'm too late. **Oh cool! Have a great time.**

We only just arrived today. Here for a few days. You at a loose end? If you can get to Tofino, come join us! There's a bus from Victoria. We've got space in the Airbnb.

Immediately, my head says, *Pity invite.* It says, *They don't really want you there.* It says, *It's a trick.*

I shut my eyes, tight, then open them again. I type, **Let me find out about this bus** . . .

NOW

TOFINO

The bus ride to Tofino the next day takes almost seven hours, but I don't mind, even though it's too bumpy to sketch properly. I sit with my head resting back against my seat, watching Vancouver Island drift by. At some point, I fall asleep, dreaming a series of confused vignettes. Eric and Flick arguing on the Capilano Suspension Bridge. Beasey lounging on the sofa in the empty sixth form common room, his glasses pushed up over his hair. A plane swooping low, wingtip gliding through the calm water of Vancouver Harbor. Me walking alone down a rainy street, looking for someone, though I don't know who or where I am. Red and blue flashing lights somewhere in the distance.

When I wake up, I've got no idea where I am. It takes a while, orientating myself first on a bus and then Canada, then Vancouver Island. I look around and realize it's a refreshment stop; most of my fellow passengers have gotten off the bus in search of coffee. I stay where I am, because my knees feel weak, my throat tight.

Later, when we arrive in Tofino to a darkening sky, I'm aching all over, tired and grouchy. I'd told Khalil what time the bus was due in and he'd said they'd meet me, but we're later than scheduled and I'm expecting to have to call him. But when I stumble off the bus, I see not just him and Beasey but Lars and Stefan, too. And beside Khalil is a girl I assume must be Heather, the one he'd detoured to Canada to see. She has bright red hair, a wide smile.

When they see me, a cheer goes up, followed by laughter. I know it's for effect, as much a joke for them to share as anything else, barely anything to do with the reality of me, but I'm beaming as I walk over to them, shrugging my rucksack onto my back. I want to say, *You're here! You came to meet me! You see me! Thank you! Thank you, thank you, thank you.*

"Hi!" I say.

"Hiya," Khalil says, still laughing. "Welcome to Tofino."

"Want me to take that?" Beasey asks, hand already extending toward my bag.

"I'm okay, but thanks," I say, letting myself look at him properly as I speak, bracing myself for the belated awkwardness I'd been so scared to confront. But when our eyes meet, he just smiles a warm, easy smile. There's a brown smudge by his nose, and his red glasses are slightly crooked.

Something inside me gives a *swoop*. Possibly my stomach, possibly my heart. Unmistakable.

Oh no.

The Airbnb that is now also my temporary home is a ten-minute walk away, and they talk over each other the whole way, telling me about their time on the Island—Lars and Stefan had come straight to Tofino from Vancouver, because they'd visited Victoria already—and what they've got planned for the next few days.

"This place is blow-your-mind beautiful," Khalil says. "It's been two days and I want to move here."

"You said that about New Zealand," Beasey says. "Not even just a town in New Zealand. The whole of New Zealand."

"I stand by that," Khalil says.

The Airbnb is right on the coast, and I'm promised gorgeous views across the water in the daylight. There's a bedroom free for me that had been, in theory, meant for Khalil, who of course has been sharing a room with Heather. (All the "friend" pretense has, apparently, been dropped entirely.) Heather is friendly and cheerful as she shows me around the house, telling me she's happy to have another girl around, making me promise to tell her if I need anything.

I unpack in the company of Stefan, who sits on my bed chatting happily about the days I've missed, asking me about Victoria, if I've been lonely on my own or if I preferred it.

"I'm so glad you came!" he says, lightly and sincerely. "We were saying, Lars and me, how it would be cool to hang out with you more."

For a moment, my brain does what it always does and wonders if he means it, if they really did have that conversation, whether it could possibly be true, but in the same moment I smile at him and he smiles back and I realize—honestly, it's like a mini epiphany—that it doesn't matter. He's saying it now, as part of his greeting in this new town in a country we're both visiting. It is a kindness, and I can be grateful and happy. It's allowed.

"Thanks," I say. "It'll be cool to hang out with you guys too."

He grins at me. "All the best people are adventurers."

Heather appears in the doorway, ducking her head around the door. "What do you fancy doing for dinner tonight, Peyton?" she asks. "We can go out, or if you're tired, Khalil was thinking of getting takeout?"

"Takeout sounds good," I say. "And I can go and get it, if

that's okay? I sat for so long on the bus, I could do with a bit of a walk."

"Cool," she says. "There's a grill nearby that does takeout. You and Beasey can go—he knows the way." When she says this, the corner of her smile twitches, but she doesn't say anything more, just bounds off into the living room, calling for Khalil and Beasey.

The idea of walking alone with Beasey is as exhilarating as it is terrifying. I find myself staring at my reflection in the bathroom for too long before we go, practicing what I'll say, how I'll apologize. But when I see him waiting for me in the hallway, and he smiles and says, "Ready to go?" the anxiety fades. It just does. There's something safe about him; the Travis I'd imagined in his face that night in the hostel was a trick I'd played on myself.

It's barely a ten-minute walk to the grill, and we've got plenty of time before our order will be ready for collection, so Beasey and I take it slowly, neither of us mentioning how I'd reacted in Vancouver, instead comparing notes on our respective Victoria trips. He tells me about the university Heather goes to, how he and Khalil had stayed in her flat and hung out with her friends. I tell him about Salt Spring Island and how I'd almost missed the boat, and he laughs and tells me that that's what travel buddies are for.

I sigh. "I know."

He glances at me, the toque he'd bought in Vancouver pulled snugly over his ears. There's a question on his face, and I know what's coming, so I smile a little, preparing myself.

"Is it okay if I ask?" he says, very cautiously.

"Why I was weird?" I'm aiming for ironic self-awareness, but I'm not sure it lands.

He shrugs, pushing his hands into the pockets of his coat. "Well, kind of, yeah. I thought we were all getting along pretty well, you know? And then suddenly . . ." He shrugs again, more awkward than I've ever seen him. "You . . . well . . . you weren't. You just disappeared."

This is a very nice way of saying, *You literally ran out on me and then avoided all of us for the next few days.*

"I'm sorry if I freaked you out," he adds when I don't say anything. "I would never have . . . you know, tried anything. If you didn't want me to, I mean."

"I know," I say quickly.

"But you went away," he says.

"That wasn't because of you," I say, hoping the dusk light is low enough that he won't notice my flaming cheeks. "It was me. I was so embarrassed that I . . . kind of freaked out a bit? And then I didn't know how to make it right again. So I stayed away."

"Because of me," he says.

"No," I say. "Look, this is all weird for me, okay? This whole thing. Being here, hanging out with you guys. I know it's easy for you, but it's not for me. I'm still trying to figure it all out."

I can tell he doesn't understand, but he nods. "Okay. Can I help?"

"You just being a nice guy helps," I say, then worry it sounds like I'm trying to flirt. "All of you. Nice people." God, I sound ridiculous. "Friends."

He's trying not to smile, and my cheeks burn even hotter. "We are your friends, yeah."

"Even though I acted so weird?"

"No one cares about that, Peyton, honest. It's not a big deal. And anyway, we're all here now, aren't we?" He waits until I nod before he says, "Did something happen before you left home? Something that made you worry about stuff like this?"

I wonder what he thinks he means by "stuff like this."

"Yeah," I say quietly.

"You want to talk about it?"

I open my mouth, but nothing comes out. I can't tell him. Of course I can't tell him. Tingles of residual humiliation alight in my chest, shame is a flood engulfing me. That's all done. It's done. It's *done*.

"Oh, hey," Beasey says, soft. "I'm sorry. You don't have to tell me."

All I need to say is, *I had some friends who turned out to be dicks, what a shame, haha*. I could make it sound like it isn't a big deal and there'd be no need to give any more details. It's normal to have fallouts, isn't it? I could just make it sound like one of them. But I can't. It hurts too much to even pretend.

"Is this the place?" I say, even though it's obvious we've reached the grill because we've come to a stop right outside the door.

Beasey nods. "I'm so hungry," he says, his voice relaxing into his usual casual tone. He gives me a small smile, so full of understanding I have to look away, and opens the door for me to walk through ahead of him.

BEFORE

aka

The one where Peyton finally has friends

aka

And everything works out

aka

lol no

"There you are." Flick's voice was a grumble as she threw herself into the chair beside me in the common room at the beginning of lunch, dropping her canvas bag on the table. It was late October, unseasonably warm, and she was wearing a short-sleeved, battered-looking Oasis T-shirt that I would later find out belonged to her mother. "I've been looking all over for you."

"Have you?" I asked, startled. I still hadn't gotten used to this; not just having a friend but *being* one. That someone might be looking for me. "Why?"

"Because I didn't know where you were," Flick said in her *duh* voice. "Eric's home sick today. Well, not actually sick. Just at home 'cause he's bored of here, he says. He does that sometimes." She rolled her eyes. "I was like, just come in for me, and he's all, you're not worth double English, and . . ."

I zoned out, even as I nodded sympathetically, because

Flick just wanted an audience, not an opinion. It still confused me how casually she shared the way Eric insulted her, as if she didn't realize it was weird. I'd thought at first she was doing it as a kind of cry for help, but when I'd asked about it she'd gotten defensive and annoyed, so I backed off.

"Where's Travis?" she asked.

"He had a free," I said. "So he's not coming back till after lunch."

"Okay," Flick said. "Cool, just you and me." She smiled, and the moment was so perfect I wanted to frame it and look at it every day. *Cool, just you and me. Smile.* "Want to go off-site for food? There are a few places down the parade."

"Sure," I said. "The deli?" They did doorstep sandwiches so packed with fillings you had to use two hands to eat them. Flick and I could sit on the wall by the parade, eating and talking. I could tease her for not eating her crusts, the way Eric did, but in a nice way.

Flick frowned. "I don't think I've got enough money for there."

"I'll pay," I said. It didn't occur to me then that the deli wasn't any more expensive than any of the other places on the parade, and the original suggestion had been Flick's, so what had she had in mind? All I cared about was the two of us sitting on that wall together.

She beamed. "You're the best. I'm so glad the boys aren't here. Let's go."

Flick-and-me time was my favorite. More than the group as a whole, more than being with Travis. For all people talk about girls needing boyfriends to validate them, no one really talks about how girls needs best friends for the same reason. Being chosen by Flick meant so much more to me than being chosen by Travis. (Maybe because Travis had been snared by me rather than chosen me, but whatever.) It's not like Flick and I had much in common—or anything really, if I think about it—but that never seemed to matter. Her attention was like sunshine, and when it was directed at me, I basked.

This was maybe because, a lot of the time, Flick didn't seem all that bothered whether I was there or not. Even when I was beside her, even when we were talking, her eyes were constantly searching out Eric in the same room, especially when we were outside of college. When he wasn't around, she was angsty, chewing on her lip, fiddling with her sleeves or the skin around her wrists. But when he was around, she didn't seem much more settled. Her energy was anxious, her smile too wide. They kissed obnoxiously on the sofa or in the corner of the room, his hands groping her body or wrapped in her hair. Sometimes they'd fight; loud yelling that filled the whole house. Flick would cry on me and I'd appease her, tell her Eric was a twat, an idiot, a dick, even as Casey rolled her eyes behind Flick's back and shook her head. I thought at the time Casey just didn't care as much as I did, that she was being bitchy and judgmental—I even *liked* being the one Flick cried on, thinking it said something about me and my worth as a friend. It took me a few months of experiencing the drama as regularly as clockwork to understand not just Casey and Flick but the whole dynamic.

In those earliest days, what I wanted was for Flick and Eric to break up so I could break up with Travis, and then Flick and I could be friends on our own. Maybe with Casey, too, if I could figure out if she liked me or not. But of course they never did break up, and the truth was Flick never seemed as interested in me as she was in those moments after a flight.

That was okay, though. It was still all worth it. Since Travis and I had become official, a big part of my anxiety had finally calmed itself down. I stopped worrying I was going to walk into the common room one day and be ignored by them all or that they wouldn't invite me for lunch. At weekends, I was with them, and even afternoons and evenings during the week, too.

We usually went to Flick's because she often had the house to herself, her mum seemingly constantly on shift. If we weren't at Flick's, we were at Eric's—he had a bigger house but more-present parents, so swings and roundabouts, as he'd say—but never anyone else's.

Mine was never an option, mostly because of my parents usually being around, but also because of what happened the first time I brought Flick round to my house, a couple of weeks after I first got with Travis, when I felt how she bristled as we walked up my driveway, saw the small frown on her face, heard the way her voice changed when she spoke.

When we got to my room I showed her the art studio my dad had made for me, converting what would have been an en suite into my cozy, white-washed haven, thinking she'd like to see the kind of drawing I did in there. But she just got very quiet, looking around. It got awkward, the two of us side by side as we walked back into my bedroom. Finally, she said, "I didn't realize you had money."

Had money. It was a phrase I didn't really understand, because I'd never thought of myself as "having money." We weren't *rich*, my family. Not in any definition of the word I'd understood before. Our house was nice and we went on holidays and both my parents had good jobs, but we weren't rich. I get now that having money and being rich aren't the same thing, and it's a distinction that requires the kind of perspective I didn't have yet. Claridge had been a grammar school and, in terms of socioeconomics, most of the kids there were like me. Or they were *actually* rich, like Amber Monroe.

"Not really," I said to Flick at the time, which was the wrong thing to say, though I don't think I realized that for a while.

She frowned at me. "I mean, yeah, you do." She gestured around my room, which as far as I was concerned was just my room. "You're lucky." She didn't say it in a way that made me feel very lucky. Besides, I was still fresh out of a five-year school experience that saw me essentially tormented. I *wasn't* lucky.

I could have told her that, but I didn't. I just shrugged and she shrugged back.

Friendship, I was discovering, didn't look like I'd expected it would. I'd imagined adventures together interspersed with emotional bonding, shared secrets and dreams, endless jokes. I thought they'd know me in a way no one else had before— especially Flick—and I'd know them in return.

But that's not how it was. For one thing, we never seemed to actually do anything or go anywhere together except each other's houses, and all they seemed to do was get drunk or high and play video games. They never really talked, either, except when the alcohol or drugs loosened their tongues, and then the conversations were rambling and ridiculous. An entire hour on why Flakes existed when Twirls were better in every way. Two on whether an afterlife existed and, if so, which scenario was most likely and, of those, where we'd all end up. ("Hell," Eric said confidently. "Every one of us." "Even me?" Flick asked. "Especially you," he said.) No one seemed to talk about their feelings or problems. No one asked about each other's lives.

A lot of the time, they didn't even seem to like each other very much. Especially Casey, who seemed to keep herself at a distance even when we were in the same room. It made me wonder if maybe I'd just been fooled all these years. Maybe friendship is just one giant con. Or maybe I really had just read too many books.

"I'm so glad college is going better for you than Claridge," Mum said to me once, the two of us watching *University Challenge* together on the sofa.

"Were you worried?" I asked.

"Yes," she said. I'd rather she'd lied. "But there was no need. You've got your friends now, and they're nice. They are nice?"

"Oh yeah," I said. "They're nice."

It wasn't a word I would have chosen myself, but I told myself I wouldn't have said they *weren't* nice, so it was accurate. What word would I have used? I wasn't sure. "Funny," maybe. "Friendly," in their way. "Mine." That was what mattered.

I didn't mind, that was the thing. It didn't matter that what I had didn't live up to my expectations; what mattered was that I had it. I would take fuggy evenings in Flick's living room, broken up by trips into the garden with Travis or runs to the off-licence that would serve us even though we were underage, so long as I was with them and not alone. I would have been whoever they wanted me to be. I didn't care what clothes I wore, what music I listened to, what drugs we took, how inexplicably sad I sometimes felt when I was back on my own.

And I didn't mind because of the moments. Moments like the earliest hours of Sunday morning, all of us together in Flick's living room. We'd reached the silly, shrieky part of our nights together, when everything was hilarious and no one in the world was having a better time.

"What kind of name is *Peyton*, anyway?" Flick asked. She got louder when she was high; more performative.

"A *great* name," I replied. I got so much more confident; smoother. I *loved* myself when I was high. In the warm fog of it all, I was convinced that my stoned self was the real me, the me I would have been if it wasn't for Amber Monroe and her merry band of twats.

(It wasn't even true. Generally speaking, I didn't like my name, because I was convinced that it had been part of the problem at Claridge. I was the only Peyton in the school, which made me stand out when it would have been so much easier to blend in.)

"Is it?" Flick said. "Is it *really*?"

"Your name is literally *Flick*," I said. "Flick! Like, flick away an ant."

"It's literally *not* literally Flick!" She was way too animated, bouncing up onto her knees, eyes wide. "It's *literally* Felicity."

"Oh, I'm so sorry!" I mock gasped. I reached out and flicked her forehead. *"Felicity."*

Everyone was in pieces by this point, including the two of us, flicking at each other and shrieking our names in increasingly ridiculous posh voices.

These were the moments when I was so happy, when it all felt so good and right, like I'd always imagined friendship would feel. When we laughed like idiots and teased each other and shared cheap frozen pizzas and took photos of Flick and me with our hair held up like mustaches and Casey played Elvis songs and we all danced to the JXL edit of "A Little Less Conversation" like nothing was wrong or could ever be wrong in the world.

Just moments, though. And that's all they were, in the end.

NOW

TOFINO

Tofino is my favorite place in Canada so far, and maybe that's because of who I'm with, but it's also because it feels exactly how you'd imagine a small beach town surrounded by wilderness, stuck right on the outer edge of the west coast of North America, with nothing ahead of it but the Pacific, *would* feel. Like time moves slower, that the right things matter more, and the wrong things matter less.

"I didn't know places like this existed in Canada," I say to Heather on my first morning in Tofino, when she and the boys have come into town with me to show me around.

"Oh yeah?" she says, smiling. "I know what you mean. It's meant to be all ice and snow, right?"

I look out across the autumnal color of Tofino, the thick green of the tree canopies. "Right."

Wilderness and sea aside, in the town itself there aren't any chains, not even a Tim Hortons. In among the clothing stores and gift shops, there are multiple art galleries, so many that I take a trip by myself out later that same day to explore them properly, taking my time, soaking it all in. I have a conversation with one of the artists, an illustrator named Patrice, who has the kind of life I can only dream of. Art, the forest and the sea. A Labrador called Salvador curled in the corner of the studio. *One day*, I think dreamily, as I walk back toward the Airbnb and my friends. *One day, maybe.*

My time in Tofino passes in a blur of bicycles and beaches, exploration and adventure. And, most importantly, *other people*. Other people who are funny and nice and don't seem to think I'm weird or annoying. We spend most of our time without a plan, cycling on rented bikes from one beach to the next to stay for a couple of hours, scattered. Some of us lying on the sand, paddling in the Pacific, looking at rock pools. At Chesterman Beach, Lars, Khalil, and Heather go surfing. Stefan buys a kite and we take turns running down the beach with it, trying to catch the wind, while Beasey takes pictures.

That evening, my second in Tofino, we light a small bonfire on Tonquin Beach as the sun goes down. Everything feels softer in the muted light, and it's so nice I want time to fold in around us, keeping us safe in the moment forever. Beasey gives me his hoodie as it starts to get cold, even though I haven't asked and I don't really need it. Of course I put it on anyway. It smells like him.

When we all get back to the Airbnb, it's late and I'm tired, but I stay up anyway to watch them all play drinking games with a pack of cards and a bottle of sambuca. I shake my head when Heather starts pouring shots.

"We won't tell anyone you're underage," she says, laughing.

"I'm not much of a drinker," I say, which is true now. But I don't say what the real truth is, which is that I don't want to be who I was before, drinking just because my friends were, numbing myself to my own unhappiness. The alcohol, the weed, the drugs that came later, they were all tricks I played on myself, masking my growing misery in imagined fun. None of it was real. *None of it*.

This is real, though. And Heather doesn't push me to drink, or make me feel stupid for not doing it, and neither does anyone

else. I stay up for a couple of hours with them, refereeing their game of Ring of Fire, before I get too tired and the novelty of being the only sober one in the group wears off. They wave as I say goodnight, singing a discordant mix of goodbye songs—I think one of them might be that song from *The Sound of Music* in a deep, Scottish voice that could be either Beasey or Khalil—until they dissolve into laughter, way too pleased with themselves. I roll my eyes, smiling, shaking my head.

When I'm in bed, I lie there for a while listening to them in the living room, their attempts to stay quiet for my benefit and the inevitable failure. It makes me think of my non-friends back home, of course it does, though I would never have willingly walked away from them, even to go to sleep, because that would have meant trusting that there would still be a place for me in the morning. I would never have been willingly sober, either.

Maybe I conjure it with these thoughts, or maybe it's just coincidence, but when I look at my phone to check the time, I see a notification that makes me sit straight up, my whole body tensing. An email from Casey. *Casey.* My heart starts pounding just from seeing her name. The last time I saw her she was rolling joints. The last time I heard her voice she was saying my name over and over, panicked. She hasn't said a word to me since then—it's just been silence. And now, when I'm safe and happy in Canada, an email.

Hey Peyton,

Hope it's okay to email out of the blue. I wasn't sure if you'd answer if I tried to WhatsApp, and I've got too much to say for that, anyway.

Obviously the first thing is that I'm sorry. I'm so sorry for what happened. It's the worst thing I've ever done. This isn't an excuse, but we were all just scared.

I was hoping you'd come back to college and we could maybe talk about it, but you didn't. I went to your house in the end and I spoke to your mum. She told me how you left and how you're in Canada now. Do you have friends there? Is that why you went? Have you been to Niagara Falls? Was it cool? Will you send me a postcard? I've never been to any other country before. You're so brave to just go like that. (Mum said if I try anything like it, she'll drag me back by my ear.)

If you don't want to reply because you don't forgive me, that's okay. I don't think I'd forgive me.

Sorry again.

Casey xx

Meanly, unfairly, I'm disappointed that the email isn't from Flick. Even with the hindsight I've been developing since I first landed in Vancouver, my Flick instinct is still rose-tinted. So stupid. Flick probably doesn't even think about me.

I don't reply, because I'm not sure what to say. It doesn't matter if Casey's sorry; it doesn't change anything. What's done is done and there's no point upsetting myself over it again.

Already my memories of my time at college are saturated with a murky dark filter. Everything just seems dull and flat and gloomy, like looking into a room with the light off.

Here, it's full color and bright light. Some time off in the future, when I think back on this adventure, I already know that's how I will remember it. Colorful. If anything, the filter in my head will probably make it even brighter.

I close my eyes and anchor myself in this moment, thinking hard about where I am. I am in a bed in an Airbnb on a Canadian island as far west as I can go. The past is the past, banished to a different time, a different land mass. I am finding my way, and I'll get there.

I lock my phone, put it upside down on the bedside table, and go to sleep.

BEFORE

aka

The one where Amber Monroe is still a bitch

aka

The advice I should have listened to

aka

NO ONE LIKES A PUSHOVER, PEYTON

We'd all been friends for maybe two or three months—Travis and me settled into our relationship, and everything going pretty okay—when I went into town with Casey and Flick. This was the kind of thing I was doing more often by then, but it still felt new and exciting, something I was lucky to be a part of.

The plan was to wander around town for a while and then go back to Flick's house before heading on to Eric's for the evening, where the boys were spending a "girl-free" day hanging out. (As far as I could gather, this involved them doing the same things they did when we were around, namely, playing video games and smoking weed.) Casey, Flick, and I had spent almost half an hour in Paperchase helping Casey choose a birthday card for her dad and then moved on to Superdrug, where Flick was bouncy happy about looking at the makeup displays. She'd disappeared off, like she did sometimes, leaving Casey and me standing in the haircare aisle in companionable silence. (I say it was companionable—who knows with Casey.)

I was staring at a display of vibrant hair dyes, wondering idly, contentedly, if I should ask Flick if she wanted to dye her hair a ridiculous color with me—something I'd daydreamed about doing with a friend for years—when I realized that someone had come up behind me and started to speak.

"Oh my God." The voice was a drawl. A loud, affected, familiar drawl that made my entire body turn to ice. "Peyton *King*?"

I could have ignored it, but I knew too well that there was no ignoring Amber Monroe. I half turned.

"Oh my God," Amber said again. She looked just the same, flanked in that moment by two boys I didn't recognize, who looked confused. The same smirk, the same mean eyes. "It *is* you!"

I hadn't said a word. She'd rendered me mute, like she always had, like nothing had changed since I'd last seen her.

"Not going to say hi?" Amber said. "So rude." She tutted twice, shaking her head. "Still walking around wasting oxygen, then? Why haven't you jumped off a bridge yet?"

"What the fuck?" Casey was suddenly beside me, spun around from where she'd been standing as distant as ever. But there she was, and her presence was huge, bigger even than Amber's. Her "what the fuck" was pitched so perfectly: incredulous but assured. "What the hell did you just say to her?"

Amber looked momentarily startled. Her eyes moved from my stricken face to Casey's glare. I saw her gather herself before she spoke again. I'd never seen her gather herself before. "Aw, Duckie, you made a friend?"

"Oh my God," Casey said, disgusted. "Fuck off, you little turd."

If I'd known beforehand that that moment was going to happen, I would have thought that Casey would be no match for Amber. But somehow, next to Casey, Amber looked smaller. And confused. She coughed out a laugh. *"Wow."*

"Do you actually think it's okay to talk to someone like that?" Casey asked. "What's wrong with you?"

"Fuck this," one of the boys muttered. "Come on, Amber."

Amber rolled her eyes at us, but I could see that she was still confused by what had just happened, why Casey hadn't been as instinctively cowed by her as I was. She sauntered off after the two boys, flipping us off when she was far enough away.

"Twat," Casey said. "Fuck girls like that, seriously."

I let out a long breath, trying to give my body permission to relax. "Casey, thank you so—"

"I didn't do it for you," Casey interrupted. "I did it because twats like that need to hear that what they do isn't okay. Otherwise they just swan around doing it to every sad fuck without a backbone."

I mean, fair, but ouch.

"Listen," she said. "People will respect you more if you stand up for yourself."

"That's easy to say," I said. "When you didn't have to go to school with her every day for five years."

"Not just her," Casey said. "I mean people like Princess Flick, too."

I blinked in surprise. "Oh—"

"Seriously," Casey said. "Don't let her walk all over you. Or any of them. Try saying no every once in a while. It'll do you good. And them."

There I'd been thinking Casey hadn't been paying the slightest bit of attention to anything that was going on between me and the group.

"So you were bullied?" Casey said, and my stomach clenched. "At your old school?" I nodded, because there was no point denying it. She considered me, her face as inscrutable as ever. "You make more sense to me now," she said.

I couldn't figure out how to reply to this, but I was saved by Flick coming back to us, beaming. "Look!" she said. "This nail varnish set is cosmos-themed. Isn't it cool?" She held it up to me. "Stardust nails! Pey-Pey, if you get this, I'll do both our nails and we'll match."

"Okay!" I said, and Casey let out a loud, obvious cough. I ignored her. It wasn't like there was anything wrong with wanting to have cool matching nails with my friend. It wasn't walking over me if I wanted the same thing.

I paid for the set—plus a nail file duo and two bottles of Dr Pepper—and the three of us headed out together.

"Shall we go back to mine?" Flick asked.

"We're *always* at yours," Casey grumbled. "No offense, but I'm so sick of your living room."

"Don't come, then," Flick said, shrugging.

"Thanks, I love you too," Casey said.

"Let's go to mine," I said. "It's closer and we can sit in the garden."

"I've got a garden," Flick said.

"My garden's nicer," I said. This was true, but it was *not* the kind of thing you said out loud, which was the very obvious thing I would have learned earlier if I'd actually had friends. I learned it in that moment though, just off the expressions on Flick's and Casey's faces.

"Great, go and sit in it, then," Flick said. "By yourself."

After a few months more friendship with Flick, I would know to roll my eyes and say, "Fine, give me that Dr Pepper back, then." But it was still too early for that, and our friendship still felt fragile, so I panicked.

"What? No. Why?"

She crossed her arms, scowling. Casey was just watching the two of us, waiting to see what would happen. "If your garden's so great," Flick said.

It was such a bizarre thing to have an argument about, and I was as baffled as I was anxious, unsure how to defend myself or whether I even needed to. "It's not that great," I said.

"Sounds like it is," Flick said. I looked at Casey, hoping for backup, which was another mistake. "Why are you looking at her?" Flick demanded.

"Casey," Casey corrected mildly. "My name is Casey."

"Oh, fuck off!" Flick snapped. She'd worked herself up, but it was over absolutely nothing, and I didn't know what to do.

"Here," Casey said patiently, taking the Dr Pepper bottle Flick was holding and uncapping it for her before handing it back. "Drink."

Flick, scowl still in place and her eyes looking somewhere off into the distance, away from us both, did. Slow sips, one after the other.

"Let's stay here for a bit longer," Casey said. "We can go to Homebase and look at all the plants and pretend we're giants in a tiny forest."

I blinked at her, assuming she was joking.

"You've never done that?" Casey asked. "You're missing out. Me and Flickers used to do it when we were kids."

"You hung out in Homebase together when you were kids?" I asked, baffled.

"Our mums are friends," Casey said. "They did loads of stuff together when we were growing up. That's how we know each other. Didn't you know that?"

I didn't. How? It seemed like the kind of thing I should have known by then.

"So much you've missed out on," Flick said flatly, a little meanly.

"Also, B&Q," Casey said. "The paint samples. Riding on those big trolleys. Remember how we used to have races and your mum got so mad when we knocked over that display of outdoor lamps?"

A smile twitched. "Worth it."

"Come on," Casey said. "We'll show Pey-Pey how it's done."

"And then we can go back to my house," Flick said, chin jutting.

Casey glanced at me, eyebrows lifting just the tiniest bit.

"Sounds good," I said.

NOW

TOFINO

The next day, Beasey, Khalil, Heather, and I go on a whale-watching boat trip around the nearby islands, which turns out to be beautiful but fruitless; not a single whale in sight. When we get back to the Airbnb, Lars and Stefan are sitting at the kitchen island, a laptop open in front of them and two familiar faces onscreen: Seva and Maja.

"Hello!" Stefan says as we walk in, beaming. "We've been waiting for you."

"All of us?" Khalil asks cheerfully, swinging the fridge door open and pulling out a carton of orange juice. He holds it up in a question to Heather, who nods.

"We have been making a plan," Seva says. "On how the four of us could share the drive to Banff." Through the screen, he gestures toward Lars and Stefan, who are nodding. "But then we were thinking about you, Peyton."

I jump, heat rushing to my face. "Me?"

"Yes, your plan to get across Canada." He very kindly doesn't use scare quotes around the word "plan." "We thought it would make sense for you to come with us, if you were interested."

My head floods with words, like all the different versions of myself have started arguing inside me. *Yes! I'm interested! No! I can do this on my own. What? No, you obviously can't. What about Beasey? What about Khalil? I wouldn't be able to help with the drive, I'd just sit there, like a child in the back of the car. What about Beasey?*

"And then Lars said," Seva continues, "that if you came too, there would be five of us, and we could get an RV."

"Make an adventure out of it," Lars adds.

My heart leaps, my head quiets.

"We would save a lot of money," Maja says. "And we'll see so much more of British Columbia and Alberta. It should be fun."

"It will be amazing," Lars says, laughing. "A proper road trip."

"Khalil?" Seva says.

"Yup," Khalil says, raising his glass to the screen.

"You were saying how you would have gone to Banff if you could hire a car?" Seva says. "You and Beasey."

Khalil smiles a cautious, hopeful smile. "Yeah . . . ?"

"Is that still true?" Lars asks. "If you could go, would you?"

Khalil and Beasey glance at each other, eyebrows rising in a mirroring question. Khalil laughs. "I mean, yeah. Wow. If you're saying you can get us there, we'd definitely think about it. Right?"

Beasey nods. "If we could get to Banff, amazing."

"If we're getting an RV, we could get one big enough for all of us," Lars says. "Are your plans flexible?"

"Flexible enough," Khalil says. "We've got a hostel booked in Portland, but that's cancelable. We haven't booked travel yet; we weren't sure exactly when we'd leave. How long are you thinking for the trip?"

"Two, maybe three weeks," Lars says. "That depends on the route we choose, who wants to come."

"We can definitely be flexible for two or three weeks," Beasey says. He's looking thrilled, like a kid who just found out school's closed for a snow day.

Khalil looks at Heather, his smile almost sad, like he knows what the answer will be before he speaks. "Any chance you could come too?"

She half laughs, shaking her head. "I wish. I can't skip out on uni for that long. I've got classes."

"Peyton, what do you think?" Seva asks. "We can get you as far as Calgary. That is where the RV will need to be dropped off. You said your grandfather was in Edmonton? That is very close."

"*Very close,*" Khalil repeats with a laugh. "Speaking in Canada terms, not British ones."

I barely hear him. To be honest, I'm speechless. I still don't think I'll actually go to see Grandad, but that doesn't seem to matter much right now.

"After that, who knows," Seva says, shrugging with his whole arms. "We can all decide what we want to do."

"So, a road trip?" I ask, and they all nod. A road trip, like something out of a film. I thought Tofino was as good as anything could get. And now this. *Oh my God*, I think. Out loud, I say, "Oh my God."

Stefan laughs. "In a good way?"

"In an amazing way," I say. "But you don't all have to change your plans just to get me to Calgary."

"We're not changing plans, we're adjusting them," Lars says. "Making them better."

"This works for all of us," Stefan adds.

"No offense," Khalil says, when I can't quite shift the uneasiness from my smile, "but if you don't come, we'll go anyway."

Beasey shoots him a look, but I laugh, relieved. It's exactly the right thing for him to say, and I relax. "I definitely want to come. How much do you think it'll cost?"

"All in? A few hundred dollars each," Lars says. "If we all go. But, overall, it'll work out much cheaper than spending nights in hostels or hotels. We can stock up on food and cook, so we save money eating out. Most of the stuff we'll be doing will be free—hiking, seeing the mountains, that kind of thing. A lot of the usual tourist things will probably be shut; it'll be the off-season."

"Is that bad?"

Lars shrugs. "We will miss out on some cool stuff, yeah."

"Expensive cool stuff," Khalil points out. "At least we'll be saving money."

"Will it be okay driving on the roads this late in the year?" I ask, imagining sheets of ice and snow six inches thick.

"I think they will be fine," Seva says. "It's actually unseasonably warm at the moment, which is good for us. Not so good for the planet, maybe, but good for us. I have lots of experience driving in the winter. I promise I will keep you all safe."

"We can share the driving," Lars adds. "Those of us with the right permit, anyway. But it doesn't matter if not everyone can drive. So long as we all contribute to the rental costs and the gas, it will be fair."

"Peyton, you must come," Seva says. "You can be our road-trip illustrator."

I almost start crying with joy right there and then. I'm struck by the feeling that this is the happiest moment of my entire life, and we haven't even done anything yet. Somehow, I keep my cool. "Deal," I say. "When will we go?"

"We will need to sort out the details," Seva says. "Everyone can think about it and confirm. We will need to get the RV, plan our whole route; logistics. A few days, at least."

A few more days, plus two or three weeks more with these people. It feels like a gift; like a dream.

On our last full day in Tofino, it rains all morning, but it doesn't matter because we spend most of our time planning, talking, and daydreaming about the trip. Everyone except Heather and Khalil, who have disappeared off to spend their last day together. I sit with Beasey on the sofa, the two of us scrolling through the tourist websites for Whistler, Jasper, and Banff to get a taste of what's waiting. I start to watch a YouTube video of the Icefields Parkway until Beasey yelps and takes my phone from me.

"Spoilers!" he protests.

As the evening draws in, we all go for dinner together in a bar and restaurant by the waterfront that turns into a club at night, sharing huge portions of chicken wings, fries, and nachos. Everyone plans to stay out, so I say my goodnights and goodbyes early, before the fact of me being underage becomes an issue, and Beasey offers to walk me back to the Airbnb. We detour along by the beach, talking about the days ahead, the road trip, what's waiting for us in Alberta.

"Do you mind changing your plans?" I ask him.

"Oh my God, no," he says. "This is amazing. I really love Canada. I hadn't expected to as much as I have. Or stay this long, either, to be honest. I'm glad to stay longer; I'll be sad to leave."

"Me too," I say. "But that won't be a while yet for me, hopefully."

"Oh yeah?" Beasey says, smiling. "You think you'll be able to carry on without us?"

I laugh, even though I've already started pushing away anticipatory flutterings of anxiety at the thought of losing the comfort and fun of these people and being back on my own again. Since I've let myself relax with them, everything has been so much better. It's been so, so nice to have people to share it all with. How *will* I carry on without them? I shake the thought from my mind. It's a worry for another day. Not for now, in the dusky Tofino night, the air cold and the moon bright on the water.

When we get to the Airbnb, I expect Beasey to throw me a wave and then ramble off back toward the bar, but he doesn't. He leans against the doorway as he talks—he's telling me about the hotel near Fort William his father runs in Scotland—gesturing with his hands, his face bright and animated.

"Have you ever been to Scotland?" he asks me.

"I've been to Edinburgh," I say.

He waves a hand. "That barely counts. You need to go back! See the Highlands. Honestly, it's like here. Beautiful and wild. I'll give you a tour."

My heart leaps. My smile is casual. "Let's finish this massive life-changing traveling experience before we start planning another one."

He grins. "Fair. Hey, are you going to be okay keeping yourself company? I could stay."

He . . . could stay? What does he mean? Stay like a friend, or stay like something else? Stay like there's potential? I think of the two of us on the sofa in the hostel back in Vancouver, his hand on my knee, and I know—I've known all along—that I didn't imagine that he wanted to kiss me. He's looking at me the same way he did then, like I'm something bright, something that shines.

"They're all waiting for you," I say.

"They'll understand."

I wonder how I'm looking at him. Because he's something bright to me, too, but it's a scary brightness, the kind that gets brighter and brighter until it explodes and destroys everything, even the good bits.

For a second, I imagine nodding, smiling, leading the way into the house. I imagine us choosing a film, inching closer on the sofa. I imagine the first kiss, which would be soft and sweet, nothing like Travis and his impatient tongue. Whispers in the dark. Coupling off like Khalil and Heather.

I want that. I do. But, more than that, I want this trip to be about more than a kiss, more than a boy, however good both those things could be. And most importantly, I can't risk what I've found here—actual friends, really good friends—on a few kisses with a cute boy. Because that's all it will be, isn't it? Beasey and I couldn't become anything, not with him midway through a trip around the world, and me—eventually—heading back to the UK.

"Nah, I'll be fine," I say, making sure to smile as casually as possible. "Your night out shouldn't be spoiled by me being seventeen."

He doesn't push me or make me feel bad for saying no. He nods and stands himself up from where he's been leaning. "Lots of sketching planned?" he asks.

"Loads," I say.

"Okay, well, keep your phone close so we can check in," he says. "To make sure you're okay."

"I'll be fine!" I say, shaking my head. "I'll just be on the sofa daydreaming about RVs and Lake Louise."

Beasey grins at me. "This trip is going to be epic."

"Promise?" I say.

"Promise."

We have to leave early in the morning to get the bus to Nanaimo, where we'll get a ferry back to Vancouver. I'm not sure what time everyone got back from the club, but it must have been late because they're all tired and groggy, especially Heather and Khalil, who emerge from their room looking bedraggled and glum. Heather's eyes are red and wet, like she's been crying. She'll be getting the bus back to Victoria, so she and Khalil are about to separate for who knows how long, maybe forever. When this semester is over, she'll be going back to Australia, and when he's done traveling he'll return to the UK. Unless one of them makes a major life change, there's no future for them. My heart aches with sympathy, but there's no way to say so without sounding weird, so I just give them some space.

We spend one night back in the hostel in Vancouver before we set off on the trip so the last few logistical niggles can get sorted out and we can stock up on supplies. I go to an outdoor store with Lars and Stefan to get what I need for the trip, now I have an actual plan with an actual destination. A destination where it will be very cold. Lars offered to come with me to help me pick out what I needed, so of course Stefan came too.

"How could you come to Canada in October without winter clothes?" Lars asks me as we walk in.

"I brought my winter coat," I say. "And I just figured that I'd work it out when I got here. Which is what I'm doing, see?" To prove my point, I reach out and pluck a pair of gloves from the display . . . $65. Shit. Very casually, I put them back.

"Besides," I add, struck by inspiration. "I didn't have space in my rucksack for bulky winter stuff."

"Peyton was being spontaneous," Stefan says to Lars, glancing at me to grin. "It's cool."

"It's irresponsible," Lars says, but not meanly. "You're lucky we're here to help. Okay, so, you'll need gloves and a hat to start with . . ."

We spend half an hour picking out what I need—including fifteen minutes of Stefan and me trying on different ear muffs and scarves, taking endless selfies, while Lars tries to keep up his *Are you done?* expression—before I go to the changing room to try on a few different tops and fleeces. When I'm in there, I let the worry that's been tickling at the back of my mind take center stage.

Because, wow, winter gear is expensive. Even with me picking out the cheapest options I could find, it's all adding up. And it's not like I have an endless supply of money. I've done a good job of putting these kinds of worries out of my head since I got here, but let's be honest, it's not going to last forever. Especially not if I have to spend over a hundred dollars on essential supplies I hadn't even considered needing. At this rate, I'll be pretty much broke by the time we get to Banff, and then what will I do? Maybe find some cash-in-hand work at one of the hostels and hope no one rats me out to the visa people?

I want to carry on acting like this adventure can last forever, that I really will be able to make it all the way across the country and say to my parents and myself and everyone, *Look, I made it. I am self-sufficient and independent, and I'm not going back to college, and I'm going to live the life I want.* But how realistic is that, really?

When I come out of the changing room, I carry my supplies to the counter to pay and push the thoughts away. Live in the moment—that's the point, isn't it?

That evening, Beasey, Khalil, Lars, and Stefan make the most of the extra night in Vancouver to go out to a bar, but I don't mind staying in with Seva and Maja, helping plan out the last few details. It's good for me to know as much about the trip as possible, so when I email my parents I can send them the full itinerary, like Mum had asked when I first told her about the plan. Still, they're unconvinced, and Mum asks me to call her to discuss it.

"Perhaps I can speak to them?" Seva offers. "Will it help them to know we are here?" He gestures to Maja, then himself.

I know what he means—that the two of them are actually adults, both in their mid-twenties, with experience, and therefore far more trustworthy than my reckless self—but all I can think about is how my dad would react if a Russian man phoned him to tell him he was taking his seventeen-year-old daughter across the Canadian wilderness in an RV.

"Or I can speak to them," Maja offers, either reading my mind or my face, and I'm relieved. "Will that help?"

It helps a lot. When Maja returns the phone to me with a smile after speaking to my mother, I can tell from her voice that Mum, at least, is feeling better.

"She sounds nice," Mum says.

"Yeah," I say. "She's great." Maja smiles at me, then points to the door to indicate she's going to leave to give me privacy. When she's gone, I say, "Doesn't it sound amazing, Mum?"

"It does," she says. "I'd still rather you came home."

"Really, though?" I say. "Miss out on this opportunity? Really?"

She's silent for a while. "Oh, Peyton," she says with a defeated sigh. "Of course I don't want you to miss out on opportunities. I want you to have the world. But I miss you, and I'm worried about you. Not just because you're in a different country, but because of what's happened to you. I feel like I don't know you."

"I'm still the same person," I say, which isn't what I mean. I mean that I don't really know myself, either, but that I've got a better chance of figuring that out here, with my friends— actual friends—in an RV on the Icefields Parkway, than I do back at home in suffocating Surrey with the friends who are not my friends. I'd explain that to her, if I could.

"If I asked you to come home," she says. "Would you?"

"No," I say.

Another sigh. "I won't ask, then." She's quiet for a moment. "I miss you."

"I miss you too," I say.

"Maybe I should have got on a plane and come with you," she says. Her voice is almost distant, like she's talking to herself rather than me. "We could have done this together."

I don't know how to respond to this, what she wants or expects me to say. Finally, I say, "Next time."

"Next time," she says.

BEFORE

New Year's Eve

aka

The mistakes are always easier
to spot in hindsight

aka

There's a reason it's illegal, Peyton: Part One

When I look back on the many, many mistakes and red flags that dot my year in college with color, trying to spot where it really went wrong, when I could have changed things, my mind always snags on New Year. In hindsight, the night is one huge, glaring red flag, but at the time, I would have sworn blind it was a great night. Everything I'd dreamed about, I would have said. Me, my boyfriend, and my friends on New Year's Eve. What more could any teenage girl want?

We went to Eric's house instead of Flick's as normal because his brother was having a party. (Eric sold it to us as a party they were having "together," but, when we got there, it became pretty clear that the party was Tyler's and we were simply allowed to be there.) Everything felt different between all of us when there were so many other people around. We stuck together, our need for each other more obvious than it had ever been or would be again, and I loved that. It was the first time, with all of them, that I really felt like I belonged.

There was an inexplicable bouncy castle in the back garden, and we sat together in it for what might have been hours, smoking and drinking and playing cards, the sounds of the party muted by the brief distance. Eric had his arm around Flick's shoulder, her hair tucked behind her ear, and he was whispering something that was making her smile wide. Casey was wearing the ridiculous tiara Callum had given her for Christmas (we'd done Secret Santa; I'd had Nico), and she kept hanging the joint out of her mouth and taking "ironic" selfies, fingers in the peace V sign. Nico and I were on our fifteenth game of Speed, way too into it, laughing together more than we ever had (he'd loved my Secret Santa present, a Linkachu T-shirt that made him snort-laugh, and he'd been friendlier to me ever since), while Travis—whose lap I was in—refereed, his fingers stroking my arm.

When it got closer to midnight, we got kicked out of the bouncy castle by a couple of Tyler's friends and went inside, squeezing into a corner of the living room together. The music was so loud we could barely hear each other, but we'd all drunk enough by then that it didn't really matter. Eric disappeared with Flick, and when they returned their eyes were wide, pupils dilated, and they were talking too fast, laughing too loud. Travis leaned over, said something to Eric, and then there were pills in his hand. He took one, held the other out to me. Did I even think about it? I like to think that I did. (That pill could have been literally anything. *Anything.*) But I know the reality, which is that I just followed Travis's lead, like I did all the time, and swallowed it down, smiling. I think I even said thank you, like a child accepting sweets.

Everything is a series of flashes after that rather than actual memories. Kissing Flick on the cheek, hugging her so tight she squeaked, telling her I loved her. Her flicking my forehead, grinning. Dancing. Laughing. Being lifted up by Tyler and spun around. The quiet cold of the bathroom, Travis and his tongue and his hands, the sound of the countdown muffled through the closed door. His fingers inside me, my hand in his jeans, his mouth against my ear, telling me he loved me, I was perfect, this was perfect. *Happy New Year!*

My next memory is waking up on the bouncy castle when the world was light again. Somehow all seven of us had made our way back there, even Flick and Eric. "God," Flick groaned. "I feel like shit." I jumped up and ran, finding my way behind the bouncy castle before I threw up. It was my first real comedown, and it was horrible, so much worse than the hangovers I'd learned to deal with over the last few months. I was shaky and cold, huddling against Travis, who gave me chewing gum and shook his head like I'd embarrassed him. *What did I take?* I wanted to ask him, but I didn't. It seemed better not to know.

When I got home—I had waited long enough for the worst of it to pass—Mum smiled and hugged me close, asked me how my first New Year with friends had gone. I told her it was amazing, just perfect, everything I'd ever wanted.

And because I was still fine, and nothing had gone wrong, I believed it, too. Or convinced myself that I did. That it was totally okay that I had somehow become the kind of person who took a random pill at a house party without even stopping to find out what it was, who couldn't even muster the nerve to ask her literal boyfriend afterward, in the cold light of day, what it had been, and tell him that she felt weird about the whole thing, and maybe it would be better if they just stuck with weed?

You never know, as it's happening, when you're becoming someone you won't recognize. With hindsight, I see myself swallowing that pill over and over, with everything that would happen ahead of me, half the choices that would lead me there already made. I don't really know if I want to hug or slap myself.

Probably both.

NOW

VANCOUVER—WHISTLER

Seva goes to collect the RV early in the morning and returns to pick us up with a broad smile on his face. It's bigger than I'd expected, but it still doesn't look big enough for all seven of us to live and sleep in for the next two or three weeks. I glance at Beasey, throwing him a surreptitious questioning look. He grins back, shrugging.

"It's made for seven, right?" he says. "Plenty of room."

"Sure," Khalil says. "But when it says it fits seven it means, like, adults and kids. Not seven full-grown adults."

I feel the smile drop away from my face. "What?"

"It'll be a squeeze," he says. "But it'll be fine. It's worth it for all the money we'll save."

He's obviously right, and I'm not about to start complaining about any of this, especially when I don't have to drive. But still.

"How many beds are there?" Stefan asks.

"Four," Maja says. "We've already planned this. One person gets a bed of their own."

"Who gets the special treatment?" Khalil asks.

"Peyton," Seva says.

"Why?" I ask, alarmed. I definitely don't deserve a bed to myself.

"You're the youngest," Stefan says.

"So? I don't mind bunking with Maja," I say, glancing at her. To my relief, she nods, like she'd expected this too. "Seva, you can have the bed to yourself," I say. "You're doing most of the driving." I'm about to add that he's also the biggest, but stop myself in time, worried he'll be offended.

We eventually agree that Maja and I will take the two beds in the back, one on top of the other like the bunk beds in the hostel dorm. As the only couple, Lars and Stefan get dibs on the double bed in the back room. Everyone else gets beds that transform at night: Seva in the kitchen; Khalil and Beasey on a sofa bed in the living area. I've never seen such a good use of space as the way the RV is put together. I take a load of pictures of it and send them to my brother, because he's the most likely to appreciate them.

It takes him hours to reply, because of the time difference, which even after all this time I keep forgetting is a thing.

Dillon:

> Remember when we stayed in that caravan in Norfolk? You hated it?

Me:

> This is different.

Dillon:

> . . . Why?

Me:

> IT JUST IS SHUT UP.

Dillon:

Dillon:

Have a great time. Try not to freeze.

As well as a working toilet, the RV also has a separate shower, which is great, though I'm already wondering just how we're going to coordinate the use of it. In the kitchen area there's a fridge, freezer, microwave, and gas cooker, and it's fully equipped with all the cookware we could need. To be honest, I'd expected the RV to just be like a bus with bigger seats, but it's not, at all. It really is like the caravan I stayed in with my family, except with a driver's seat. It even has towels and bedsheets for everyone.

It is the coolest thing I've ever seen. I don't even care that it's cramped and we'll probably drive each other mad within a day.

We stop off at a grocery store on the way to the highway to stock up on food and supplies for the journey. It's a mission, trying to negotiate what everyone wants compared to what we all actually need, but we get there in the end. Sort of. We've still somehow ended up with an ungodly number of marshmallows.

"Look at this beast," Lars says, grinning, when we get back to the RV. "It's amazing."

"We should give it a name," Seva says.

"Justin," Beasey, Stefan, and I all say at the same time. We look at each other and laugh.

"Trudeau?" Beasey asks us both.

"Bieber," Stefan and I say in unison, then laugh again.

"We're not traveling in an RV called Justin," Khalil says.

"Too late," Beasey says.

"Everyone in," Seva says, smacking his hand happily against the side.

Our first overnight stop is going to be Whistler, which is a town and ski resort a couple of hours' drive from Vancouver, including stops, along the Sea to Sky Highway. I sit myself in the passenger seat next to Seva, who grins at me, and look at the physical map he's got folded up by the dashboard in case there's a problem with the satnav.

"Excited?" he asks me.

I just beam back, so wide I don't need to say anything, and he laughs. "Whistler is a good first destination," he says. "It won't be a long trip, this first leg."

"Ease us into RV living," I say.

He grins. "Exactly."

"You've driven an RV before, right?" I ask. When he nods, I say, "When?"

He tells me about a road trip he'd taken a few years ago with an old girlfriend across the United States. The motor home was smaller, he says, perfect for two. I ask if it was better than Canada and he laughs. "Different. Just as beautiful, in places."

It occurs to me as we talk that I barely have to think when I'm with Seva; it's almost like being with Dillon. I never worry about how I'm coming across, whether I'm going to say the wrong thing or embarrass myself. Maybe because I trust that, even if I did, it wouldn't matter. As we talk, I nuzzle happily in against the uncomfortable seat, watching the road in front of us, British Columbia unfolding itself as we leave the urban bustle of Vancouver behind. The Sea to Sky Highway begins by winding along the coastline at sea level, with the mountains on one side of us and the sea on the other. It's like we've stepped inside a postcard and started driving in it. Later, we'll move farther inland and higher, through the old growth rain forests until we reach Whistler, over two thousand feet above sea level, our first official destination.

On the way there, we make our first stop at Porteau Cove, on the shores of the Howe Sound, to take pictures and stretch our legs. I sit on some driftwood on the small beach and watch as Lars and Stefan take pictures of each other attempting handstands. I mean to sketch, but I end up just sitting, taking it all in, until Beasey sits himself down beside me, handing over his phone.

"Look, I got a great one of you," he says happily.

In the photo, I'm in profile, staring out across the water toward the mountains ahead, unsmiling but steady with concentration. My hair is a bit all over the place and my hoodie sleeves are bunched up, but I look so calm; peaceful, even. I don't know what to say, so I jump up, holding my phone.

"Let me get one of you," I say. "Look like you don't know I'm here."

Obediently, he stares out across the Howe Sound with a ponderous expression on his face. I allow myself a second to take him in through my phone screen, how much I like his face, how just looking at him makes me feel calmer. The kind of things you can't say out loud, or even to yourself, without sounding cheesy.

In the second I take the picture, he turns to grin at me, and that's the shot I get. His laughing face, the sand, the sea.

It takes us another hour to get to the RV park and campground near Whistler where we're staying, which I imagined to be something like a caravan site in the UK but, happily, isn't. For one thing, the view is classic Western Canada dialed up to ten; we're high enough to be able to look out over a sweeping vista of trees while the white-peaked mountains tower over us. And for another, it's a pretty hands-off site. No entertainment hub with karaoke nights and a restaurant here. It's just a handful of RVs, the bare essentials of washrooms and a camp store, and the wilderness.

Seva, the only one of us who's driven an RV before, takes care of the hookups, showing the rest of us how to connect the electricity and water as we nod attentively. Beasey and Khalil are keen to be involved, asking Seva to show them over and over, while Lars and Stefan disappear off exploring, and Maja scopes out the campground facilities.

"Watch out for the bears!" Khalil calls after them.

"Bears?!" I repeat, alarmed.

"You'll be fine," Khalil says. "Bears don't have much of a taste for English runaways. Too highly strung."

I can't help laughing. "Thanks."

"Make sure you are always with one of us," Seva says, so seriously I balk and Khalil's cheerful grin falters. "It is best if none of us is ever alone, especially you."

"Can't argue with that," Beasey says. "Good life advice in general, not being alone." He smiles at me. "Right?"

I could say, *Sometimes you don't have a choice.* I could say, *Depends on the people.*

I smile back. "Right."

BEFORE

My seventeenth birthday

aka

Good days, bad decisions

aka

There's a reason it's illegal, Peyton: Part Two

I turned seventeen on a Wednesday in February, the first birthday I'd been able to celebrate with friends since primary school. Mum encouraged me to have them over to our house, but I said I'd spent years' worth of birthdays at home, and I wanted to spend this one somewhere else. She said she understood and gave me money so we could all go out somewhere for dinner together. I gave the money to Eric and told him to get us "something good," basking in my own bravado, buoyed by the way he smiled, impressed, and looked at me with something like respect.

At college, Flick draped birthday bunting round my shoulders like a scarf and handed me a card. "Sorry about not getting you a present," she said. "Obviously my friendship is gift enough."

This was clearly a joke, but it cut too close to the bone for me to find it funny. I tried to smile. "Obviously."

That Friday night we all stayed at Flick's, where they presented me with a chocolate cake made by Casey, festooned with way too many candles. They sang for me, and when I got teary I tried to say it was because of the candle smoke. After Flick's mum, who had stuck around to wish me a happy birthday, left to go to work, Eric produced the "something good" he'd promised me. Cocaine.

"Holy fuck!" Nico said.

Eric dropped a party hat on my head. "Only the best for Pey-Pey."

"Didn't you get that with *my* money?" I asked. "So, you're welcome."

He laughed. "Everyone say thank you to Pey-Pey for getting us a present on her birthday."

They let me go first. It was my birthday, after all. And so that was me on the celebration of my seventeenth birthday, kneeling on Flick's living-room floor, head bent over her coffee table, my boyfriend holding back my hair, snorting cocaine for the first time. I think there might have still been chocolate cake crumbs on the table, because it made me sneeze, which made them all laugh. It took a few minutes for the high to hit me, which made me think I'd done it wrong until I suddenly stopped doubting anything and simultaneously understood the word "euphoria" better than anyone in the world ever had. "I get it!" I said, over and over. "I get it now!" I also said, "Holy shit! Holy shit! Why don't we do this all the time?" Over and over.

Travis was laughing, and he looked so gorgeous, more gorgeous than he ever had. It was like I had new eyes. "You're adorable," he said.

"I *am* adorable!" I said.

It didn't last, though. It felt like it came and went in an instant, leaving me hollow and sad, way too quickly, worse than I'd been before. I wanted more to get it back, but Travis shook his head at me, unusually protective. "Once is enough for your first time, Pey," he said. He kissed my nose, which he'd never done, and held my hand. Travis wasn't a fan of coke—he said it was too expensive for what you got—and the whole time we were together I never saw him take any from Eric.

Was it fun, taking cocaine? Sure, for about five minutes, and then it was shit. And it was shit for way longer than five minutes. It was shit every time I thought about how I'd done it; how horrified and disappointed my parents would have been if they'd known; how horrified and disappointed I was with *myself*, for how I was suddenly a person I wasn't sure I even recognized. Sometimes it would come into my head out of nowhere, *Peyton! Cocaine?!* and my skin would prickle and burn with shame and confusion.

And yet I still did it again, didn't I? Not for a while, but the next time I had the opportunity, I did. And just look what happened then.

NOW

WHISTLER

What we find out, pretty quickly, is that we've chosen the wrong time to visit Whistler, because a lot of the activities and attractions, like the gondola that travels between the two highest peaks, are closed.

"What a shame," Beasey says, looking giddy with his obvious relief. "We won't be able to dangle almost fifteen hundred feet in the air in a tiny cage. Woe! Such woe!"

"This is what you get for doing Canada in October," Lars says, shrugging. "The great in-between."

"It looks so cool though," I say, sighing. "Oh well. I'll just have to come back one day."

"Hell yeah," Stefan says, grinning. "We'll have a reunion. Five years' time, all seven of us in a Justin 2.0. December. We'll have a Christmas tree. Fairy lights around the windscreen."

"Promise?" I say hopefully.

He ruffles my hair and I duck away, batting him off. "Promise," he says, laughing.

The good thing is that the lack of tourist attractions means we have more time to spend on the natural ones. We all agree to do something called the Train Wreck Trail, which is a short and easy hike that includes a suspension bridge—Beasey makes a face at me, but the bridge isn't that high and he keeps his cool—over the Cheakamus River to the train wreck site. There are seven old train carriages—boxcars—scattered among the trees like they, too, had grown there. They're all covered with years' worth of colorful, vibrant graffiti, and it's like nothing I've ever seen in my life. I love it so much I actually bounce on my feet. I have to stop myself clapping my hands like an excitable sea lion. But it's just so cool. It's *so cool*.

"How did this actually happen?" I ask, looking around for a place to sit or even lean, reaching for my sketch pad.

"I don't want to know!" Lars protests. "It's cooler if we don't know."

"It's magic," I say.

We take so many photos between us, even managing a group selfie (only Seva's arms are long enough to get us all in shot) with one of the boxcars behind us, a splash of hot pink and orange against the rusting brown.

Later, when we're back in the RV, I sketch myself standing atop one of the boxcars with the trees stretching high up to the sky above me, my arms held aloft. I call it *Train Wreck on a Train Wreck*.

"Can I see?" A German voice comes from beside me, and I look up, surprised, to see that Maja has sat down on the sofa at some point and I hadn't even noticed. God, that's embarrassing. I get so engrossed when I'm sketching.

"Sure," I say, turning my sketch pad so she can see.

A smile lifts her face, the unconscious kind that means the person really means it. It's my favorite type of smile, especially when it's sparked by someone looking at my drawings. "That's great," she says. "Very cute. Even though you aren't a train wreck, of course. I wish I could draw."

"Everyone can draw," I say.

"I wish I could draw *well*," she corrects herself, laughing. "Like you. Like this." She points to my sketches. "There's so

much expression in your drawings. I remember when I took art at school, everything I tried to draw always looked so flat. Is this what you want to do? Be an artist?"

"An illustrator," I say. "That's the dream. But my parents say that I should be more realistic. They say, keep art as a hobby, get a proper job."

She makes a face. "Parents."

"I know, right?" I say. "What do you do, when you're not traveling?"

"Dream about traveling again," she says, smiling. "I'm a financial administrator. Oh, Peyton, please don't make me talk about my boring job." She covers her eyes with her palm. "You'll make me sound so dull."

I can't help laughing. "Sorry."

"Canada must be a great place to be as an artist," she says, settling herself back against the sofa. "All the scenery is so beautiful."

"Definitely," I say. "Though I usually prefer drawing people."

"Even better," Maja says. "You have all of us." She laughs, gesturing toward Lars and Khalil, who are trying to play a game of makeshift tennis across the length of the RV with two frying pans and some balled-up socks. "Right?"

I grin back at her, almost hugging my sketch pad to my chest with the happiness of the moment. "Right."

In the evening, we all have dinner together in Whistler Village at a bistro before everyone starts talking about going out to find a bar or club in the town, and I feel so very, very seventeen. I keep quiet, not wanting to spoil the party, until they move on to discussing who will go back to the RV with me and keep me company, which is 100 percent mortifying.

"I will," Beasey says. Khalil snorts, Beasey ignores him.

Out of the corner of my eye, I see Maja give Seva an *aww* look, and I feel my cheeks flame. But I can't exactly say no—I don't even want to say no—so I nod and smile.

Beasey and I walk around Whistler Village for a while before we head back to the RV park, admiring the full spectrum of autumn in the colors of the trees: reds, oranges, golds, greens, and every shade in between. I try and take pictures, but it's getting dark and it's not the same.

We stop off at a Dairy Queen to get a Blizzard Treat each, even though I protest that it's too cold—"Oh my God, you're in Canada," he says. "Acclimatize. Ice cream in October!"— and argue over which one to get before landing on Reese's Peanut Butter Cup (him) and Mint Oreo (me). We've already ordered when he asks me if I've ever had an Orange Julius, which is like a kind of orange milkshake, and when I say no he insists we need to get one each of those, too.

"Aren't you meant to be being frugal?" I ask. "Haven't you still got half the world to see?"

"Some things are worth the money," he says. "Overpriced North American specialties are worth the money."

"Are they, though?" I ask, dubious.

"Peyton," he says. "For the rest of your life, if anyone ever says to you, *Have you ever had an Orange Julius,* you'll say, *You know what, yeah, I did. When I was seventeen, in Whistler Village one evening with my friend Beasey as we headed back to our RV.*"

The smile on my face is uncontrollable. "That's what I'll say?"

"Yep," he says, so confidently. "Don't think of it as buying a drink. Think of it as making a memory."

"You're quite weird," I say.

"Thank you!" he says, delighted.

When we get back to the RV, we bulk up with our gloves and hats because it's cold, piling blankets into our arms and going to sit outside the RV to feel the chill and smell the air with an Orange Julius apiece in our laps. Beasey is talking about Khalil going bungee jumping when they were in Australia, how he'd almost done it himself but couldn't make the leap.

"Do you wish you had?" I ask.

"Massively," he says. "But that's easy to say now, isn't it?"

It's almost eleven when I get a message from Dad, asking if I'm free for a phone call. I'm surprised and then worried, wondering if he's calling with bad news. What if something's happened to Mum or Dillon or Grandma? My worry intensifies as the thoughts flood in, reminding me that I'm on the literal other side of the world, that if something happened to someone I love, I couldn't just be there—I'd have to travel. Oh God, what am I doing here? Why didn't I think this could happen?

I go into the RV to make the call, my heart thundering with panic. When he answers with a distinctly unpanicked, "Hello, Peyton," it's not enough to calm me down.

"What's wrong?" I demand. "Has something happened?"

"Nothing's wrong," he says. "What do you mean?"

"Is Mum okay?"

"Of course she is. I would tell you if she wasn't."

"And Grandma?"

"Everyone's fine, love." The "love" softens us both and I blink back sudden senseless tears. "We're all fine."

"Okay, good," I say, sighing out my anxiety, sinking down onto the passenger seat at the front of the RV. "Good. What do you want to talk about, then?"

"It's been a while since we spoke," he said. "I wanted to hear your voice and make sure you were doing okay."

"I'm doing great," I say. "We're in Whistler right now."

"The ski resort?"

"Not in the actual ski resort, but near there, yeah."

"I remember Whistler," he says. "Beautiful place."

"You've been?"

"Many years ago," he says. "I went to a conference in Vancouver for work and they pulled out all the stops. Flew us to Whistler in a seaplane."

"You never told me that," I say.

He laughs. "You never asked."

"Why didn't you tell me when I got to Vancouver?"

"Because I was frantic with worry that my daughter had run away," he says. "I wasn't going to start reminiscing and offering tourist insights. Anyway. How is your trip? Are you keeping safe?"

"Yes, Dad. Everyone's looking after me really well. You don't have to worry."

"I do," he says. "I wanted to ask you—you haven't gone to Canada because cannabis is legal there, have you? I've been researching."

I roll my eyes at the steering wheel. "Oh my God, Dad, no."

"Are you sure? You don't have some kind of drug problem?"

"I told you, I only did them at home because of my friends. Who weren't actually friends. I haven't touched them since, I swear. And I don't want to, not ever again."

There's a silence. A distrustful, skeptical silence.

"Don't you trust me?" I ask.

"No," he says shortly.

Great. That warm, friendly conversational tone lasted long.

"Dad!"

"I trusted the daughter who was sensible and honest," he says. "The one who wouldn't dream of jetting off to the other side of the world, dropping out of college in the process, taking my money without asking first. How can I trust you? I hardly feel like I know you."

"You did the same thing," I point out. "You did the exact same thing when you were basically my age. You went traveling, too."

"No, I did not," he replies, so tense that I know he's trying to stop himself shouting at me. "I did not at all do the same thing. I had a *plan*. I funded my own trip. I paid my way."

"I'm going to pay you back for the plane ticket."

"That's not the point at all."

"Is this why you called?" I ask. "To have another go at me?"

"I called because I wanted to speak to you," he says. "But that doesn't mean I'm happy with what you're doing. You know that. I want you to come home."

"You're making me not want to come back—do you realize that?"

"For Christ's sake, Peyton, don't be such a child."

"I'm not."

"Yes, you are. If you want me to believe you're mature enough to handle this, don't be petulant." I don't reply and he waits for a while before he says, "I'm expecting you to come straight home when you get to Banff."

"Well, I won't," I say. Petulantly.

"Have you made a plan? A detailed plan?"

I'm silent. The time after Banff seems hazy and distant, like it doesn't really exist. I don't want to think about what happens after this, when I won't be with these people anymore, when I'll be alone again, and all the goodness I've finally found ends. I swallow. "I don't know yet."

"That's not okay."

"Please don't get mad again."

"I'm not mad; I'm concerned. You're not really thinking you'll see your grandad, are you?"

"No," I say.

"Well, maybe you should," he says, surprising me. "Maybe that will make things a bit clearer for you, one way or another."

What a weird thing to say. "I don't even know him."

"Neither do I," he says flatly. "But, nevertheless, he is family to you. If you really don't have a plan and for some reason still refuse to come home, at least go and see him."

"Won't he turn me away if he doesn't know me?"

"No," he says. "Under these circumstances, he'll probably be thrilled. Anyway. I shouldn't have said any of that. Just come home to your actual family and your real life. Your place at college is hanging by a thread—"

"Dad!" I shout, actually shout, into the phone. I don't even know why, but I think it might be something to do with the words "your real life" and what they've done to my heart. "*Listen* to me. I've dropped out. It's happened. I'm not coming back to finish the year, okay? You can't make me. I don't care about any of those subjects. I'm not going to do anything with them. There's no point in me forcing myself to do something I hate just because you want me to."

"Peyton—"

"*No*, Dad. We can't keep having this argument over and over." There's motion through the window and I suddenly see

Beasey's worried face, peering in at me. I try and control my voice. "Listen, it's late here. I should go to bed."

"Of course." Dad's voice is quiet now, almost defeated. "Peyton . . ." For a moment I think he's going to apologize, but he doesn't. He says, "Goodnight."

When I go back outside, Beasey is looking anxious, but he doesn't say anything, just waits for his cue.

"My dad," I say, possibly unnecessarily. "He's not happy I'm still out here."

Beasey's eyebrows go up. "No?"

"No."

I sit back down and he does too, listening quietly as I recap the conversation for him until I get to the bit about Grandad, at which point he makes half an interjection, then stops himself.

"Go ahead," I say.

"I thought the plan *was* to go and see your grandad," he says. "Isn't that what you said?"

"He's in Alberta, yeah," I say. "But I'm not actually going to go and see him."

"Why not?"

"I don't even know him," I say. "He's not that kind of grandad."

He looks baffled. "Then why did you say you were going to?"

"Well, I told border control so they'd let me through and wouldn't think I was just trying to get into the country to . . . I don't know, do whatever it is they think people without legit reasons to enter do. And I mentioned it to you guys because you were all so freaked out that I didn't have a plan."

Beasey looks at me for a long moment, his expression part confused, part incredulous. "Jesus," he says eventually. "You really have no fucking clue what you're doing, do you?"

This is clearly true, but I'm immediately defensive anyway, especially because of the unBeaseylike use of "fucking." "I'm traveling," I say.

"No, *we're* traveling," he says. "You just turned up in a foreign country completely unprepared and got lucky."

Also true. "That's not fair."

"What are you going to do when we've all moved on?" he asks. "How are you going to look after yourself?"

"I can look after myself," I say, stung. "I'm not incompetent. This whole trip with all of you has been amazing, but that's because I like you all, not because I need you."

He looks dubious.

"You think I should go home, too?"

"No!" he says. "Of course not. But maybe have a clearer idea of what you're going to do, yeah."

"I will," I say. "I'll make a plan. But not right now. I just want to live in the moment." I hesitate, then let myself say, "With you. And everyone else. That's enough for now, isn't it?"

His expression softens into a smile. "Yeah," he says. "That's enough for now."

When everyone gets back, I can tell by the way that they smile at us that they're expecting something to have happened between Beasey and me. I'm embarrassed, and it makes me wonder if Beasey had had some expectations of his own when he offered to stay with me tonight. But he didn't try anything, not even the hint of a move, so I decide to not worry about it.

He can't be my boyfriend, because we'd have no future, and we couldn't be anything casual, because we're in an RV with other people. So it doesn't matter that when he stands close to me my skin tingles and I get little electric flashes of what it would be like to kiss him. In another life, maybe the two of us could have been something, but this is this life, and that can't be.

Besides, the last time I had a boyfriend, that boyfriend was Travis, and now that's all I can think about, lying in the dark in the RV, unable to sleep. Travis and our relationship. Trying to trace a line from the me I was with him to the person I am now—the imaginary me I could be with someone like Beasey. The problem is that I still don't really understand any of it, even in hindsight.

For one thing, our relationship covered almost none of the bases I'd read about and seen in films. We didn't have the honeymoon phase of being all over each other, not being able to get enough of each other, starry-eyed and smiley. We didn't dance around "I love you" until a big emotional moment brought it to the surface. We didn't date, or even go on dates. I never met his parents. He didn't write me love letters or kiss me under the stars.

So what did we have? We were a couple, after all, for an entire year, and it can't just have been about sex (for him) and his friends (for me). I think about how I drew little comic strips for us, *The Adventures of Peyton and Travis*, which he loved, his cheeks and ears pinkening when he smiled down at the cartoon versions of us. (Who were definitely having more fun than we were, safe in the pencil lines of their cartoon lives.) Sometimes he could be sweet; even soft. He called me Pey instead of Pey-Pey, which I liked because it felt like something that was just ours.

But I didn't love him, and he didn't love me, and I knew that even as we said the words to each other. And, honestly, I still don't understand how I could have spent a year with someone I didn't love, didn't particularly even like that much. Now that it's all blurred into memory, I find myself thinking, *But what did we talk about?* We must have talked sometimes. What did we do the times we were alone, when we weren't having sex? But I guess the truth is that we weren't really alone all that much, and when we were, we had sex.

God, sex with Travis. My memories aren't exactly golden, but more than anything I think I feel sorry for him; for both of us. He didn't know what he was doing, did he? And I never told him, just let him talk to me how he thought he was supposed to, touch me like he'd seen men touch women in videos online. I should have tried to tell him or show him, and I didn't, because I didn't really care, did I? Not about him or how good he was as a boyfriend, because I thought it didn't matter. It wasn't ever really about him, and maybe on some level—if I believed that Travis had levels—he knew that.

This is when I can't help myself from trying to be fair. To remember that there were moments when he was good; sweet, even. The time he brought me a little Tupperware box, lined with a tea towel, full of brownies that his mum had made, because he thought I might like them. When he dried the rain off a bench I was about to sit on with the hoodie he'd been wearing moments earlier. How he stroked my hair when I dozed with my head in his lap, stoned and sleepy, while he played video games. How he shut Eric down that time he made a joke about how they could "share" or "swap" Flick and me for a night. He could have played along, been part of the joke from the inside and left me on the other side, but he didn't, and I appreciated that. My point is, there were moments. But they were just that: moments. And a tiny number, really, over almost a year. Like sprinkling a handful of hundreds and thousands over a giant bowl of shit.

Besides, let's be honest, I could easily come up with plenty of moments when he wasn't good, or sweet, or soft. Like how he'd say, when I was annoying him, "Don't be a needy little bitch," and I'd stutter and apologize and shake my head because if there was anything—*anything*—I truly did not want to be, it was a needy little bitch. How sometimes, when we were with our friends, he'd roll his eyes at me if I said something he thought was stupid, or—worse—roll his eyes at Eric. When I'd message him and he wouldn't message back for hours. How on four different occasions we'd arranged for him to pick me up before school and he just forgot, so I had to get the bus and just be late. How he'd look at me with such bored disdain when I'd lose it and yell at him and I'd end up crying, all that buried frustration and disappointment rising to the surface and leaking out of my face. (Then he'd sigh and apologize, wrap me up into a hug, kiss me until I gave in, his tongue in my mouth and my head going, *Boyfriend. Boyfriend. Boy. Friend.*)

I try to remember if it felt as depressing at the time as it feels in retrospect. I was high for a lot of it, for one thing, so a lot of the time it just didn't matter. I think for most of it I was just *grateful.* So fucking grateful that these people were willing to be my friends, even if that friendship didn't much look like the kind of friendship I'd actually wanted or imagined. If I broke up with him, I'd lose them; that was clear.

It was what had happened with his last girlfriend. Maybe if I hadn't kissed him in the kitchen that first night at Flick's and chosen him as my route in instead of trusting they'd be my friends regardless, things would have been different, but I did, and they weren't. So I had to believe he was worth it. What other choice did I have?

I stay awake for a long time in the RV, letting the thoughts run and run through my head. When sleep finally comes, I dream of him. He's squinting at me through a window; I'm sitting on a bus. "Pey?" he says, voice muffled, and I shake my head, say, "No—that's not me." I turn away to see that the bus is empty, rows and rows of empty seats, and when I look back he's gone too. I'm alone.

Maja has planned a proper hike for the following day, and she's enthusiastic when we all wake up in the morning, asking who wants to come.

"You can't come to Whistler and not hike," she says. "God made this place for hiking."

"I thought he made it for skiing," Stefan says, drooped over the table, eyes still half closed.

"Not in October," she says. "This is hiking weather."

"What's the hike?" Khalil asks. "We were thinking of kayaking today." He gestures at Lars and Stefan and Beasey, who all nod.

"Hiking later," Lars says. "We're saving our hiking energy for Jasper and Banff."

"You can build up the energy again," Maja says. "But okay." She rolls her eyes, then smiles at me and Seva. "You two?"

"I will be sleeping," Seva says. "I need more sleep."

Maja's face has dropped a little in disappointment.

"What's the hike?" I ask. "I'll come."

She shows me the route she's chosen, which is a hiking trail to Rainbow Lake. "I did some research," she says. "This seems the best one for us at this time of year. It's a decent hike."

This turns out to mean, I find out once we've started walking, that it will take about six or seven hours. I've never spent that much time one-on-one with anyone who wasn't family, except maybe Travis, who doesn't count. Despite my low-key concern, though, I'm excited. The pictures she's shown me look gorgeous, the weather is crisp and fresh, and if nothing else it will be nice to spend some time away from the RV and the boys.

The trail takes us through deep forest, over bridges, past gigantic trees and waterfalls. My feet begin to blister after a couple of hours, but Maja is prepared with a mini first aid kit, handing over plasters when we stop for a drink of water. I close my eyes as we sit so I can listen to the sound of the forest, the birds, the wind.

"Do you do this kind of thing a lot?" I ask when we start walking again.

"Hiking?"

I nod.

"Yes, when I can. I want to do the Pacific Crest Trail next year, if I can get myself ready and save enough money."

"Is that a long one?"

She laughs. "Yes, it's long. Over two and a half thousand miles. It's several months' worth of walking."

"Wow!" I say, instead of what I'm thinking, which is, *Why?*

"It's a dream of mine," she says. "But we shall see. Have you done much hiking before?"

I shake my head. "Not really. We used to do big family walks when I was younger. My dad is big on walking. We did Snowdonia—you know, in Wales?—a couple of times when I was a kid, but we haven't done anything like that for years."

It makes me feel guilty thinking about Dad and how we used to go on those family walks. I haven't even thought of them for years. Maybe, when I get home, I can suggest we try hiking together again. Maybe all of us, as a family. We could do Ben Nevis or something.

"My boyfriend and I did Snowdonia," Maja says. "We did each of the UK peaks."

"You have a boyfriend?" I ask in surprise, wondering why she hasn't mentioned him before, and thinking about how well I'd thought she and Seva were getting along.

"Not anymore," she says. "My boyfriend at the time. Ex now."

"Oh," I say.

"We were together for a while," she says. "Happily, I thought. But he found somebody else. Sometimes, that happens."

"I'm sorry," I say, inadequately.

She shrugs but doesn't reply. I wonder if it's okay to call her ex a dickhead.

"Is that why you came to Canada?" I ask.

"Yes," she says. "We always talked about doing a big hiking trip here. We have friends near Banff that we planned to see. I was feeling very lost in the life that was left without him back home, so I decided to take the trip myself. My friends are waiting for me in Banff and I think it will help a lot to see them." She smiles at me. "Good people make bad things survivable."

I nod.

"So tell me, Peyton. What brought you all the way out here?"

Something about where we are, how peaceful it all is, how casually open she just was, how unobtrusively friendly she's been to me this whole time—it loosens me, and I talk. I tell her slowly as we make our way through the forest about the bullies at Claridge; the loneliness; Travis and Flick, and how having them hadn't made the loneliness go away. That's as much as I say, though; I can't bring myself to tell her just how bad it got, how I changed, what I did. I just focus on the bullying, how deeply and profoundly it hurt me, in a way I worry I will always carry.

"There should be a different word for it," I say. "*Bullied*. It makes it sound so trivial."

"It doesn't," Maja says.

"It does, though. It's such a soft word, like the kind of thing you should just laugh off and get over. When I said to my parents, *Some kids are bullying me,* I think they just thought it was normal. Like, just something that everyone goes through at school at some point. There are so many words for this kind of thing in adulthood, you know? Like 'harassment' and 'abuse.' But because it's kids hurting other kids, it's all called bullying. I don't get why that's okay. They . . . they destroyed me. Day by day, over the years."

I'm just at the point where I feel like I might start crying when we arrive at Rainbow Lake, and I stop talking, gasping out a laugh instead.

"Oh, wow," I say.

Maja lets out a happy sigh. "Worth the walk, yes?"

We find a spot by the side of the lake and take out the lunches we'd packed that morning. For a couple of minutes, we eat in companionable silence, until Maja says, "I'm sorry you were bullied. That's a terrible thing to experience at such a young age, when you're finding out who you are. It's like . . ." She considers. "Like taking a cake out while it's mid-bake and punching it."

I surprise myself with how loudly I laugh. "That's exactly what it's like."

"The cake will still taste good, though," she says, pushing the analogy. "It will be an excellent cake."

I laugh again. "Well, I hope so. I'm sorry your boyfriend went off with someone else."

"Me too," she says. "It was devastating. But I try not to take it too personally. You can't set your self-esteem by other people. It is never your fault if people don't see what's good in you." She wipes the crumbs off her hands onto the grass in front of her, like she hasn't just said something profound that I'm going to file away in my head to bring out every time I remember Amber Monroe and her sneer.

"It's hard not to do that, though," I say. "Listen to what other people think, I mean."

"Of course it's hard," she says. "Hiking is also hard. But look." She gestures out toward the vast lake. "The rewards."

I smile. "True. I just wish . . . I just wish it was all a bit easier. Other people, you know?"

"If everything was always good, no one would ever learn anything."

"Doesn't seem like the lessons are worth it."

She shakes her head. "They always are. I believe that. You're going to have so many wonderful, enriching relationships of all kinds in your life, and they'll all be better because of what you've learned so far."

It feels nice to believe this could be true, for there to be a reason for the bad stuff that happened; lessons to be learned rather than just mistakes to regret. Maybe one day it'll all just be stories I'll tell, snippets from an unhappy time. Maybe some of them will even be funny rather than tragic. Maybe in a few years I'll be able to laugh about it. Something like The Punch, that could be funny, if I told it in the right way. I thought it was funny at the time, didn't I? Or, at least, I told myself I did.

BEFORE

The Punch

aka

Hey, Peyton, remember that time you got punched in the face?

aka

You could make a blanket out of all these red flags

It must have been about a month or so after my birthday that the punch happened. We were all our usual mix of drunk and/or high. I have a vague memory that we might have been playing Monopoly, or even Risk, though that seems unlikely, requiring way more brain cells than we possessed on those evenings. It was late into the night, probably past two a.m., and we'd reached the loudest point of our time together, the kind of time when Flick and Eric would start either dry-humping on the sofa or screaming at each other across the room.

That night, they were putting on a show. Eric told Nico that Flick had "the best tits" in the county and she shrieked, smacking him, retorting that, actually, they were the best in the *country*. It got even louder, her cupping one in each hand, thrusting out her chest, a wide, sloppy grin on her face, Eric asking—yelling—"Who told you that? Who told you?" and then Nico telling her she should show us all so we could judge, and of course, being Flick, specifically being drunk and/or high Flick—she did, whipping up her top and bra in one motion for a short-but-long-enough flash. Eric, groaning: "Fuck's sake, Flick," but proudly, a shit-eating smug grin on his face. Nico: "Pretty nice, yeah." Me, my tone too full of admiration: *"Flick!"* And then Travis: "Jesus, you're such a slut."

Do you know what kind of hell can break loose when no one is sober in a group, there are no adults of any kind around, and one guy insults another guy's girlfriend? Well, I'll tell you: It's a volley of swears from the boyfriend, swiftly returned by the insulting party, as someone's glass—impossible to know whose—flies above all our heads to smash, loud and dramatic, against the wall. The insulted—Flick—sitting motionless, her expression betraying her mortification even as she tried, so painfully, to laugh. Callum telling everyone to chill out. Eric lunging at Travis, the flying of fists. Me, out of some bizarre unearned protectiveness, trying to pull Travis to safety.

So who got a fist in the face? Yep, that would be me. And I mean right in the face. Eric's entire fist smacking into my cheekbone so hard I stumbled backward, tripped over Flick's shoulder, and ended up on my back on the floor, staring up at the ceiling, which was distorted by a kaleidoscope of stars.

"Holy fucking shit, Eric!" I remember Casey's voice, her hand pulling on mine. "You stupid shit!" I was upright but still sitting, her hand touching gingerly at my face. "Peyton? Peyton!"

"I'm fine," I said, through a mouthful of blood.

I really was. I was so high I couldn't even feel the pain in my cheek or my tongue, which had got caught between my colliding teeth at the moment of impact. All I cared about was the fact that all my friends were clustered around me, horrified and worried, saying my name. Flick was in tears, asking me over and over if I was okay, alternating between nibbling her fingernails and smacking Eric, who'd gone very quiet, eyes round and startled. Callum and Nico talking over each other about boxing and how the face is made to take punches and, *"You'll be fine, won't you, Pey-Pey?" "Pey-Pey's tough as shit."* Casey reappearing with an ice pack (frozen peas wrapped in a tea towel) and pressing it to my face, telling everyone else to shut up.

Once they finally accepted that I was fine, we all laughed about it. A lot. There were some dramatic re-enactments, mostly done by Callum and Nico and given a score out of ten by me. Eric apologized, once in front of everyone, very loudly, and once more in the kitchen later, quietly, *"I get carried away sometimes. I'm a dick."* (I'd wonder, later, and often, whether that was how he apologized to Flick all those times he was mean to her, or if he just never did.) Travis checked my face after everyone had calmed down, kissed me more gently than he ever had and called me a diamond. It wasn't a word he could pull off, but I loved it anyway. I even felt like a diamond that night—sparkling and so strong. Wanted. Invincible.

But then I woke up the next morning in my own bed with a screaming pain in my cheek so bad it made me stumble to the mirror, panicked. The bruise was a color swirl of black and blue, spread from the corner of my swollen eye down across my cheek to near my jawline. I was still in the clothes I'd been wearing the night before, and there was blood on my T-shirt that I hadn't even realized was there. My makeup was smudged, my eyes glazed, my head aching. I didn't look like a diamond. I looked like a breakdown.

Maybe that should have been the wake-up call, but it wasn't. I couldn't let it be. It was all fine, I told myself. I was now the central part of an anecdote that quickly became a private joke, one I treasured. I'd never been a part of a private joke outside my family before. All the grubby details—why Eric had been punching anyone, the fact that we were all high out of our minds in an empty house at seventeen, the blood on my dirty T-shirt, the collision of fist and bone—were forgotten in favor of the re-enactments that got more and more absurd each time, more and more distant from reality. Even I mostly forgot how I'd felt that morning in my bedroom, sober and alone, when I looked at myself and saw the naked misery wrought across my face. You wouldn't think I could forget something like that, but I did. You can convince yourself of anything if you try hard enough, if you want to be someone enough.

For a while.

NOW

WHISTLER—JASPER

We leave the next morning for the next leg of our trip. The drive from Whistler to Jasper is a lot longer than the one from Vancouver, but we're all a bit more used to the RV and each other. It feels like we're properly in it now, our road trip adventure. We take three days to do the whole journey, stopping off regularly on the way to see as much as we can. At Joffre Lakes, the water is such an unreal shade of blue I feel like I'm hallucinating. I don't even try to sketch it, because there's no point. I just stand and stare.

We have no Wi-Fi when we're on the road, and there's no TV in the RV, so we spend our time together talking and playing cards as a group or in pairs. Someone sits up front with Seva—usually Maja or me—keeping him company. There's always music pumping out from someone's phone or laptop—the playlist we created together before we left Vancouver runs for three hours, which is long enough for it not to matter when it starts to repeat. After a few days, Stefan uses the Wi-Fi at an RV site to download *The Bridge*, and we—him, Lars, Beasey, Khalil, and me—binge the whole thing for the next couple of days, clustered around his laptop, subtitles on.

It's not all idyllic, obviously. Seven people in one RV is too many, and we're on top of each other more often than we're not. We all irritate each other for various reasons—I get annoyed when I feel like they're babying me, which is a lot.

Khalil hums when he's bored, which infuriates everyone. Lars and Stefan sporadically break into bursts of Swedish at each other in tones that vary from moody to outright fury. Maja occasionally snaps at us all for acting like children. Basically, we bicker. Constantly.

We try and combat this by stopping as often as possible, way more than the breaks we'd factored into the road-trip plan. Sometimes, when the air starts to spark with irritation, Seva will pull over and bark at us all to "Be with nature! Go and have the awe!" We pile out obediently to go and have the awe. (There is literally always something to have awe at from the Trans-Canada Highway.) Within days, this phrase has meme-like status within our little family. Happy? "I have the awe." Unhappy? "I do not have the awe." Want someone to go away? "Fuck off and have the awe." And so on.

We usually get to the RV sites in the late afternoon rather than drive for as long as possible, which surprised me at first until Seva explained that big animals like deer and moose can be out in the roads, which can make driving more dangerous at dusk. At the campsites there are shops and laundry facilities, as well as better showers than the one in the RV. We share the various RV chores between all of us, except Seva, because he does most of the driving.

Our last overnight stop before we get to Jasper is Wells Gray Provincial Park, where there are dozens of waterfalls and the whole place seems to hum with the sound of rushing water. It feels almost alive with it. We explore a couple of the waterfalls together as a group before dividing off. Beasey and I wander off on our own and, much as I love our RV family, it's blissful. It's so quiet, just the two of us. So easy. We take our time hiking the couple of hours to Moul Falls, which we chose because there's a path you can walk that takes you right behind it. Right behind an actual waterfall. Like a Disney film.

"Robin Hood," Beasey says, nodding, when I say this, and I honestly don't think he could have said a single thing that would have made me love him more than I do in that moment. So cheerfully, so confidently. And then when he adds, "Good that you're thinking of that and not thinking of the second Jurassic Park film like I was," I laugh so hard I snort.

I'd thought we'd get some amazing pictures standing behind an actual waterfall, but it's too dark, though we both try with different camera settings. It's just the two of us in the cold and damp, his arm snaking around me as I shiver. If I could cut this moment separate from the rest of the trip and our lives in general, I would turn to face him, lift my chin, and lean into the inevitable. We'd kiss and it would be the most perfect, romantic thing ever: our bodies would heat up so we'd forget about the cold, his glasses would steam up, he'd whisper my name between kisses and oh my God, I want to kiss him, I want to kiss him so badly, but you can't cut moments away, there's no such thing as a kiss in a vacuum. Kissing him would mean consequences, and that would mean—

"We may as well get a selfie," Beasey says. His voice is completely normal, which is a relief to the practical part of me and a disappointment to the rest of me.

"Go on, then," I say, turning so I'm facing the right way.

We end up with a photo of us both with strained, shivery smiles, straggly wet hair sticking to our faces, looking like we're standing in a slate wet room with bad lighting.

"Oh well," I say.

"Oh well," he repeats, then laughs. "We'll just have to remember it, like the old days."

*

Later, we meet back up with the others and head to the nearest town, Clearwater, to explore before settling back in the RV for the night. Between us, we've seen thirteen waterfalls, and my ears feel like they're still ringing from the sound of rushing water. I want to tell them how *alive* I feel, how I've never felt so alive, not really, but I don't know how to say it without it coming out cheesy and self-consciously dramatic. I mean it, though. It's like every part of me has woken up. Which may, if I'm totally honest, have something to do with that moment with Beasey behind the waterfall, when I'd imagined us kissing and my body had reacted as if we really were. What would have happened if I had kissed him? He would have kissed me back, I know it. And yes, there would have been consequences, but maybe they would have been *good* consequences . . .

I lie awake in the dark that night when everyone else is asleep, letting these thoughts—increasingly delicious— wind through my head. After a while I calm myself down by reminding myself that the friendships I've made here are the most important thing, especially with Beasey. His is basically the best friendship I've ever had, and however much I like his face, however much I want to kiss him, it's just not worth risking that. Especially not as risking that would mean, in consequence, risking everyone else. I run through all their faces in my mind, this proof that I can make and have friends, good friends.

And then the first thought, treacherous and quiet, creeps into my head, scary enough to trigger my anxiety and leave me lying with my eyes wide open in the dark, trying not to spiral into a panic attack. Coldness has seeped in, filling my chest. *What if it's just here?* What if me making and having actual friends is some kind of Canada thing? Maybe everyone can make friends here. Maybe it's like how people queue in England because that's just what you do. Like, a cultural thing. I've been thinking that this trip has marked some kind of change in me and my life, proof that my loneliness before was not some state of my existence I'd need to get used to but just a sad, painful period I had left behind. But what if it isn't? What happens when I go home—I have to go home, don't I?—and leave behind these friends I've made, and the me I was with them, too? What if going home means returning to exactly the life I thought I'd left behind?

I don't feel at all like the same person I was then, who did the things I did. But I am the same person. That version of me is still in me. Under the right circumstances—or the wrong ones, I guess—who's to say I wouldn't be her again? *I wouldn't*, I tell myself. I'm stronger now; I understand things now I didn't understand then.

I try to breathe in slowly through my nose, like we learned once in that session at school about breathing techniques if you or someone you know is having a panic attack. What was it? In through the nose, out through the mouth? And I'm meant to count, aren't I? Oh God, forget it.

I reach quietly into the bag I'd hung from the corner of my bunk and withdraw my bottle of water, taking little sips until I calm down. I'm being ridiculous. Of course I've changed. I won't go back to the old life because I'm the one in charge of it. I can make sure it won't be like it was. It's like Maja said when we went hiking—I've learned from those experiences. I'll be better able to spot the red flags as they happen, instead of pointing them out in hindsight.

Besides, it wasn't like it wasn't obvious then. I can remember how it felt when things started to change with my friends, how it got harder to ignore how I really felt. I just wasn't brave enough to face up to what that meant, and I would be now. I try to reach into my memories, letting myself remember that last summer we shared, how my unhappiness had started to grow into something I couldn't ignore. Maybe it was because I'd spent so much more time with them, or maybe because it had been long enough by then that the novelty of having friends had worn off and I began to see them for who they were instead of who I wanted them to be. I wanted more of my alone time back, which was weird, because I'd always thought I didn't like being alone. I started leaving earlier, going home instead of staying at Flick's or Travis's. I'd get home too high to sleep, retreating instead to my studio, where I drew unPeytonlike landscapes of imaginary places in the kind of big, bold colors I didn't usually use. In the mornings, sobered up, I'd stare at them in consternation, looking for myself in the lines, finding a stranger.

There were also things that happened within the group that made a difference. Callum got a new girlfriend who seemed mostly bored by us, sitting on the sofa examining her nails while he tried to hang out with us as normal until he eventually gave up and chose her company over ours. This shifted the dynamic slightly, but it was more affected by the other person who also got a girlfriend: Casey, who was really the moderating force of the group, started going out with a thin-lipped, dark-haired slither of a girl called Grace, who we met only once before Casey spirited her away from us. A couple of weeks later, when Grace came up in conversation, Eric made a reference to "muff-diving" that made Casey—

stoic, unflappable Casey—cry right in front of us, before she grabbed her bag and left. I didn't get then why she'd been so upset by what I'd thought was just Eric being Eric. Crude, dickish, but essentially harmless. Later, when I met up with Casey at the Clarks where she worked that summer, she said, "I know why Flick didn't say anything, but why didn't you?" and I was both confused and flattered that she'd thought I would.

To be fair to my former self, I was a bit distracted around that time because my period was late. Late enough to send me into a spiral of actual terror at the thought of being pregnant, not just with any baby but a baby who was half Travis, potentially tying me to him for life. My terror was so huge, in fact, that it was impossible for even me, still high on the fumes of denial, to ignore the fact that I barely liked him, let alone loved him. Even after my period came—I cried with relief—I could barely tolerate him touching me for a while, which confused and annoyed him, and we argued. A lot. I should have left him, but I didn't; I couldn't. It was clear to me that doing that would mean losing all my friends, and I just couldn't even fathom being alone again.

The final thing was Flick and Eric. They'd always been loud and annoying together, either kissing obnoxiously or arguing, but over that summer—or maybe it hadn't changed and I'd just begun to notice it more—the arguing got worse. Eric was often grumpy, and he'd snap more at Flick even when she wasn't trying to wind him up, insult her without using his usual softening, teasing tone. Once, toward the end of the summer when we'd all spent a suffocatingly hot day inside, drinking and smoking, he spilled his drink on her dress and she yelled at him, smacking her hand against his arm, and he grabbed her by the shoulders, shoved her backward and slammed his fist into the wall, right by her head. I still remember the way she jerked her head instinctively away, like she'd done it before. How that one movement had chilled me more than the look on Eric's face, the sound of his fist connecting with the wall. It was Travis who'd pulled him back, yelling, "What the fuck are you doing?" and I'd tried to comfort Flick, but she wouldn't let me, shaking me off, telling us all it was fine, she was fine, everything was fine.

It frightened me. I think it frightened all of us. But no one talked about it, least of all Flick, even later on. *"You don't understand,"* she'd say. *"You don't know him like I do."* And then, if I pushed, it was me she'd get annoyed with. She could be mean if she wanted to be, and I couldn't handle mean, so I backed off.

The night of that particular incident, when I was lying with Travis in his bed—he'd been soft and sweet with me after what had happened, even affectionate—he said into the quiet, "Eric really loves Flick," and I said, "Okay." He said, "I love you," and I wanted to say, "Okay," but I didn't, I said, "I love you too," and were we both lying, or was it just me? I stayed awake long after he'd fallen asleep, listening to him snore, wondering how I'd gotten there.

So yeah. It wasn't a golden summer. If anything, it was a dulling summer, a tarnish on what I'd so desperately wanted to believe was something shiny. What happened was inevitable, really. I can't pretend I hadn't known, somewhere inside me, what was coming.

NOW

WHISTLER—JASPER

"Guys!" Seva's voice, a high-pitched yelp, sounds from the front of the RV the following afternoon. By the time we've all hurried over to him, he's already pulled over, gesticulating with excitement.

"What's wrong?" Lars asks, alarmed.

"Bear!"

We all pile out of the RV—I can't help hanging back, nervous, until Beasey grins reassuringly at me and promises that he won't let me get eaten—and see that there's a couple of cars also pulled over near us, their occupants leaning out of windows.

"Where?" Maja asks.

Seva points, and finally I see. It's an actual bear. A real live Canadian bear, just clambering away between the trees near the road, like it's normal. Like there's no road at all, like humans don't exist.

"Wow," I say, right out loud.

"I have the awe," Lars says.

"So much awe," Khalil agrees. "Awe in abundance."

When we're back in the RV, clattering away toward Jasper again, I sketch the bear over and over again. In one sketch, he's waving at us, all gawping at the side of the road. I caption it *THE AWE*.

*

Before we cross the border into Alberta, we stop off at a Tim Hortons for coffee and snacks. It's still early; cloudless but cold. Beasey joins the queue with the others, and I hang back near the door, pausing as I connect to the Wi-Fi. It's nice being disconnected while we're traveling, but I have to admit, getting back online when we make stops like this feels like being plugged back into the world. As soon as I'm connected, I send the email I'd drafted the night before to my parents, telling them all about the trip since I last spoke to them, Wells Gray, the bear. I'm about to read the emails that have accumulated since I was last connected, when an Instagram notification slides into view at the top of the screen: **flickabrick has tagged you in a post.**

My heart feels like it's jumped right out of my chest. *Flick.* Tagging me? Why? What post? How does she know about this Instagram account?

I don't tap on the notification, just watch it slide back up the screen and away. I'm waiting for my heart to calm down and the weird, uneven feeling of approaching tears to leave me. There should be a word for when you feel like crying without crying; like how you can be nauseous but not physically sick.

I used to look at Flick's Instagram all the time when we were friends, back when I didn't have an account of my own. She was "low-key annoyed" that I was "too good for Instagram" but she seemed to accept my explanation that I thought it was a waste of time.

Of course I hadn't added Flick when I'd started my adventurer account after I first arrived in Canada. I haven't even looked at hers the whole time I've been away. How has she found my new account?

I leave the queue and head out the doors back into the car park, where I lean against a railing and open Instagram to go straight to my notifications. I click on her post and it opens, filling my screen. Flick, exactly as I remember her, half smiling at the camera with her arm held up crooked to her forehead. At first I'm disorientated, because there's a drawing on her arm, the one I did for her so close to the end—my drawing of the phases of the moon. I can hear her voice in my ear as real as if she'd come to stand beside me. "Pey-Pey! It's amazing!" But how can it still be there, months on? Why hasn't it washed off by now? And then, almost in the same moment, just as I scroll down to read the accompanying text, I realize.

flickabrick

> Finally 18 and got my FIRST TATTOO! It looks incredible, thanks @inkartsurreywest for the ink and @peytontheadventurer for the design. SO happy with it!

I stare at the picture for a long time, taking in her familiar smile that is not quite a smile, the way her eyes are not exactly sad, but not happy, either. She's wearing a black T-shirt and black skinny jeans just visible at the bottom of the frame, a black baseball cap that I recognize as Eric's on her head. She looks sober. I hope she is.

I scroll lower to see the replies, which are mostly wishing her happy birthday, telling her the tattoo looks amazing. Someone with a handle I don't recognize has said, **That design is gorgeous!!** Flick has replied, **I know!! My friend is a literal artist :)**

That's when I start crying. Big, ugly sobbing, right there in the Tim Hortons car park. I drop my phone into my lap and give in to the tears, letting them fall into my hands, wet and hot. *My friend is a literal artist.* Every time the phrase runs through my head, the tears resurface. That's how she thinks of me, still? Her friend? This is her way of telling me that? No phone call, no message, just a tag on an Instagram post weeks after she abandoned me.

I get it, though. It's so Flick. For all I've been telling myself that we shared nothing over our year of friendship, I did know her. I can feel that knowing, just looking at her face through the screen. It's such a weird sensation, like a pull from the past. A tug somewhere inside me, saying, *Remember?* And I do.

They're all still there, living their lives, having birthdays, going to college. Maybe I've been able to pretend to myself while I've been away that that all stopped happening, but it hasn't. I can't make the rest of the world stop, no matter where I am, how far I go.

I really feel it then, the fact that I'm on the other side of the world from her, from all of them. And not just them, but my family, who I love and miss and didn't mean to abandon. My whole life. Is it still there, waiting for me, in a generic town in Surrey? Would I have it back, if I could?

No. I scroll back through her feed, past the multiple photos of her and Eric, the selfies, the group shots—until I get far enough to find myself in the images. Long enough ago that she couldn't tag me, but there I am. I existed in that life with her. I come across a photo of all of us where I am snug against Travis, smiling giddily out at the camera, his arm around me, a confident grin on his face. Looking at Travis doesn't give me the same kick of emotion that I get looking at Flick, which makes no sense but also makes all the sense in the world. My hopes had been pinned on Flick, not him. He may have been my romance, but he had never held my heart like she did. There should be a word for friend love. It burns as hard, just in a different way.

"Peyton." The voice is soft, questioning, and I look up, wiping my eyes. It's Seva, coffee in hand, concern on his face. "You are okay?" he asks.

I love how he phrases this question. *You are okay*. "Yes," I say, smiling, wiping at my face. "I'm okay."

"I can get Beasey," he says.

"I'm fine," I say. "This is an old sad."

Seva nods, understanding. "Ah," he says. "The worst kind." We're both quiet for a minute. "Is there anything I can do?"

"No," I say. "It's enough that you asked."

BEFORE

My friend is a literal artist

aka

Remember how you did actually
like each other, sometimes?

aka

The nice memories hurt the hardest

I wasn't thrilled about starting year thirteen. As much as the summer had been a bit of a let-down, it was still better than being at college, having to sit in classrooms for most of the day, taking notes, preparing coursework and then doing coursework.

Still, it didn't take long to find myself settled back into the usual routine. Back to seeing my friends every day, sitting with them in the same spot in the common room, trying to do my reading for English while Flick chattered on happily beside me. The workload seemed to have doubled—I'd kept up four subjects instead of three on my parents' advice, which I realized after about two days was a mistake—and my time to myself shriveled away. Between the demands of college, my friends, and my boyfriend, I barely had time to do anything on my own except sleep. My studio was practically gathering dust. My sketch pad went unopened for days.

Sometimes, I daydreamed about faking illness for a week so I could just sit alone in the blissful silence of my bedroom and sketch or paint or do literally anything creative. I would tell everyone I was ill, even my friends, even Travis.

But I didn't. I was too worried about what everyone thought of me. Even after all that time, even through my disillusionment with my friends, there was still a part of me that was worried they'd forget about me if I was out of sight for too long.

Basically, it had been a year, but very little had actually changed. I was still the same neurotic ball of anxiety I'd always been, except instead of worrying about how I could get people to like me, I worried about what I'd inadvertently do to make them stop. People *I* didn't even like. It was exhausting.

Casey was still spending most of her time with her girlfriend, so it was usually just me and Flick spending time together with the boys and without. Flick had started talking about getting a tattoo, showing me design after design until she remembered "Hey! You draw!" and asked me to design one for her. The problem was her flightiness; she'd love a design on Monday and hate it by Thursday. She'd be certain she wanted it to involve flowers—a daisy chain round her ankle, a rose on her inside hip—then dismiss flowers as "too girly."

"You're impossible," I said. "Whatever you get, you'll be bored of it within a month."

"Ugh, you're right," she said, resting her head on her crossed arms. "I'm the worst. You should just not listen to me at all; design something for me that you think is good for me and I'll get that."

"Oh, no way," I said. "I'm not falling for that."

"Please?" She fixed me with her most beseeching look. "Seriously, what would you choose for me, if you had to?"

I thought about it, giving her a slow once-over. She sat up and squared her shoulders, grinning, lifting her chin and turning her head so she was in profile.

"How about one of those moon-cycle ones?" I said. "You know, like, the phases of the moon? That's very you. Changeable."

"Show me," she demanded, shifting closer in her chair. I pulled up the browser on my phone and did a quick search, handing it over so she could see. "Oh, cool," she said. "Like, on my arm?"

"Sure," I said.

Flick leaned down to her bag, rooted around and pulled out a black pen. She pushed it toward me, pulled up her sleeve, and rested her arm on the desk between us. "Try it," she said.

"Right now?" I asked, laughing despite myself.

"Yes! I'll see how I like it."

"What if I screw it up?"

"You won't," she said. "I trust you."

I think that might have been the nicest moment of our entire friendship. The two of us together—I don't know where everyone else was—in the common room, sober and relaxed, not performing for anyone or each other. Her stating so simply that she trusted me, smiling when I touched the pen to her skin and made little hissing noises to imitate an imaginary tattoo needle.

For all the memories that make me sad from our time together—and there are lots—for some reason this is the one that makes me saddest. I don't know what it is that makes happy memories more painful with hindsight after a relationship breaks down, but it's real.

That can't have been long before the end, because Flick still had my design inked on her skin the night everything went so wrong. I remember catching a flash of it when she reached up to fold her hair into a temporary ponytail and her sleeve dropped away to reveal it.

"I love it," she'd said that day in the common room, looking down at her arm with something like awe. "Pey-Pey, it's amazing!" She shook her head. "God, you're so fucking talented."

"Wear it for a while before you get it for real," I said, trying to control my beam of pride. "I can top it up for you when it fades."

We had different classes that afternoon. When the bell rang, she hugged me, still giddy-happy, and we went our separate ways.

NOW

WHISTLER—JASPER

Later, when we cross the border into Alberta—according to the satnav—I make Seva stop the RV so I can say goodbye to British Columbia.

"We're still in Canada," Khalil says.

I roll my eyes at him. "Obviously."

I'd hoped there'd be a *Now Leaving British Columbia* sign, perhaps with an accompanying *Welcome to Alberta!* sign, so I could photograph them, but there's nothing. I'm disappointed, and I say so as everyone spills out around me. Stefan bounces on his feet, smiling; Beasey rolls his neck, closing his eyes.

"We're on the wrong route for a sign like that," Seva explains.

"They can't exactly line the highway with them," Khalil points out. "That would be weird."

"Draw one," Maja suggests. "With all of us."

I take a whole page and draw the highway running through the middle of it. On one side, I write *BRITISH COLUMBIA* and add a couple of waterfalls, the gondola at Whistler we couldn't ride, some mountains. On the other, I write *ALBERTA,* with lots more mountains. I add cartoons of all seven of us, standing by Justin the RV, looking off in all different directions, like we're waiting to see what will happen next. At the top of the page, on the BC side, I write *NOW LEAVING . . .* and at the bottom, on the other side . . . *NOW ENTERING.*

"My ears are not that big," Stefan says.

"They are gigantic," Lars says affectionately. "So big. You can see them from space."

I decide to take it as a compliment that they no longer feel the need to tell me how good my drawings are. A boundary of friendship crossed where things are less grandiose but smaller, quieter; more familiar.

Everyone piles into the RV while I stop outside to take one last look at the view, smiling against the wind, breathing it all in. And then I hear the scratchy clunk of a door closing, and I turn in time to see the RV pulling away from the roadside, away from me.

It takes about four seconds for the RV to stop, the door to swing open, and Khalil's laughing face to appear. Four seconds. But in those beats I see the RV getting smaller, disappearing into the distance, leaving me behind. I see myself stranded on the side of the road, left. Abandoned. Alone in a foreign country with no bag, no money, no phone. No friends.

I can't tell you what it does to my body, those four seconds. The panic is like nothing I've ever felt, visceral to the point of physicality. I am ice cold and white hot at the same time. My hands burn. I think I let out a whimper.

I stumble toward the RV, willing my legs into motion— they feel wobbly, like they don't quite belong to me—and step up beside Khalil, who is still grinning, not getting it yet, not seeing in me what they have all just done. "Gotcha," he starts to say, but he falters midway through and it tails off into a confused question. The boys, who had been laughing, stop, bewildered. Maja's face falls in understanding as she takes in mine, even as the boys still look baffled.

"We were just joking," Lars says.

"We wouldn't actually leave you," Stefan adds, but it comes out uncertain, like he thought it was so obvious he doesn't know how to say it properly.

My body is pulsing with the sobs I know I'm not going to be able to contain. I am going to cry beyond all normal crying, and I can't do it in front of these people, but there's nowhere to go. I tell my feet to move and manage to make it to the bathroom, swinging myself inside and locking the door. It's just in time, because the sobs burst out of me, loud and mortifying and uncontrollable. I try to stop myself, crushing my hand against my mouth, squeezing the other into a fist and smacking my leg. *Stop, stop, stop.*

There's a voice outside the door. Scottish and male. Worried, insistent. My name, repeated. Apologies. "Please come out?"

I can't reply, and the voice goes away. I still haven't gotten control over myself when there's a different voice at the door, female and German. Calm. "Peyton? The boys have gone. It's just me."

I unlock the door and let it fall open to reveal Maja. She's not frantic with worry, just solid and steady. "I didn't know they were going to do that," she says. "I would have told them no. I'm sorry they upset you. They thought it would be funny."

It *would* have been funny, that's the thing. For basically anyone else. It's just me who's spoiled the joke, and that's not their fault. I know that, rationally. But there's no room for rational in me right now. The residual panic is just too loud.

God, they must all think I'm so pathetic. A pathetic, whiny baby.

"Come outside," Maja says. I haven't said a word, and I know it's weird. "Fresh air will help."

I leave the bathroom and follow her outside. She sits me down on a patch of grass, pats my shoulder, and then opens an arm to me. I let myself fall into it, the tears I'm still trying to suppress coming out in humiliating little squeaks.

Softly, Maja says, "It's okay to cry. Don't try to stop yourself. Just cry."

"It's stupid," I manage.

"It's not," she says. "Let it out."

So I do. I imagine the dam inside me crumbling, the tears spilling. I cry into her shoulder and she hugs me with one arm, not saying a word, just occasionally patting. I don't know where the boys are but I sense they aren't far off.

The whole thing is beyond mortifying. But still, when the tears finally stop, I actually feel better. Sated, even. I wipe my eyes. "Sorry."

"It's okay," Maja says again.

"I totally overreacted," I say. My breath is still coming out scratchy, choked in my throat.

"We all get emotional sometimes," she says. "Especially if . . ." She looks at me, and I know she knows. Not the specifics, obviously, but that whatever's brought me here is the same thing that has just set me off. "If there's pain," she finishes.

I nod, and we're both quiet for a while.

Finally, she says, "It might help you to talk about it."

I know she's right. So I do.

BEFORE

The night happened almost a year to the day after I'd first gone to Flick's house, which is some bullshit symmetry. It started badly, and got worse.

The plan had been that I'd go to Flick's earlier to hang out, but I'd had to cancel that bit because I had an essay to write for English that I hadn't been able to finish on time. She was annoyed and didn't try to hide it, complaining that I wasn't there when she needed me, that she had "stuff" she wanted to talk about with me. I knew that "stuff" meant "Eric," but not in a way that meant anything would ever change, and she just wanted me to nod and make sympathetic noises. **Shockingly, I have a life outside of you,** I messaged.

Flick:
Bitch.

Flick:
Please come over :(

Me:
I'll be over later, OK? Promise. Let me work.

She didn't. Over the next few hours, she messaged me constantly, whining about Eric spending too much time with the boys, how she was lonely on her own, how her friends didn't care about her, that her hair was too straight, her bum too flat—she knew because Eric complained about it—how he expected more head than she gave, how much did I do it, did I hate it?

Replying or not replying didn't seem to have much of an effect on the frequency of these messages. Even when I turned my phone around so I wouldn't see the screen light up, I couldn't stop myself flipping it over to check.

These are not real problems, I told her, when I'd only written about four paragraphs in two hours and her messages were making my teeth grind with irritation.

Her reply was a four-word sulk: **You're a real problem.**

When I got to her house later, bringing with me an appeasing three bottles of wine that would otherwise have been drunk by my parents, she was excited to see me, apologetic about "overloading" me with her "neediness." For about ten minutes. Until Eric arrived. Then, I was all but forgotten.

"I thought you wanted to talk to me," I said to her in the brief minute it took for Eric to go to the bathroom.

"I did," she said. "Earlier. You didn't, remember?"

Her irritation with me made no sense, at least not as much sense as *my* irritation with her made. We were snappy with each other for the rest of the evening. She kept rolling her eyes at me, hard-faced, but still drinking the wine I'd brought. *Why are we friends?* I thought. *Seriously, why?* I'd thought it before, multiple times, but that time it was without any kind of affection.

I made the mistake of complaining about her to Travis when he arrived, the two of us alone in the kitchen, which only made things worse, because he defended her. "Since when is it a bad thing for her to want to talk to you?" he asked, mouth full of tortilla chips. "Thought you loved that."

"That's not the point," I said. "Obviously. And even if it was, you're meant to be on my side."

He frowned. "Why?"

"Because I'm your girlfriend," I snapped. "Remember?"

"I've known Flick since we were kids," he said. "And you're just being a bitch." He raised his eyebrows at me, tortilla chip crumbs round his mouth, and walked out of the kitchen.

I leaned back against the counter and looked at my blurred reflection in the fridge door, thinking about the first time I'd been in this kitchen, how excited I'd been to be in Flick's house, how it had felt to kiss Travis for the first time. All of that excitement and potential, for what? For being here now, one year on, having to put up with both of them, and the group in general? I would never really be part of what they all had together, that was clear. They had too much history and they didn't like me enough to displace it or override it. I would always be an extra. And hadn't that been enough, for a while? Enough to ignore, anyway.

I got drunk, taking one of the wine bottles for myself and hiding it behind my chair. Travis and I had another mini argument in the garden, sloppier this time because of my wine and his weed. I said some horrible things and so did he. I told him I hated him, and he rolled his eyes. It was a half-hearted replica of the kind of fights Flick and Eric had, and I was so aware of it in the moment, embarrassed for both of us, but especially myself. I kissed him to distract us and we had sex right there in the garden, behind the shed, as if that would make anything better.

After, still breathing hard, he smiled at me. I said, "I still hate you," which was so mean of me and, despite everything, I still feel bad about it.

He didn't say anything, just shook his head, zipped up his jeans and walked away from me, back into the house. I watched him go, thinking about leaving. I could walk right home, finish the English essay that was still incomplete, be sensible. It was too late to try making new friends at college, but maybe I could just see out the year on my own. Friendless again.

No. I couldn't.

I went back inside and sat with Travis, whispered that I was sorry. He kissed me but we didn't talk. I drank more. Later, Eric went out to meet his brother in the driveway and returned smug and obnoxious, the way he got when he had coke.

"Pay up," he said to us. "This shit isn't cheap."

I still could have left. For the record, I could have left.

"I don't have any money," Flick said.

"Not you, babe," he said.

Same old, same old. "I do," I said. Flick glared at me, then tossed her hair as she went back into the living room. I rolled my eyes at Eric and he smirked back at me. "If I pay extra, do I get extra?"

He raised his eyebrows. "Damn, Pey-Pey. Look at you."

"Eric!" Flick's voice, impatient.

"Sure," Eric said to me. "Let's settle up later, though. Got to deal with Flick."

"Of course you do," I said, and we shared a look at her expense that I hadn't earned and shouldn't have encouraged. I was annoyed with Flick, but she was still my friend, and Eric was such a dick. I'd become mean, somehow. Mean and small.

I had also not earned the cockiness I felt when it came to

the cocaine, blithely asking for extra like I had any idea what I was doing. What was I trying to prove, anyway? Or maybe I wasn't trying to prove anything. Maybe I was chasing something instead—something that would make all of this better, or at least make it make sense.

Maybe I would have been fine if I'd just stuck to the one line. Maybe none of it would ever have happened, and I'd have made up with Flick and we'd all have carried on as normal. I would still be at college and Travis would still be my boyfriend and I would still call them all my friends.

But I did do the second line. And a third. Surreptitious, with Eric, in the kitchen that was somehow the site of so many of my terrible decisions. I bounced through the house, joyful, throwing my arms around Travis, kissing him. Everything was good again, so good, including me. I was exactly where I wanted and needed to be. These were my very best friends, my squad, and I was a champion.

It didn't last long enough, of course. The happiness was so temporary. The weird thing was, though, that this time the rest of my body didn't calm down when the euphoria passed. The energy didn't dissipate—it doubled. My whole body felt weird, actually. Wired. Weird. *Wired*.

My heart was going really fast. *Really* fast.

"Why's it so hot?" I asked the room, but no one responded. I wasn't sure if I'd actually spoken out loud. I got to my feet and made my way across the room, stumbling out into the hall, through the front door, into the garden. It was raining and I closed my eyes, trying to control my breathing, which seemed to be happening a lot faster than usual, or was that my heart, too? I put my hand to my chest, trying to blink away my confusion. *Thump, thump, thump.*

"Close the door, Pey-Pey." Someone's voice, someone nearby. "It's fucking raining."

My heart was going even faster. Was I breathing or not breathing? I'd closed the door, I was inside the house, but now I was looking at the floor, which was weird, because why would the floor be this high?

"Pey-Pey?" Motion near my head. "Where's Travis? Someone get Travis. Pey-Pey's being weird." Fingers on my skin. "Fuck, she's really hot. Pey-Pey?" Worry. "Pey-Pey?" Panic. "*Fuck!* Eric!"

". . . probably just passed out."

"No, something's wrong—"

"Shit, oh fuck. Peyton?" A shake. "Peyton? *Eric!* Did . . . see . . . she had? Fuck, fuck, fuck."

". . . been drinking . . . not supposed to . . . taking coke."

". . . all been drinking . . ."

"How much . . . we all . . . though? Fuck, why . . . stop her?"

Loud. More voices. Shouting. Hysterical. Hands on my face, my arms. Something cold and wet splashed over me.

"Nico!"

"It might wake her up!"

More hysteria. Someone crying.

"Oh my God, oh my God!"

"Shut up, Flick!"

"You shut up!"

My eyelid lifted open, then dropped.

"We have to get her to hospital."

"How? You going to drive like this?"

"I'm calling Mum."

"*No,* Flick!"

A clatter, a shriek. "Ow!"

"Don't be an idiot. You know what will happen to us if we get caught with all this shit?"

"*Fuck!* Why's she shaking like that? Oh my fuck, is that a fit? Oh fuck, oh fuck."

"Someone call a fucking ambulance."

"Everyone *shut up,* I can't think."

"Peyton? Peyton? *Peyton!*"

Everything black for a while. Then being lifted, held in someone's arms, my head lolling back. Cold air, rain. Outside. Why? Trying to open my eyes but my *head.*

Being put down. Down on the . . . on the what? Cold and wet. Hard. Concrete. Pressing my forehead against the pillow. No, curb. Mumbling, "What?"

"Fucking *go.*"

"We can't just leave her here!"

A soft voice, near my ear. "The ambulance is coming, Pey."

"*Flick!* Where are you go—you can't—"

"You'll be okay—it's okay."

"*Go!*"

"Shit, shit, shit."

Running footsteps, running away, away from me. The rain on my face, stirring me out of the dark, but still something quiet deep inside me, saying, *Stay down. You don't want to be awake for this.*

I still don't remember much of anything after that until I woke up to the harsh light of the hospital the next day. I had the sense more than the memory of a flurry of people all around me, talking to each other or me, I wasn't sure. Being poked by needles and one question on repeat. *What did you take? What did you take?* Either I told them or they figured it out, because when I woke up I was, at least physically, fine. Numb, hollow, confused. Dry-mouthed. But fine.

And then there were my parents, alternating between fury, worry, and—this surprised and confused me—shame. "This isn't how we raised you," they said. I knew this meant the drugs, though they didn't say so specifically. They wanted me to confirm who it was they should blame, but I didn't tell them. I still thought I should be loyal, that's the thing. I thought they were still my friends. Even when Mum said, as if the words hurt her, "They left you in the gutter." Those are the words she used. The gutter.

Maybe I should have cried when I understood what she meant, that my only friends had abandoned me on the side of the road when I was clearly having some kind of extreme, potentially life-threatening episode, but I didn't. I felt numb. Just entirely numb, physically and emotionally. The memories surfaced slowly, swimming back to me through the sludge of my addled mind. The sound of running footsteps away from me. The flashing lights reflected in the puddles on the road. The low voices of the paramedics.

But, mostly, a feeling. One that started there on the roadside in the dark and the rain and never went away. Abandonment. Like loneliness, but worse. Like rejection, but deeper. I felt it then and I've carried it with me ever since, even as I've tried to outrun it by crossing oceans and continents. Some feelings have staying power, though. Some feelings last.

NOW

WHISTLER—JASPER

I tell Maja in a jumble of confused, embarrassed shame, the two of us sitting on the grass together on the roadside in Alberta. She listens quietly, and at some point I realize she's holding my hand and maybe it should be weird but it isn't—it's nice. She doesn't interject with gasps or protestations or commentary—that wouldn't be very Maja—she just listens.

"I guess . . ." I say, my voice a little hoarse. "I guess they had to leave me, right?" Hearing the story out loud for the first time, I find myself needing to defend them, searching for reasons I've been overreacting all this time. "They would have got in so much trouble, and . . ."

"No," Maja says. "They didn't have to leave you at all, and they shouldn't have done. That was very wrong." She says this like she knows I need to hear it. "What did they say, when you spoke to them later?"

"They didn't," I say. "Speak to me, I mean. No one even checked I was okay." I think of Casey's email, weeks after the fact, too little too late. "The only one I spoke to was Travis, and that was only to . . ." My voice gives out. The memory of that awful phone call, after I'd gotten home from hospital, charged my phone, waited for the screen to fill with messages and stared in shock when they didn't come. Travis's guilty, defiant voice when I finally called him. How he'd shrugged off the silence of him and his friends in the face of what all my lifelong hopes of friendship—"Which I get isn't fair on her; I do know that." How when we were friends I'd lost all sense of myself, trying to be exactly what they wanted even though I—and they, probably—didn't know what that was.

When I'm finished, he says, very carefully, "What is it you want from her? From them?"

"I don't know," I say. "I really don't. Nothing, I think. I mean, a real apology would be nice, but it's way too late to mean anything. Or otherwise some kind of explanation, like a debrief of our friendship. Why they even bothered with me. What they thought of me, really. But you don't get that stuff in real life, do you?"

"Why does it matter what they thought of you?"

"Of course it matters."

"Why? Do you think they're thinking this much about what you think of them?"

The question throws me. I'd never even thought about it. "Well . . . no. But they don't have the issues I have. They've always had friends."

"The issues you have are even more of a reason why you shouldn't be thinking about what they thought of you."

"Beasey, they were the first friends I had since primary school, which doesn't count."

"Of course that counts—"

"And before them, everyone hated me. I had *no* friends, okay? I told you that. So what was wrong with me before, was it still there? Did they just not care about it? Or maybe they didn't see it, and then they did, and—"

"Won't you listen to me?" Beasey breaks in, frustrated. "There's *nothing wrong with you*. You haven't had any issue making friends here, have you? Whatever went wrong before, it wasn't because of you. It just *was*. I know this is easy for me to say, but you have to find some way of letting that go, or it's going to really screw with the rest of your life."

"It's different with traveling friends, though," I say.

"Yeah, people are even more likely to just pass you over if there's no connection," he says. "People aren't nice for the sake of it just because you're traveling. If they like you, they're nic*er* and they try harder. But they still have to *like you first*. And we do like you, all of us. You're not going to have trouble making friends when you get back to your 'real' life. Can you just trust me on that?"

"But why didn't I have them at school?" I know as I'm saying this that he can't answer, but I say it anyway. "Why? Everyone has friends at school."

"I don't know," he says. "School is such a weird, artificial environment. You put, what, thirty kids in one class, all the same age, all from the same place? That will never happen again in your life. It's not how life *is*. If you think about it, it's weirder that you *would* make lasting friendships there. I don't think you should beat yourself up about that time of your life. It doesn't say anything about you."

"It does, though," I say. "It's nice of you to say that, but it does."

He shakes his head. "Don't read too much into the school bit," he says.

"You and Khalil met at school," I point out.

"Sure," he says. "That's how we met; it's not *why* we're friends."

"Why are you friends, then?"

He manages to both frown and smile at the same time. "God, I don't know. That's such a big question. It's history,

yeah. We've been through a shitload together. We like a lot of
the same stuff. We have a lot of shared values, even though
we disagree about a lot of things, which is important. I guess
we just . . . Look, I'm trying to think of this in relation to
this specific conversation and to you, and how I feel about
my other friends, and I think the main thing is connection.
Sometimes you connect with people, and it all goes from there.
I think that's the most important part of any friendship. It's
why sometimes people can meet and have nothing in common
on the surface but become great friends. So even when we
were eleven, Khalil and me were like, *Yep. You're my kind of
person.*"

"And so I just didn't connect to anyone?"

"Or they didn't connect with you," he says. "Because of
a load of weird school politics that goes on; because they
thought for some bizarre reason that they shouldn't. And you
did have friends at college. Clearly they weren't great friends,
but that can happen. Friends aren't always good."

I think about that first time I spoke to Flick, the way I'd
been able to joke with Travis so quickly. Was that connection?
Or was it just my all-consuming need? How could I tell the
difference? Did it even matter?

"I just want to say," Beasey adds, his grin reappearing,
"that I'm not an expert. I'm hearing myself and it's like I
think I'm some kind of friendship guru?" He laughs. "Totally
not. I've literally never thought about this subject this much,
ever."

"It's good, though," I say.

"Yeah?"

"Yeah. Makes sense. Connection."

He nods enthusiastically. "You can connect with people

from all over, you know. They don't have to be the same age or from the same place. And family, too. I've got cousins who are like my mates. Am I helping? You can tell me to shut up."

"You're helping a lot," I say. "Sorry, I know I'm weird about this stuff. It's just such a big thing for me."

"I get that," he says. "You don't have to apologize."

"What did you think when you first met me?" I ask.

Beasey considers this, and I know it's because he's wondering how honest to be, how to phrase what he's thinking. "You seemed . . . lost," he says. "And you had such sad eyes."

"I mean apart from that," I say.

He laughs. "I don't think you can 'apart from' if it's being lost and sad. Those are pretty fundamental things."

"Don't say that," I say. "That's shit, isn't it? You're basically saying I was pathetic."

"I'm obviously not," he says.

"You are. If there was nothing else to me except those two things, I'm basically a stray dog."

He laughs again, even though I hadn't been making a joke. "Peyton."

"What?" It comes out combative, even though he's been being so nice to me and the last thing he deserves is a snap.

"You're obviously not a stray dog," he says.

I look away. *He is not trying to hurt me*, I remind myself. *He is on my side.*

"This is hard for you—I get that," he says. "I shouldn't be flippant. Look, what can I say except I like you and I'm your friend? I can't speak for any of those people, just me. Okay? Can that be enough?"

"Of course that's enough," I say, because it's more than

enough, and I'd be an idiot to risk the best friendship I've ever had because I'm still burned by the crap ones. But my heart still hurts at how easily he recalls me being lost and sad, that it was that obvious. Maybe it still is? I could ask him, but I decide I've been needy enough for one conversation.

I tell him I'm starting to get cold, and we head back to the RV, where we find that the others have set up a campfire and are waiting for us, bag of marshmallows at the ready, mid-conversation about the Canadian Rockies. I'd told Maja it would be okay for her to tell the rest of them the gist of why I'd been so upset, and I'm a little nervous of how they'll react, but all that happens is that Stefan says, "You okay, Peyton?" and I say, "Yes, thanks." And that's it—we move on.

NOW

JASPER

We spend our time together over the next few days in and out of the RV, exploring what we can in Jasper, which is a bit limited by it being off-season. On our second day, Lars, Stefan, Beasey, and I all go to the planetarium together. "Why would I go to look at a screen of the night sky when I can just look up?" Khalil asks, but I love it because it feels like the kind of thing I would do back home in my ordinary life, with normal, permanent friends, instead of my temporary gang of travelers in the kind of setting that demands your attention every single day. I like the splash of ordinary in the adventure.

There are a couple of art galleries still open, and Beasey and I spend some time mooching through them—that's the word he uses, "mooching"—while he asks me more about my own art, what I'd display if I had a gallery of my own. I feel closer to him—to all of them—since my mini breakdown and their understanding. Like they watched my emotional baggage explode all over the highway, but instead of leaving me to pick it all up myself, they've shared it between them. I feel so much lighter. I've been smiling all day.

"I'd rather work with paper," I say. "Illustrate children's books." It's a dream I've never shared with anyone. "Or graphic novels, even."

"So, storytelling art rather than . . ." He pauses, searching for the word in his own head. "Aesthetic art?"

I know what he means, so I nod. "I guess so."

"That'll be amazing," he says.

"If it happens, yeah," I say. "But that's a big if."

"Nope," he says confidently. "It's a when."

I try to roll my eyes, but I'm smiling. I give his arm a little shove and he laughs, leaning over to put his arm around my shoulder. When he squeezes me playfully against his side, I have to stop myself snuggling in and staying there.

That night, the sky is cloudless, so we head out on a mini hike, wrapped up in our coats with extra blankets, to stargaze. Jasper is a dark-sky preserve, so I'd been expecting to see more stars than I'm used to, even for Canada, but the reality of it— an impossible number of stars spread out above us, making the night sky look less like pinpricks of light through a dark blanket but a living sea of stars—is something else. There's depth I've never even known was there. It makes me feel a bit weird, to be honest. It's so eerie, and I've never felt so small.

"I've never seen stars like this," I say. "Not ever."

"In the Highlands—" Beasey begins.

"Oh, are you from the Highlands?" Khalil asks.

"Fuck you," Beasey says good-naturedly. "I was just going to say that there are some good dark-sky places in the Highlands, too."

"Didn't you go to the same school?" I ask, confused. "Isn't that how you met?" I turn to Khalil. "Aren't you also from the Highlands?"

Khalil looks lazily over at Beasey. "Do you want to try to explain your complicated family life?"

"I'm from the Highlands," Beasey says. "Parents divorced when I was eleven; I had to move with my mum to Aberdeen."

"Where he met me," Khalil interjects.

"Where I met Khalil," Beasey agrees. "When I left school, I went back to live with my dad to work at the hotel he runs."

"That doesn't sound that complicated," I say.

"Let's just say neither of my parents liked me wanting to be with the other one," Beasey says. He shrugs and looks away, then says, "Weird how you can sum up something in one sentence that just strips out all the emotional shit, right?"

I'm not sure what to say. I glance at Khalil, who says, "I worked at Beasey's dad's hotel too, for a while. It's true; the Highlands are beautiful." He gives Beasey's shoulder a small, affectionate nudge, then smiles at me. "Hey, one day, when the three of us are back in the UK, everyone should visit."

"Amazing," I say.

"That should be the reunion," Beasey says, brightening.

"Sounds perfect," Seva says.

"I'll be there," Stefan says, nodding. "Let's make it a plan."

"Speaking of plans," Lars says. "Have you figured out what's next for you yet, Peyton?"

Instantly I tense, like the words themselves are a test I haven't prepared for. Because of course I haven't figured it out. I haven't even really thought about it. Why would I, when everything here is so good, beyond good? I have Canada and friends and an RV. And, more than that, I have *myself*. The person I'd always hoped I'd one day be, given the right circumstances, the right people.

"Aren't you going to see your grandad?" Stefan adds, when I don't say anything.

"Peyton doesn't need to think about that now," Beasey says.

"Time's running out, though," Khalil says.

"You should stay in Banff with Lars and me," Stefan says. "Work at the ski resort, like us."

"I wish," I say. I wish *hard*. "I don't have a work visa."

"What about you, Seva?" Khalil asks. "Do you know what you're going to do when this is over?"

"Toronto," Seva says, yawning. "My new job starts next week. I will fly from Calgary the day I drop off the RV."

"See?" Khalil says to me, pointing at Seva. "A plan."

He's teasing in a warm way, but I still shrug and look away, because I think if I talk I might do something embarrassing like cry. Why are we suddenly all talking about what's next when now is so good? I don't want to think about everyone scattering across the continent, how little time we have left together.

Seva calls it a night after ten more minutes, and we all head back to the RV together. Beasey and I hang back, walking behind everyone else. He drops his voice low.

"Sorry about them getting at you about your plans," he says. "They're just worrying for you."

"I know," I say. "I'll be fine, though. I've actually been thinking about the stuff you said before about my grandad."

"Yeah?"

"Yeah. Maybe I *should* go and see him. I've never been this close to him before. And he's an artist—did I tell you that?"

"No." He looks baffled. "If he's an artist, why wouldn't you want to see him?"

"It's just not a thing in my family. I've never even met him. We barely talk about him, except if my grandma's complaining about him, or my dad is telling us not to turn out like him. But now I'm thinking that it doesn't have to be like that? Maybe I should meet him; find out his side of the story."

"What's the side that you know?"

"Basically that he walked out," I say. "When my dad was a kid."

"And he moved to Canada?" Beasey says. "You have a family member that ran away from their life to Canada?"

I roll my eyes. "No—calm down. This isn't a parallel-lives story. He ended up in Canada. Settled here about twenty or thirty years ago, maybe? Before I was born, anyway. But he moved around a bit before then, I think."

"Maybe not parallel lives, but I'm seeing some similarities here."

I shake my head. "Imaginary ones."

"But that must be why you came here, right?" he asks. "Because he's here? I was going to ask you why you chose Canada, of all the places in the world. It makes more sense now I know about him."

"It wasn't him," I say. "He barely featured. I guess maybe him living here made the whole country seem less . . . I don't know, abstract, than other places. But I would have chosen here anyway."

"Why, though?" he asks. "And actually, as I'm asking, why did you leave at all?"

"You know why," I say, surprised. "I told you about what happened."

"Yeah, but how did that turn into getting on a plane and running away?" I open my mouth to protest, and he laughs and says, "Or whatever phrasing you want to use."

I think about those days after I'd gotten back from the hospital, how lost I'd felt, how pointless everything seemed. Pretending to go to college and then just going to the library instead. The night before I'd left, sitting in Dad's office, staring at the globe. It's like remembering someone I don't recognize.

"It's kind of hard to explain," I say.

He smiles. "Try me."

BEFORE

The leaving

The first thing was the hairdresser.

It was a Friday, six days after I'd left hospital, and I was spending another afternoon when I should have been at college just wandering around town. The sign outside said they were taking walk-ins.

Fancy a change? 20% off first appointments.

"What can I do for you?" the hairdresser, whose name was Chloe, asked me, meeting my eye in the mirror.

"I actually don't know," I said. "But I don't want this."

When I was a kid, I had blond curls. I was cute then, all big brown eyes and wide smile. The blond grew out, the cuteness faded, and my smile got smaller and smaller until secondary school killed it. I wanted that Peyton back. The happy, hopeful Peyton.

I showed her a photo of child-me on my phone that I'd found on Mum's Facebook account. "Can you do a seventeen-year-old version of that?" I asked. It sounded like a pretty stupid request, but she understood.

"Sure," she said. While she worked she asked me, "Why the big change?" and I told her about Travis and my friends who weren't my friends, how everything had turned out so wrong.

"I don't know what to do," I said.

"Sounds like you need a change," she said. In the mirror, she smiled at me for the first time. "People always start with their hair."

"Do they?" I imagined all the people she must have had in that chair, wanting to be transformed.

"Oh yeah," she said. "Makes sense, doesn't it? It's the quickest way to feel—or, at least, look—like a different person. And if it doesn't work out, it's only temporary."

I nodded.

"But," she added. "It's only surface. That's the thing. It's not *real* change. If you want things to be different, you've got to go deeper."

Chloe was right, of course. Hadn't I done this exact thing before college? Changed my hair and expected everything else to change as a result? If I wanted more, I needed to do more. Go deeper. Find the root of the problem and rip it right out.

"How?" I asked.

She shrugged. "I don't know, love. It's your life."

That wasn't my moment of epiphany, but I think it started there. Someone telling me that my life was my own, which is so obvious, yet so easy to forget. My life wasn't the college my parents made me go to or the subjects they chose for me. It wasn't the friends I'd latched on to out of panic and loneliness. The boyfriend I loathed but thought I needed. My life was me, and I was the only constant thing in it I could depend on.

Chloe made me close my eyes while she finished and blow-dried my hair so she could give me her "reveal moment." When I opened my eyes I saw myself transformed, as I'd hoped. My hair blond, bright and cheerful, not tempered by lowlights, framing my face in wide, confident curls.

"Is this what you had in mind?" she asked me.

"It's perfect," I said.

I went home to an empty house, my parents out for an anniversary dinner they'd considered canceling before I'd convinced them to go. My happiness at my transformation lasted for about an hour, then faded, like all highs do. I missed my friends. Or, more accurately, having friends. I didn't want to, but I did.

I went into Dad's study and slunk around the room for a while, walking so close to the bookshelves that my elbow rubbed along the spines of the books. When I'd done the full circuit twice, I slumped into Dad's ridiculous OTT leather chair—the one I hadn't been allowed to sit on as a kid and that was probably still technically off limits—slouching low so my legs dangled over one arm of the chair, my head crooked against the other, eyes gazing up to the ceiling. I stayed like that for a while, trying to summon a feeling, an emotion I could latch on to. But there was nothing, just a blank space. Was this it? Had I finally lost the last part of me that felt? That cared enough *to* feel?

I kicked myself up into a proper sitting position and reached forward to open one of the desk drawers. I opened another, and then another, until I found what I'd only been half expecting to find: a bottle of whiskey, three-quarters full. I uncapped the bottle and took a slow sip, closing my eyes against the burn. *Thanks, Dad.*

It helped, that whiskey. It made time slow and my skin warm. When I thought about Travis, he seemed smaller somehow, so distant from this room and me in this chair and the bottle in my hand. *I am real. I am here.* I flipped through the jotter on Dad's desk, eyes scanning vaguely for my own name. I finally found it in the top corner of one page, an idle scrawl.

Peyton—Bude? ASK.

I squinted at the scribble for a while, assuming at first that I was misreading Dad's handwriting. The whiskey had slowed my usual thought streams, so it took me probably longer than it should have done to realize that Bude was the name of a town in Cornwall, the very-far-away home of my grandmother. Ask who? Me, if I'd go? Grandma, if I could stay? He wanted to send me away. Banish me to the far corner of Cornwall, make me somewhere else's problem.

But no, I was going off the deep end. I was in the middle of the school year; I couldn't leave college. My parents wouldn't really send me away, however disappointed in and confused by me they were. The note was probably old anyway, and nothing to do with what was happening right now. No one was going to make me leave. My heart calmed. I drank some more whiskey.

And then three thoughts trickled in, one after the other. The first was, *I wish I could leave, though.* The second was, *Cornwall isn't far enough away.* The third was, *Who cares if it's the middle of the school year?*

They were great, those thoughts. They warmed me right up, made my nerves dance. I smiled at them as they circled around me. I imagined myself packing a bag and walking out of the house, closing the front door behind me, getting on a bus that would drive me right past college, out of town, across Surrey and to the airport. I'd get on a flight somewhere.

Where? Anywhere. Just . . . anywhere. I'd cross time zones to get there and I'd leave everything hateful and sad and painful behind. I would finally—*finally*—escape.

I sat up and leaned over to look at the globe Dad kept by his desk, the ridiculous ornate one he bought himself for his fortieth birthday. I spun it slowly, closing my eyes like I used to when I was a kid, and let my finger drop. *Wherever it lands, I will go.* I opened my eyes. My finger was resting somewhere in the middle of the South Atlantic.

I drank some more whiskey. I thought, *Fuck you, then.*

Where would I *want* to go? I sat back on the chair, tucking my knees up under my chin, crossing my arms around me. Far. That was the first thing. The most important thing. Thailand, like Dillon did the summer after his first year at uni. Argentina, right on the lowermost tip. Nepal. Somewhere in the Arctic, or Antarctica; whichever is the one you can visit. The world was so full of places that weren't where I was. I pulled out my phone and opened a browser, typing, *Where would I be if I was furthest from home?* The website I clicked on asked for my country, my city. It told me the furthest I could be, some twelve thousand miles away, was a town in New Zealand.

New Zealand, that would be all right. I could go to New Zealand. I could go and never come back. A few more taps and I was looking at flights. Almost a grand for a one-way ticket, leaving in eight hours. For a moment I was so full of longing, so desperate with it, that time suspended around me and I just . . . *ached*. I needed to be on that plane. I wanted to walk onto the tarmac of an airport in a city on the other side of the world and know that no one, *no one*, was going to laugh at me or misunderstand me or hate me or hurt me or even fucking *know* me.

I looked back at the globe and put my finger on the small, shriveled island I lived on, then leaned around and put my other hand on the other side—New Zealand. Also a small island. I wondered if I'd have the same problems if I lived there. I ran my finger back over the globe, over oceans and continents and borders, until my fingertips touched again over Europe. So much world. So many countries. So many people.

God, imagine being that far from everything wrong. Wouldn't it all seem so small? I could send postcards to everyone that wouldn't miss me. *Look,* I'd say. *I made it.*

My eyes were wet and burning. I went back to Google. Where do people go to get lost? *Bali. Iceland. South Africa. The Alps.*

Where are people happy? *Finland. Norway. Denmark.* (The Scandinavians are clearly onto something.) The first non-European country on the list was Canada.

Where do the nice people live? Another list. *Canada.*

Of course. Canada's known for being nice. It's like its thing. I gave the globe another spin and traced my finger across the length of the country. That would be a good place to get lost. That giant country where people were nice.

One flight, that's what I should do. A one-way flight to Vancouver. That, Google told me, was nearly five thousand miles away. Far enough, not quite as scary-far as New Zealand. English-speaking, apart from Quebec. Safe.

Fuck it, I could do it. I could do anything I wanted. I could pack a rucksack with nothing but clothes and my sketch pad and just *go*. I could do some old-school backpacking. That was still a thing, right? Make my way from one end of the country to the other, like a challenge. I could start in Vancouver and end up in . . . I looked at the globe again. St. John's, Newfoundland.

And at some point, and I really don't know when or how it happened, I stopped thinking "I could" and started thinking "I will." And then it was "I am." And there I was on the British Airways website, looking at flights, mentally packing my bag.

And in the back of my head, the steady beat of *I have to get out of here or I will die.* Honestly, it was like a drumbeat. A warning and a promise, and it didn't even scare me, that was the thing, because it was so *true.* I felt how true it was. I had to get out of there or I wouldn't survive. That's the real answer of how I got here. Everything that had happened—all the bullying, and college, and Travis and the drugs and being so fucking lonely for so long—all led to that moment and that thought.

So I know that it sounds like I did it on a whim, that I didn't think it through, and I'm only seventeen and it was a stupid thing to do and at some point I'll have to go home and face the consequences and all the same problems will still be there waiting for me when I get back, yes. But all of that? It doesn't matter. Because I had to get out of there or I would die.

NOW

THE ICEFIELDS PARKWAY

The next afternoon, it snows. I'm nervous about how it will affect the roads, but Seva shakes his head. "This is nothing," he says. "Barely a flurry. If it was a snowstorm, I would be concerned. But this will melt quickly at this low level. Not a problem."

When the snow stops we go on a walk together because I want to see Jasper in the snow, and Seva wants sweet treats from Tim Hortons. We've been walking for less than five minutes when I slip on a hidden patch of ice and stumble, very gracefully, toward the ground. Luckily, Seva catches me before my head collides with the concrete. He lifts me to my feet, muttering something in Russian.

"I'm fine!" I say, brushing down my legs.

"You are so reckless," Seva says, smiling affectionately, shaking his head. "You should watch how you walk in these conditions. I can drive the RV, but I cannot steer you."

I laugh. "You don't need to protect me. I can take care of myself."

"We *all* feel protective over you," Seva says. "You are like the group's baby sister."

"Baby?" I repeat.

"Younger," he amends.

"Hmmmm," I say. "This isn't fair, anyway. I didn't grow up in wintery conditions. I'm still learning. You know how often we get proper snow like this where I live? Like, never." I turn to look across our small section of Jasper, covered in white. "Not like you," I say. "You must have had this all the time. Right?" When he doesn't answer, I add, "Does this remind you of home?"

Seva's forehead crinkles and he shakes his head, unsmiling. "You mean Russia?"

"Well, yeah."

"I do not think of Russia as home," he says. "Not for some time."

"Oh," I say awkwardly. "Um. Sorry. Where . . . where is home, then?"

Seva is looking out across the snowscape, the soft frown still on his face. "I do not know yet," he says. "I'm still looking."

Can I ask? Is there any way to ask without being rude? I'd had a vague idea that Seva's backstory was going to be exciting. A spy, maybe. A political exile. The kind of thing you don't bring up, so I'd been careful not to pry.

"How long have you been traveling?" I ask.

"Seven years," he says. "I have not been traveling the way Beasey and Khalil have; it has not been an adventure. I have been finding work and staying where I can to earn money, then moving on when a visa demands it. I have been back to Russia a few times when I had no choice, worked there for a while, and then left again for the first place I could."

Carefully, I say, "So you *can* go back?"

A smile twitches on his face. "Ah, you are thinking I am some sort of exile? Of course."

I flush an immediate, guilty red. "Well, I . . ."

"Too many films," he says, teasing. "Too many books. No,

nothing exciting like that. I can return whenever I please. I just do not please."

"Why not?" Quickly, I add, "You don't have to tell me."

He looks at me, then away. "It is a sad story."

"Oh." I feel like I've wandered into a territory I don't belong in. "You don't have to tell me," I say again.

"My mother and sister were killed," he says, and my heart lurches. "Not in an exciting way. A car accident. The kind that happens every day." He flicks his hand in the air as he says this, like a shrug, though there's a deep pain in his face that makes me hurt just to see it. "My father and I were not close, and their deaths made that worse. He remarried and made another family, and I left." He glances back to me. "You see, it is very mundane. The kind of story that happens everywhere, all over the world."

"I'm sorry," I say. "Has it helped, being away?"

He nods. "Yes, very much. My sister, she wanted to travel. I used to tease her for that."

"What was her name?" I ask.

He smiles and looks properly at me. "Yana. You remind me of her. I was not sure if I should say, but you do. She was seventeen. Bold, like you."

I'm about to say, automatically, *I'm not bold!* But I stop myself. This isn't for me; it's for him.

"I feel protective," Seva continues. "Like a brother. For you."

"That's why you came up with this plan?" I ask gently. "The motor home, and driving us all this way?"

"The world is not always safe," he says very quietly. "Not even somewhere like this. You seemed as though you felt lost, and that can be a dangerous thing. I saw a way to help, and so did everybody else."

I'm not sure how to feel. I'd sensed, on some level, that Seva saw me as a little sister, like most of them did, but I hadn't realized quite how deep that went. It's a nice thing to be cared for, of course, but I'd hoped we'd all been having this adventure together because we liked each other. Not because they thought I needed protecting.

But I *have* needed protecting, haven't I? Who knows where I would have been without them.

"I have upset you?" he asks.

"No!" I say quickly. He just told me about his tragic life and I'm going to be upset because they've all been so nice to me? No. "I was just processing." I smile at him and make robot hands. "Meep morp."

He laughs.

"Beasey said that too," I say, putting my hands back down to my sides. "That I looked lost. I didn't realize it was that obvious."

"Perhaps if you had had a plan," Seva says, quite drily. "But there you were, seventeen, on the other side of the world from where you should be, looking at us with such bafflement when we asked where you were going. In Canada! In October!"

I feel my face start to redden again. "Okay, don't rub it in."

"One day, you will see someone like that and you will help them," he says. "You will be glad to do it, as we have been for you."

"You must think I'm really silly."

"Silly? No, not at all. Why do you say that?"

"For coming here for, like, nothing. Running away from my easy life just because I fell out with some friends."

Seva shakes his head. "That is not what you really think,"

he says. "And it is not what I think. You are dismissing your own unhappiness, and there is no reason to do that. I know you must have been deeply unhappy to feel you had to leave. That is not a small thing. I understand. It is how I felt."

"God, Seva, yours was so much worse—"

"No," he interrupts me. "That is a pointless game to play. Pain is not a hierarchy. It is like . . ." He considers. "A reservoir. It all comes from the same place. Sometimes the volume changes, but people can drown in three inches of water. You and me, we have had very different lives, but we have this in common—the unhappiness and the leaving. There is a whole world. You do not have to stay where you are unhappy."

I look at him, taking in his familiar face, so serious and soft at the same time. I'm struck by a sudden gratitude that he has shared his story with me, that he's opened up. There's so much trust in it; a depth of friendship I had once only imagined and never dared attempt with anyone at home. I want to hug him. Instead, I say, "You're a really good brother."

"Better now than I was," he says. "As soon as I was no longer a brother, I became the best one I could be."

"You're still a brother," I say.

NOW

JASPER—BANFF
THE ICEFIELDS PARKWAY

The Icefields Parkway—or Highway 93, technically—is 144 miles of epic, connecting the two national parks, Jasper and Banff. As a straight drive, it would take about three hours, but we've allowed ourselves two full days to make all the stops we want, plus a third day for Lake Louise before we finish our trip in the town of Banff and everyone goes their separate ways. Aka the breaking of my heart.

The highway is a wide, smooth road framed by mountains from basically every angle. Everywhere you look, there are mountains, trees, lakes, glaciers. We stop a bunch of times just for gawping/photo purposes, but our first actual stop is at Athabasca Falls and canyon. A little farther on there's a lookout, apparently known as Goat Lick, over the glacial blue of the Athabasca River, winding beside a sea of trees stretching all the way to the mountains in the distance.

"Imagine if you lived in Banff and worked in Jasper," Lars says dreamily. "You could make this drive every day. It would be your commute."

"Don't you think the magic would wear off, though?" I ask. "If you were doing it twice a day, every day?"

"Not for me," Lars says. "Every day, I would stop right here, and I would say, *Wow!* I would see it in all colors, all seasons."

Stefan is smiling affectionately, nodding. "I will say *Wow!* with you," he says.

Lars grins at him—the kind of grin that is just for the two of them—and takes his hand.

"You should do it," I say. "And set up an Instagram for it. You can call it 'The Daily Goat Lick.' Oh! Or make one of those a-second-a-day videos."

Lars groans. "God, now I want to do it even more, but I can't, and now I'm sad."

Later we stop at the Columbia Icefield where, if we'd only come a few weeks earlier, we'd have been able to do the Glacier Skywalk, which is a glass-floored walkway built into a cliff edge hundreds of feet above the valleys and waterfalls below. But it's closed for the season—Beasey fails to hide his relief—and I'm disappointed until Khalil suggests we pool the money we would have each spent and use it to go out for dinner in Banff.

"I'm going to have to come back one day a bit earlier in the year, aren't I?" I say.

"Yes," Stefan says.

"We all are," Khalil says.

I try to imagine myself in a few years' time, when I'll be old enough to come back without anyone yelling at me to come home. Maybe I'll have a boyfriend with me or, better still, a friend. A best friend, a permanent one. I'll tell them all about this trip, the things we saw, how loads of stuff was closed because I'd accidentally come in the off-season. They'll say, *But was it still worth it?* and I'll say, *Yes, yes, yes.*

There's never a moment on our journey when there isn't a view that wouldn't look out of place on a postcard, but there are also specified places on the route to stop to experience The

Awe in full. At the Stutfield Glacier Viewpoint, we sit around a picnic bench together in almost total silence, all of us trying to take just one picture that captures even a slice of The Awe. We all fail, and one by one we give up and just sit.

We spend the last couple of hours of daylight walking up to Parker Ridge, hoping for a good sunset. We don't get much of one—too many mountain peaks in the way, though there are some nice colors sweeping across the sky—but the view is worth it anyway, right over the Saskatchewan Glacier.

"If someone came by with a gun and said, *Spell 'Saskatchewan' or you're dead,*" Beasey says, conversationally, "how many of us do you think would survive?"

"What a way to go, though," Khalil says. "A spelling test."

We take our time before we head back to the RV, a few of us lagging behind to take in the view for longer. I end up at the back of the group beside Lars, who had sat beside me as I sketched, his attention on his phone. As we walk, slow and companionable even though the two of us haven't spent much—if any—one-on-one time together, he reaches into his pocket and pulls out a pack of cigarettes and a lighter.

"I didn't know you smoked," I say in surprise.

Lars takes a hold of the cigarette between his teeth and quirks a smile at me. "Lots you don't know about me."

"Seriously, how can we have spent the last couple of weeks in an RV and I didn't realize you smoked?"

"I keep it away from the RV," he says. "I try to be a considerate smoker. Do you mind? I can save it for later."

"No, go ahead," I say.

"You want one?"

I surprise myself by wanting to say yes, to feel that camaraderie again of smoking with a friend. "No, but thanks."

I watch as he lights, closes his eyes, inhales. "So what else don't I know?"

He smiles again and opens his eyes, exhaling. "I can play the drums."

"Really?"

"At home, I'm in a band."

"Seriously?"

"I also box."

"You box?"

He's laughing. "See how people can surprise you?"

"Your life is so cool," I say. "A boxer in a band traveling with your boyfriend to the most beautiful place in the world to ski for a while. That's amazing. I wish that was my life."

He shrugs, looking away from me as he inhales again.

"Didn't you say you lived in the UK for a while?" I ask, trying to remember a conversation from early on in the RV. "Was that because of the band?"

"No, the band came after that," he says. "I was in the UK to work for a while. I like to be away from home."

"Why?"

He looks directly at me, our eyes meeting. "Do you really want to know?"

"Sure, of course."

"My parents are homophobic," he says. "At home, I'm closeted."

I say the stupidest thing. "I didn't realize Swedish people were homophobic."

"'Swedish people,'" Lars echoes, making quote marks with his fingers, "are not homophobic. My parents, who are Swedish, are."

"Of course, sorry," I say, horrified with myself.

"They think Stefan is my traveling friend," he says. "Much like Khalil and Beasey; platonic. When we travel together, we can be together freely. Stefan and I met when we were both in England, and we've tried to find ways to be together since then. I returned to Sweden for him. But he has no issue with his family, and I do mine, so it makes things very difficult." He taps his cigarette, dusting the ground with ash. "When we travel, we're free."

"I'm sorry," I say. Sorry for the situation, but also sorry for the fact that it's taken me this long to find out something that must be so fundamental to him as a person, especially as we're nearing the end of our time together. I realize, too late, how much I've taken Lars and Stefan's presence for granted, never asking them anything beyond the basics. I've been so passive as a friend, and that's only halfway there, isn't it?

God, I've come so far, but I've still got so much to learn.

Lars glances at me, a small smile quirking on his face. "Maybe if things were different," he says, "I wouldn't be here, with you and everyone. This is an adventure, and I love it all. Don't be sorry. This bit is good."

I think about what Seva said, all those weeks ago in the Vancouver hostel, about how everyone who travels is running from something in some way. Maybe that's only half right. Maybe it's more true that everyone is looking for some kind of freedom.

It's not safe to drive in the dark at this time of year, so once we make it to the RV site we settle down early. Tomorrow, we'll have to go back on ourselves to properly see some of the spots we missed, but that's better than parking illegally overnight—"boondocking"—and hoping we don't get caught and/or arrested. Maja and Seva go off together for a walk in the moonlight, and the rest of us play cards for a while before Lars and Stefan decide they want some time alone. Khalil says he wants an early night—I see the look he gives Beasey—and Beasey and I are left alone together in the quiet of the RV. Of all the times we've been alone together, separating ourselves off to go for a walk, sharing our conversations, and how nice it's all been, it feels different somehow to be alone like this in the cozy warmth of the RV. It feels intimate. Not that it can actually be intimate, obviously, not with Khalil only a few feet away behind what is just a very thin wall. But still.

"How do you like the Icefields Parkway?" he asks me. "Is it everything you wanted?"

It's such a casual question. There's nothing in his delivery that suggests he's asking anything else. But suddenly, crushingly, I realize that no, this isn't everything I wanted. I didn't know what I wanted before, but I do now. I want to be kissing. I wish we *were* kissing. I wish we'd been kissing the whole entire time, thin RV walls and all. I wish I'd let him stay with me that night, way back in Tofino, that I'd thrown caution to the wind instead of worrying, that we'd spent this whole journey together. Actually *together*. It feels so suddenly obvious. Of course that's what we should have been doing. And now it's too late.

Somehow, my voice comes out normally when I speak. "Yeah, it's amazing. I know it's maybe not the best time because of tourist stuff being closed, but it's so beautiful, I don't even care."

"I can't even imagine it being better at any other time of year," he says.

If I kissed him, he would kiss me back, I know it.

"What are you going to do after Banff?" I ask. I don't really want to know. I still don't want to let myself think about him moving on, but I have to remind myself that it's going to happen. Otherwise I will absolutely lean forward, put my lips on his and—

"Me and Khalil are talking about taking an extra couple of days there," he says. "To make sure we're planning the best route on from here."

"On to the US?"

He nods. He doesn't look happy about it. *Don't go to the US!* I want to say. *Carry on through Canada, with me.*

"Have you figured out what you're going to do?" he asks me.

"Yeah, I'm going to go and see Grandad," I say. "I'm so close, and I did basically use his existence to get through border control. I should say hi."

Beasey smiles. "Just say hi, just like that? Pop up to Edmonton, as you're passing?"

I shrug. "I guess so."

His smile fades into a soft frown. "On your own?"

I look at him, his familiar, lovely face. "Yeah. It'll have to be."

"I don't think you should do that on your own," he says. "You've never met him; what if he's a dick?"

"Then I'll leave."

"That still doesn't seem . . ." He trails off, uneasy. "I could come with you?"

"No, you couldn't. You can't just detour to Edmonton; you've got to move on."

"I don't," he says. "Our plans are so flexible, especially now."

"You should talk to Khalil," I say.

"Well, if we're going to spend an extra couple of days in Banff, it doesn't matter if I detour to Edmonton with you, does it?" he points out.

"And just leave Khalil behind?"

Beasey doesn't reply. We just look at each other. Quietly, he says, "The thing is, I'm not sure I'm ready to say goodbye to you."

My heart freezes, then begins to pound, heavy and slow, in my chest. Hope and dread and excitement and desire and *he has the nicest face in the world.* Involuntarily—honest—I lick my lips. I see his eyes flicker to my mouth, then back to my eyes, the pink in his cheeks clear even in the dark light of the RV.

"I . . ." My voice gives. I try again. "Me neither."

Slowly, he nods. "So . . . I should . . . maybe . . . talk to Khalil."

If we both leaned forward, right now, we could be kissing. And it would be an amazing kiss, I just know it. Somehow, I just know—

There's a clatter outside the RV, the low rumble of Seva's laugh, the door handle moving. Beasey leans back and smiles a small, understanding smile at me as the door opens and Maja walks in ahead of Seva, already unzipping her coat.

The moment is over, but the possibility is still hanging in the air, lifting my smile, softening Beasey's eyes.

When I say goodnight to them all and go to bed, I feel it, warming me up from the inside. The smallest hope of a maybe.

In the morning, we're on our way again. We try to catch a sunrise from the Cirrus Mountain viewpoint, where the Jasper and Banff national parks meet, but though the view is spectacular anyway, the changing light doesn't make much difference. Maja and I go on another hike together, but just a tiny one this time, to explore the Mistaya Canyon, already iced over in parts, and its rushing water and rock formations.

"You'd think I would've got tired of waterfalls by now," I say. "And yet . . ."

She smiles. "And yet," she echoes. "I wish we could have been here a little later, when it will be all ice. I've seen photos, and they looked amazing."

"Next time," I say.

As we get closer to Lake Louise, we stop off at a number of smaller lakes. One is called Peyto Lake, where I sit cross-legged on the concrete at the viewpoint to sketch a self-portrait: me sitting on a boat in the lake, surrounded by trees and mountains. Even if I had all my colors from home instead of just my graphite pencils, I still couldn't capture the almost-eerie greenish blue of the lake, but this sketch is just for me, anyway. I write *PEYTO* and then *LAKE* on either side of my head, as if I'm blocking a missing *N*.

"Shall we start calling you Peyto?" Lars asks.

"For, like, two more days?" I ask. "Go for it."

"It sounds like a Pokémon," Beasey says. "Peyto."

"Says *Beasey*," I tease.

He laughs. "All right, *Peyto*."

I'm smiling. It's so much better than Pey-Pey.

The next day is Lake Louise day. I'd imagined us all doing some kind of great hike to reach the lake, but it turns out the big day hikes aren't really possible at this time of year because of the conditions.

"What kind of conditions?" I ask. "Too icy?"

PEYTO LAKE

"Avalanche risk," Seva says.

"What? Really?" I say, alarmed. "Actual avalanches?"

"Not a worry for us," he says. "Because we won't go up high."

"There are a couple of low-elevation trails we can do," Maja says. "We can combine them. We can do the Louise Creek Trail from the village to the lake, then do the Lakeshore Trail around part of the lake." She smiles at me. "Don't worry. It will still be epic."

"You've given me a taste for hiking!" I say. "I was imagining . . . what's the word? Peaking?"

"Summiting," Maja says, laughing a rare proper laugh. "And not at this time of year in this part of the world with your experience, no."

We start early to make the most of the day. There's snow on the ground—not so much that we can't do the walk, but enough that I'm glad we decided not to attempt any of the higher-elevation hikes. I probably wouldn't have made it fifteen minutes without slipping on ice and breaking my leg.

The Louise Creek Trail isn't actually that long, but it takes us a while because we have to be careful on the icy stretches. At one point, Stefan's feet go flying out from under him and he skids on his side a couple of feet down the incline of the path. When Lars helps him to his feet, he's wincing, testing his weight on both feet.

"You are okay?" Seva asks.

Stefan nods. "Just about." He rubs his elbow through his jacket, his face still one big wince. "This better be a good lake. I want ultimate Awe."

And of course that's what we get. It feels like it takes a long time to get there—particularly if you count the rest of the entire trip—but when we do, it's like everything I've seen and felt up to now rolled into one. I'd thought that it might be a let-down—or, at least, an anticlimax—after seeing it in so many pictures and learning it by heart, but it's not. It's amazing. It's not frozen over yet, as it will be, come the proper winter season, but it's getting there.

"You know, normal water is going to be spoiled forever for me now," I say. "I'll look at the sea and be like, *You think that's blue? I'll tell you about blue.*"

"'Blue' isn't even the word," Lars says. "They should invent a new word for this color."

"Louise Blue," Stefan says. "Louise Bluegreen."

We take our time at the lakeshore, even though it's bitingly cold. The good thing about it being the off-season is that it's not crowded with tourists as it would have been if we'd come during the summer or later in the winter when it will be completely iced over. It's just our little RV family and a handful of strangers, all of us sharing the view and the cold.

I give myself the time to stand at the shore, looking out across the vast, impossibly turquoise lake. I think about all the pictures I've seen, how right now I am *there*—I am *here*. This place exists all the time, when the camera is there and when it isn't, when I'm in Canada and when I'm at home where I belong. It was here before all of us, and it'll be here long after we've all gone. Before someone called it Lake Louise, it was here. When there's no one to remember it ever had a name, it will be here. It is as forever as forever can be.

I think about all the countless thousands of people who have stood and will stand where I'm standing, maybe feeling as small as I do right now, re-evaluating their own small problems and priorities. They'll take the same pictures as we all have and show them to Instagram and their friends at home and say, *It really was that blue!* I feel weirdly fond of all these strangers I'll never meet that I have this thing in common with. I actually want to cry a bit, but I'm not even sure why, because I'm not sad. I'm deeply, perfectly, happy.

"Selfie?" Beasey's voice comes from behind me, and I turn, smiling, to nod. He puts his arm around me like it's normal, like he does it all the time, and I lean into him, like it's normal, like I do it all the time. He holds his phone out in front of us. "Smile," he says, but soft and quiet, a whisper into my ear, like a kiss. I smile wide.

NOW

BANFF

We have one more day together with the RV before Seva has to drive it to Calgary to drop it off, and we spend it driving around the Vermilion Lakes, just outside Banff town. Everyone is a little subdued, the usual energy muted. I think we're all feeling that this the end of something special. The only time we'll all ever be together in this place, sharing our slice of Canada.

After, we all take the Banff Gondola up to the top of Sulphur Mountain—even William "No one said there'd be this many bloody gondolas" Beasey—where we're rewarded with panoramic views of Banff and eat lunch for the last time all together, looking out over the mountains.

All too soon, it's time for the goodbyes to start. We all go to the Fairmont Springs Hotel—which looks like an actual castle—and spend our last hour with Maja, who has plans to meet her friends there. We walk around the grounds and down to the Bow River, where there's yet another waterfall. I tell Maja that I'll miss walking with her, because I know she isn't sentimental and I don't want to make her feel awkward by saying what I feel, which is that she's been an incredible friend to me, and I'm so grateful, and the rest of my life will be better because of that. She hugs me tight, like she knows.

"Maybe we'll see each other again?" I say, embarrassed by the earnestness is my voice.

"Of course we will," she says, so matter-of-factly it makes me smile. "Come to Germany. I'll show you the Black Forest. We'll eat strudel together."

It feels wrong to be back in the RV without her. Especially as we're only really in it long enough for all of us to collect the bags we'd already packed the night before. Seva stops the RV outside the hostel we'll be staying in without him, and the round of hugs begins. I start to cry.

"Aw, Peyto," Lars says. He hugs me, and Stefan joins in on my other side, sandwiching me between them.

I wipe my eyes, embarrassed. No one else seems close to tears. But even anticipating the end coming hasn't stopped its arrival feeling sudden.

"You're going to be so lonely in the RV," I say to Seva.

He smiles. "It will be very quiet." The drive to Calgary, where he's going to stay for a night before flying to Toronto, will take a couple of hours. "I will see you in Toronto," he says when he hugs me.

"Promise?" I say.

"I promise," he says.

The idea of making it across Canada without all of them feels a little easier, knowing I'll have a friend in Toronto.

When the RV has disappeared around a corner, it's just me and the boys left, and we head into the hostel together to check in. The boys are all sharing one of the dorms, and I'm on my own in the girls dorm. It's empty when I get there, which makes the loneliness I feel even worse. I try to shake it off—I'm going to be on my own in a lot of hostels if I'm going to make it farther across Canada—but there's no escaping the thoughts of life post-RV now. It's already happening.

There's a knock on the open door and I glance behind me

to see Beasey smiling in the doorway. "Hey," he says. "I'm going to do a load of washing while the laundry room is quiet. You want to come too?"

"Sure," I say. "Give me a sec to get sorted."

He nods. "I'll see you down there," he says.

I look down at my bulging rucksack, which I've barely had to really think about since we'd got the RV and I hadn't had to carry it on my back from place to place. Now it's going to be my closest companion for the next God-knows-how-long. Maybe I should give it a name.

When I get to the laundry room, Beasey is there on his own, sitting on the long ledge built into the wall, waiting patiently with two cups of tea. "I keep thinking of Seva on his own in the RV!" he says, holding out one of the cups to me.

I take it, then immediately set it down to start loading up one of the machines. "I know; me too. It's not that far to Calgary, though. Just a couple of hours, right?"

"Maybe even less, depending on how the roads are," he says. "I bet he misses us, though."

I try to smile, keeping my eyes on the instructions on the wall, keying in the program to the machine. How can he be so cheerful and ordinary? Doesn't he care that this is all almost over? All we have left is a couple of days, max, in Edmonton. I know all of this has meant more to me than the others, but I'd hoped it still meant a lot to him.

I push the coins into the slot and the machine chugs into life.

"Are you okay?" Beasey asks me. "You seem really sad."

"I am sad," I say. "Of course I am. Having to say goodbye to everyone . . . it's awful."

"Well," he says. "I've kind of been thinking about that."

I look at him, a flicker of hope in my chest. We hadn't had any real time to talk since we were last alone in the RV together. "Yeah?"

"You know, I've never been to Toronto," he says. "Or anywhere in Eastern Canada. They say Montreal is incredible." When I don't say anything, because I can't, he says, "Maybe we don't have to say goodbye yet."

And then we're kissing. Completely out of nowhere, *finally* kissing. And not a soft, gentle, questioning kiss, either. It's a full-on, tongues mashing, hands in hair, legs entwining kiss, right up against the row of washing machines. We break apart, suddenly, at the same time, both gasping. His glasses are almost hanging off his face. "Holy shit," he whispers. "Hooooly shit."

"Yeah," I say. I'm thinking, *Travis and I never kissed like that.* "So." I casually smooth down my hair. "You were saying something about Toronto?"

He laughs, and it's adorable. I want to kiss him again. Why weren't we doing this all along? Why are we doing it now, when this is probably all about to end? I think about our beds in the dorms. Could we . . . ? No. *No, Peyton. Get a grip.*

"I wasn't sure you . . . you know," he says. "Liked me like that."

"Of course I do," I say. "I just . . . This is all temporary. God, even if you *did* come with me, this would still be temporary. I shouldn't have . . . We shouldn't have . . ."

"Don't spiral," he says, his hands still at my waist. "We can figure this out."

"Would Khalil even agree to carry on traveling in Canada?" I ask. "Don't you have a plan?"

"I can talk to him."

My heart sinks. I want to just be kissing again, the kind of kiss where thinking is impossible, but I can't stop my head snagging on the words. "So you haven't yet?"

"He knows about Edmonton," he says. "Me going with you to see your Grandad. He was okay about that. He's going to hang out with Lars and Stefan while I'm there, but he could just come with us, and we'll all carry on together."

"Okay" isn't exactly enthusiastic, though, is it? Why do I have a feeling that Khalil won't be happy about this idea at all?

"You should talk to him."

"I will," he says.

"When?"

"Later," he says. "We were thinking about going to one of the bars, so I'll bring it up then. In the meantime . . ." He glances at the washing machine. "There's a while left on this cycle."

I can't stop myself smiling. I tilt my head, moving closer to him, lifting my hands up to loop around his neck. "Is there?"

I'm back in my dorm room, sorting through my freshly clean clothes, when I find a T-shirt of Beasey's in the pile. I smile down at it, pressing it to my nose to smell it like I've wandered into a cheesy rom-com—unsurprisingly, it just smells of washing powder—and put it aside while I pack everything back up. When I'm done, I wander down the hall to the dorm room he's sharing with Khalil to return it to him.

I can hear their voices through the partially open door, not exactly shouting but unmistakably tense, angry. Argument voices, even fighting voices. I stop.

"You can't be fucking serious." Khalil, sharp and annoyed.

"What's the big deal? We said we'd be flexible. Go where we wanted, if something cool came up." Beasey, irritation in his voice even though he's trying to use his placatory tone.

"I *have* been flexible!" Khalil snaps. "We *have* gone where we wanted when something cool came up. That's why we've ended up here. But we can't carry on randomly traveling across this country when we're meant to be going in the literal opposite direction. The later it gets, the more this screws up our plans."

"Mate," Beasey says.

"Don't call me mate—I'm fucking angry."

"Mate," Beasey says again. "One week in Toronto."

"We've got to *get* to Toronto first, remember?" Khalil says. "Fuck, Beasey, you know how much time—and *money*—we've spent on this detour? We haven't worked since Australia. We carry on like this, I won't make it further than Mexico."

"We wouldn't even have come to Canada if it wasn't for you and Heather," Beasey says. "You want to talk about detours?"

"A couple of weeks, that was meant to be," Khalil says. "A country we hadn't seen. And now we've been here over a month, and yeah, I'm glad we've seen Banff and it's all been great, but this isn't a see-as-much-of-Canada-as-possible trip— it's a see-the-world trip. Heather was a detour. You're making Peyton a whole new plan."

I'm long past the point where I should have walked away and let them have their argument in private, but of course I'm still there, leaning against the wall, T-shirt in hand, shamelessly eavesdropping.

"This isn't about Peyton," Beasey says, unconvincingly.

Khalil barks out a sharp laugh. "Oh, fuck *off*."

There's a long silence. Maybe this is the moment I should

casually walk in? No. It'll be obvious from my face that I've overheard them.

"Listen," Khalil says. "We can swing down into the States from here. Head to Portland, then carry on like we planned down through California. But if we go to Toronto, we're on the wrong side of the continent."

"We could do the East Coast instead," Beasey says.

"I've done New York before," Khalil replies. "We agreed the route would take us west, not east. What about the Grand Canyon? Vegas? San Francisco?"

"Fine, then we can fly."

"We've flown enough! We're meant to be keeping our flights down to an absolute minimum. Yeah, we said we'd be flexible, but we're still meant to have a basic plan. Look, I like Peyton. She's great. But you can't derail our entire trip because of her. You want to go to Toronto? Fine. Go. I'm going to the States."

Shit. My heart has started hammering. I clutch my elbows, fingers digging in against my skin.

"Our number one rule was we wouldn't separate."

"I don't want to separate."

"Fuck, Khalil." Beasey's voice is tense and sharp. "You can't throw an ultimatum at me like that."

"It's not an ultimatum; it's a fact. I'm going to the States in two days. You can choose to come with me or not. Right now, I'm going to find somewhere to get a drink."

"Can we talk about this?"

"We just did."

I duck into the nearest doorway—it turns out to be a cupboard—just in time to avoid being seen by Khalil, who walks past as he pushes his arms into his coat. He's shaking his head.

When he's gone, I duck out of the cupboard and go to their room, pausing outside until Beasey looks up from where he's standing in the middle of it, like he hasn't moved. He blinks in confusion when he sees me. I hold up the T-shirt.

"I took this by mistake," I say. "Just . . . bringing it back."

He tries to smile. "Thanks."

I expect him to ask me if I'd heard, but he doesn't. I guess it's obvious. After a moment he sits down onto one of the beds and I sit beside him. We're both quiet until I say, "You should go have that drink with him."

"Yeah. I should, shouldn't I?" He glances toward the doorway, then back at me. "You'll be okay staying here at the hostel?"

"Yeah, of course; I'll be fine. I've got Wi-Fi and my sketch pad." I smile at him, but he can barely muster one back. "Listen," I say. "If you have to leave with Khalil, I'll understand. You don't even have to come to Edmonton, if this is too much."

"No," he says. "We're going to Edmonton. But after that . . . I don't know." He shakes his head in frustration. "I just don't know."

NOW

EDMONTON

In the morning, Khalil is as friendly as ever toward me but noticeably cold toward Beasey as we all eat breakfast together. Lars and Stefan, who are staying in the hostel for a week before moving into the accommodation they've been allocated for their job, are talking about spending the day exploring the bars in Banff, trying to decide if they've "seen enough nature" to make it acceptable. Khalil has pulled out one of the maps of Banff and is planning a route with them, the three of them in good spirits.

"First one to fall on the ice buys the drinks," he says.

We all go for a walk around Banff town together, the snow now thick on the ground and the roofs of the chalets and buildings, then have lunch at a ramen place before Beasey and I have to go and get our bus.

"You going to miss the Rockies?" Khalil asks me after we've done our first goodbye hug.

I'll miss him more. His dry smile, his understated affection, how he looks at me like he can see my thoughts but still likes me anyway. There's magic in having a friend like that. "So much," I say. "Will you send me photos every day before you leave?"

"Sure," he says. "And you'll send me pictures of Toronto, yeah?" I nod, and he hugs me again. "See ya, King," he says. "Stay safe, okay?"

Lars and Stefan give me another Swedish sandwich hug—this time, I swear Stefan gets a little tearful—and then all three of them stand and wave as we walk away. I let myself go ahead and cry as Beasey puts his arm around me and squeezes, but by the time the bus arrives for our first leg of the journey, to Calgary, I've calmed down.

"How many hours do you think we've spent together in a moving vehicle now?" I ask once we've sat down.

Beasey smiles. "Not enough."

My skin is tingling just being around him. I want to kiss again. Oh my God, I want to kiss again.

"So I spoke to Khalil," he says after a few minutes, breaking the silence.

I tense. "Yeah?"

"Yeah." He's quiet again, clearly trying to decide what to say. "He's going to the States whatever happens. In a couple of days, that's where he's going."

I'm not surprised. It had been clear from what I'd overheard that Khalil's mind wasn't going to be changed. "Okay," I say.

"And I just . . ." He swallows, shakes his head and looks out the window. He looks so sad. "I don't know what to do," he says finally.

"Okay," I say again. It's pretty clear what he'll do, at least to me, which is go with Khalil like they'd been planning for years. What's going to take the time is Beasey deciding for himself that that's okay. "Let's just do Edmonton," I say. "Everything else can wait."

"But you and me—" he begins.

"Can't be a thing," I say.

"I want to be there for you," he says.

"You are!" I say. "That's why you're on a bus going on some

wild grandad chase with me. And I'm very glad about that."

He turns his head so our eyes can meet properly. "Yeah?"

I nod. "Very glad."

I duck my head into the curve of his shoulder and we watch the snowy mountainscapes of Banff slide past through the window. At some point one of us—I think it's me—does the chin tilt, and we're kissing like two people shouldn't kiss after they've all but agreed that they have no future, not even a short-term one. We kiss like we have all the time in the world.

And we don't, which is why getting off the bus into the freezing Calgary sleet is such an unwelcome jolt of reality.

"Oh my God," I say, burying my face into my scarf as far as it will go. "This is horrible. How long until the bus?"

"Er . . ." Beasey says. "Half an hour?"

"Oh my God," I say again. "Can we at least find somewhere warm to stand?"

We find a Starbucks—there are at least two within sight of the bus stop—and huddle inside for the next twenty minutes, using our cups more for their hand-warmer qualities than for the coffee within. Before we leave to get the bus, Beasey buys us two more coffees for the journey and two cinnamon rolls, which cheers me up.

"Has anyone ever told you that you're a cinnamon roll?" I ask.

"No," he says. "Is that a good thing?"

I smile. "It's a very good thing."

When we get on the bus, I take the window seat and he settles down beside me. "I miss the RV," he grumbles.

"Me too," I say. "I wonder how Seva's getting on in Toronto." Saying it reminds me that soon enough *I'll* be in

Toronto, far away from Beasey, and being as cute and cozy together as we are now is only going to make things more painful later. "We shouldn't kiss anymore," I say.

"Definitely not," he says. "No more kissing."

We kiss all the way to Edmonton.

By the time we get to the city, my legs are aching from all the sitting, and my chin is chafed with stubble rash. It's another hour on another bus to get to the actual town Grandad lives in, which is a little way out of the city, and it's already evening, so we decide to stay for the night in a hostel and make the trip in the morning. It feels strange being in a hostel alone with Beasey, without our friends, not so much a continuation of our adventure but something new. Short-lived, probably, but new.

I'm nervous about the bed situation, but I don't need to be. He gets a bed in the men's dorm; I get one in the women's. No problem, no temptation, no further confusion.

We go to a diner for dinner and take our time, making the most of the free refills, talking about everything except the fact that it feels like we're on a date when we shouldn't be because that's nothing but a road with a dead end. I don't know what Beasey thinks is going to happen after we've visited my grandad, and I don't want to ask, because I don't know either. I don't even know what I want to happen. There are two things in my head. One is *Toronto*. The other is *Beasey*.

"Are you going to call ahead or anything?" Beasey asks. "To your grandad?"

I shake my head. I hate calling people on the phone at the best of times, let alone an estranged grandfather who could be going senile, for all I know. Just thinking about trying to explain who I am and what I'm doing—"I'm Peyton. I'm your granddaughter. I wondered if I could pop in while I'm in the province?"—makes me feel embarrassed and anxious. I don't know why it seems less terrifying to do it in person, but it does. At least then I'll be able to take some cues from his facial expressions.

"What if he's not there?"

"He will be," I say confidently, as if I have access to information that Beasey doesn't, which I don't. But it honestly hadn't occurred to me until this moment that Grandad might not be home. He could be in the middle of his own travels, for all I know. I try to shake off that particular worry; if he's not there, there's nothing I can do about it. May as well at least check. It's not like it'd be the end of the world if I didn't see him, anyway.

The next morning, we set off early and get to Grandad's house—a bus and a decent walk away—before eleven a.m. The house is huge, at least twice the size of the one I grew up in, with floor-to-ceiling windows to make the most of the view across a lake just a little way over in the distance.

"Nice spot," Beasey says.

"No mountains, though," I say. "If I was going to have a house with a view in Canada, I'd want there to be mountains in sight."

His smile is understanding. "Fair enough. You going to knock?"

"Give me a minute," I say, breathing in slowly to calm my nerves. I'm trying to imagine how I'll describe all this to my dad later, when it's just a memory. *So we got there, and the house was beautiful, right out in the countryside . . .*

I jog up the driveway and push the bell in one smooth

motion so I don't have time to second-guess myself. Beasey lets out a yelp of surprise and hurries after me, reaching my side just as I hear the rattle of motion behind the door before it opens to reveal my grandfather. I know it's him from the photos on his gallery website. He looks like a taller, thinner, grayer version of Dad.

"Hello," he says. "Can I help you?" His accent is thoroughly Canadian; no hint of British in there at all.

"I'm Peyton," I say. I'm about to say, "Peyton King. I'm your granddaughter," all dramatic, because some moments, like meeting an estranged family member, call for drama.

But before I can, he smiles. "Ah, Peyton," he says. "Come on in."

Behind me, I hear a tiny, "Oh," of surprise. My mouth has dropped open. Grandad has already backed away, gesturing for us both to come inside, like all of this is normal.

"You don't seem surprised to see me," I say, trying to adjust my expectations of this visit with what's actually happening. I follow him inside, glancing at Beasey behind me for reassurance. He looks as confused as I feel. I'd thought I'd have to explain myself more, at the very least. To be honest, I'd been expecting him to turn me away.

"I'm not," Grandad says.

"You knew I was coming?"

He chuckles. "Isn't it funny that you, my British grand-daughter, have turned up on my Canadian doorstep out of the blue, and yet it's you that seems surprised?"

"How did you know?" I press.

"I spoke to your father," he says. "I'm sorry—I assumed you'd know that."

What the actual. "He told you I was coming?" Dad spoke

to Grandad? How did he even know I'd decide to come here?

"No, he said you were in Canada and that you may turn up unexpectedly. And here you are." He's still smiling—almost smugly, I think, though that may be me putting that on him—like he's pleased with how he's handling this. "Would you like some tea?"

"I thought you didn't talk to each other."

"We don't," he says. "It was the first time we've spoken in quite some time. But he's a good parent, unlike me." He smiles like he thinks this is funny. Dark funny, but still funny. "So he set the bad feeling aside for one phone call. For you."

"What did he say?"

"That you were feeling very lost, that he wanted you home but you wouldn't come home. He said that you probably wouldn't make the trip up to Edmonton, but asked that if you did, I'd be kind to you. I don't know why he'd think I wouldn't be, but there we go. Here you are, and I am very pleased to see you, and you are very welcome." He smiles at me. "Look at you! You're fully grown. How old are you?"

"Seventeen."

"Oh. Well, not quite fully grown, then. I'm sorry to have missed your life." He says this so matter-of-factly that it throws me. "But Canada is a big country, and England is far away."

That is clearly not the reason why the two of us have never met, but there doesn't seem to be much point in saying so.

"I'm sorry, who are you?" Grandad says to Beasey. "I've been waiting for you to introduce yourself, but I'm quite curious. Peyton's father didn't mention anyone else."

Beasey flushes an immediate red, his eyes blinking behind his glasses. "Oh. Sorry. Um. I'm William. William Beasey."

DESTINATION ANYWHERE   269

"I see," Grandad says. "Well, let's all have some tea, shall we?"

The kitchen he leads us into is big but sparse, almost too clean, like it doesn't get used much. "So tell me," he says, gesturing for the two of us to sit down at the table. "Why did you come to Canada?"

"What did my dad tell you?" I ask.

"That you'd run away to Canada without warning," he says. "Something about how you want to be an artist, how you'd had some trouble at school. Is that right? I wasn't really very clear on his explanation, to be honest with you. I hoped you might enlighten me."

"Well, I didn't run away," I say. "And yeah, I want to study art, and my parents won't let me. I felt like I was *stuck*, being at home, you know?" He nods, very emphatically. "In a life I didn't want. And I didn't have any friends," I add. "And I was miserable, so—"

"So you thought you'd make your own way," Grandad says approvingly. "You knew the world was out there, so you stopped waiting for it to come to you."

I hesitate. That's pretty true, but it sounds different, somehow, out of Grandad's mouth, in that tone. "I guess."

"Smart," Grandad says. "That's bold. Carving a life for yourself where you don't *need* friends. Relationships, friendships, they're all ties, that's what they are. They have their value, of course, don't get me wrong. But some people, the free spirits, they *can't* be tied. It's unnatural."

Beasey is frowning openly, his whole forehead bunched into itself. I'm just confused.

"Artists," Grandad continues. "They are put on this earth to reflect it. To bring a new perspective, a different way of seeing, of thinking. How can you do that when your priorities are dictated by other people?"

"Plenty of artists have families," Beasey says mildly, which is as close as Beasey gets to being rude. "Husbands, wives. Kids."

"So did I," Grandad says. "For a while. And you know what it made me? Miserable. I know that sounds terrible to you. It sounds terrible to most people. But it wasn't them; it wasn't their fault. That's something your father could never understand," he adds to me, like this is an aside. "He's always seemed to take it very personally. But I *had* to go—that's the truth. I didn't leave because of them. I left because of me."

This is starting to sound scarily, dangerously close to my own logic for getting on a plane, coming to Canada, hitching a ride in an RV across two provinces. *I had to go*, I've been telling myself.

"Do you regret it?" Beasey asks.

Grandad considers. He really does; he takes the time to think about it, which is how I know that he isn't a terrible person. Maybe this whole conversation would be easier if he was, but when I look at him—really look at him—I see sadness. It's etched in every line on his face. The deep kind of sadness, settled in to the point that he probably doesn't even recognize it for what it is anymore. "No," he says eventually. "Sometimes I . . ." His voice has gone soft. He coughs. "I wish I did, to be perfectly honest with you. I wish I had the capacity to love other people as they wanted to love me. But, as I said." He shakes his head. "Not everyone is built for that kind of life. I needed to be solitary; to be independent. And I have been, and I've had my art, and it has sustained me."

"Have you been happy?" I ask.

"That is a childish question," Grandad says, but not unkindly. "Happy is not the point."

I feel a hand on my knee. Beasey's gentle fingers, reminding me that he's here with me, that we're together, and happy, and that *is* the point. The whole entire point.

Grandad asks me about my time in Canada, and I tell him about Vancouver and Vancouver Island, the RV, the Icefields Parkway. I expect Beasey to chip in with anecdotes, but he mostly stays quiet, listening to me talk, eyes on my face.

"It's been great," I finish. The word doesn't seem like enough, but I'm not sure any would. "Really great."

"So where is your next stop?" Grandad asks.

I glance involuntarily at Beasey, who's looking down at the table. "Toronto," I say.

"Great city," Grandad says, pleased. "I lived there when I first came to Canada. Are you flying there from here?"

"I'm actually not sure yet," I say. "Whatever's cheapest, I guess." Whatever is the decision I don't have to make right now. Whatever keeps me with Beasey for a little longer. "I guess that means flying? Or maybe a lot of buses."

"Not at this time of year," Grandad says. "You don't want to be on a bus. You should get the train."

"The train?" I repeat.

"It's the best way to see Canada," he says.

"Isn't that expensive?" I say.

"And *long*," Beasey adds.

"Yes, on both counts," Grandad says. "Three days, but they'll be life-enriching ones. And for you, Peyton, in particular." He beams at me, like he's actually my grandfather in an emotional way instead of just a biological one, like he's proud. "An *artist*. And as for the money, don't worry about that. I'll pay."

"What?" I say, so sharply it comes out rude. But seriously. *What?*

"I have plenty of money," he says, shrugging. "And, as you know, not many people to spend it on. I'll be happy to help you out with this, if you'd let me."

"Did you talk about this with Dad, too?" I ask, trying to get a handle on the conversation.

"No," he says. "If I was trying to garner favor with your father, I would put you on a flight home. But I'm not going to do that, because I understand what you're doing. Your father doesn't; that was clear. I think this is a wonderful thing you're doing, seeking your own freedom. I'd like to contribute."

Why does him saying he understands make me feel like I understand it all a bit *less*? Like his support is the wrong support to have?

"Why would you just give me loads of money like that?" I ask.

"To be clear, I'll pay for a ticket," he says. "I won't be giving you any actual money." He hesitates. "Unless you need it? Do you need money? I have plenty of money."

"You said that already," Beasey says, and I pinch him under the table.

"Look, why don't you have a think about it?" Grandad says. "Whatever you decide, you should have some kind of a plan. Toronto is a long way away. I would feel better—and I know your parents will too—if I can be sure you will be arriving there safely. I'm very aware that I've not been a part of your life, but nevertheless I *am* family, and I do feel some responsibility for you. I'd like you to leave here with a ticket booked on some form of transport and an itinerary of some kind."

Beasey and I look at each other. His face is saying, *Well?* and I'm pretty sure mine is saying, *Wtf?!* Neither of us says anything, and it's just fringing on awkward when Grandad coughs and looks at his watch.

"I tell you what," he says. "I've got a Skype meeting with my agent in ten minutes. It shouldn't take long. Why don't the two of you have some tea and think about what I've suggested? Then we can discuss when I come back."

We nod, and he shows us where the tea bags are before he excuses himself to go to his office. Beasey boils the kettle while I dither with a couple of mugs, waiting for him to start the conversation. But he doesn't, so it's up to me, when we're sitting at the table with two mugs of tea, to ask what he thinks.

"I think you should do it," he says.

"Really?"

"Yes. That train journey will be epic. Why not? Take his money."

I lower my voice, even though Grandad is on the other side of the house and won't be able to hear me. "He seems like a bit of a dick, though."

"So? Even more of a reason to take his money. Just be like, *Cheers, Pops.* And ride in style to Toronto."

"But what about . . ." I trail off, hesitating. "What about you?"

He's quiet for a moment, his face full of the confusion that must be in his head. "I wish I could come," he says eventually. "God, I really wish I could. I'd love to see Toronto with you. Maybe even get further across Canada. I've heard Nova Scotia is incredible. But . . ."

"But you can't," I finish.

"I can't," he says. "Khalil and me . . . we had a plan. I have to see it through. I *want* to see it through. There's so much we haven't seen yet. It's not that I don't—"

"I know," I interrupt. "You don't have to explain."

"I've been thinking, though."

When he doesn't continue, I prompt, "Yeah?"

"The train isn't for three more days. Tuesday, right?"

"Yeah," I say.

"I could hang around here for three more days," he says. "Khalil would be fine with that."

I laugh to stop myself getting tearful. "Would he actually?"

"Yeah. He gets this. Remember why we even came to Canada in the first place? Heather?"

"Am I your Heather?"

I hate myself for being cheesy, but then he says, "No, you're my Peyton," and it's so hideously cringey we both start laughing, almost hysterically.

When we've calmed down, he says, "Look, what I mean is, maybe we can just have right now."

"Right now?"

"Right now. These three days before your train. You and me in Edmonton. We'll have an entire relationship in three days. No questioning it, no worrying about whether it's a bad idea. Just you and me, actually, properly together."

"For three days."

He looks at me. "For three days."

We can do a lot of kissing in three days. A lot of . . . well, more than kissing. My whole body is tingling.

"And then . . ."

"You'll go to Toronto," he says. "On the train. And I'll . . ." He hesitates, then exhales. "I'll go and meet Khalil and we'll get back on track. But we don't have to think about that now; that's what I mean. What have we got to lose, really? We have to separate either way. So we may as well make the most of the time we have. Besides, isn't this what traveling is all about?"

"Living in the moment?"

"Exactly."

"Is this just a line to get me to have sex with you?"

He laughs in surprise, glancing around to check the kitchen doorway as if Grandad might have appeared and he needs to be embarrassed. He even lowers his voice when he replies, "Jesus, no. If you don't want to have sex, we obviously won't have sex."

"But you want to?"

He's smiling when his eyes meet mine. "Yes, Peyton. I do want to have sex with you."

The tingles in my body ignite. Fire spreading through me, to the tips of my fingers.

"But that's not why I'm saying all this," he adds. "That would just be . . ."

"A bonus," I finish.

His mouth twitches. "A bonus," he repeats, a little unsteadily.

We look at each other for a long moment. It feels physical, that stare. Like he's touching me, though we're sitting apart. I swallow. "Sounds good," I say.

None of us speaks when Grandad drives us back to Edmonton. Beasey is staring out the window, contemplative, in the back seat. I'm in the passenger seat, watching the road. In my bag is the travel pack Grandad has made me: my train tickets, travel itinerary, details of the hotel he's booked for me in Toronto. I'm feeling a little shell-shocked. I'm not sure what I'd been expecting from dropping in on my estranged Grandad, but it wasn't this.

It seems like there's a lot we could be talking about, but we're all silent. After five awkward minutes, Grandad puts the radio on.

When we get to Edmonton, he clears his throat and says, "Where's the best place to drop you both off?"

I'd thought he might suggest taking us for dinner, or at least going with us for dinner, but he doesn't. I glance over my shoulder at Beasey in the back seat, who is clearly thinking the same. "The hostel?" I ask him.

"That's probably best," he says. "We can figure out where to go after that."

Beasey says a quick goodbye, gets out of the car, and heads into the hostel ahead of us, leaving Grandad and me to say our goodbyes. The last few hours have been a bit overwhelming, and I don't really know what to say. "Thank you" doesn't seem like enough, but also like too much, in a weird way, if I think about my dad.

"I'm glad you came to visit," Grandad says. "If you're ever back this way, come by again."

I nod. "I will."

"Good luck with your travels," he says. "And finding out whatever it is you feel you need to find out. Enjoy Toronto, and the train."

"I will."

"I can't know what goes on between you and your parents," he says, surprising me. "Or why you really did feel the need to make this trip. But let me say this." He pauses, then says, "I wasn't a good father to your father. But he is trying to be one to you."

For a second, it's like my throat closes up. I try to smile.

"Well, goodbye, Peyton," he says, quite formally. He pats my shoulder, which could be sweet but is mostly awkward.

"Bye—" I mean to say, "Bye, Grandad," but it doesn't feel like it would be right to call him Grandad out loud. Feebly, I repeat, "Bye."

There's a sad, dry understanding in the way he smiles at me. "Look after your dad for me," he says.

I tell him I will and get out of the car, throwing an awkward wave behind me that I don't think he even sees before he drives away. I head into the hostel entrance, where Beasey is waiting.

At reception, Beasey books three more nights, this time for both of us in one room. One room with just us, no one else. Just us and one bed.

Turns out, it's not one bed. It's actually bunk beds again, which we realize only once we've walked into the room.

"Oh," we say at the same time, then both start to laugh.

"Oh well," Beasey says, tossing his stuff onto the floor and reaching for me, one hand on each of my hips, pulling me toward him.

"Oh well," I echo.

He kisses me, and this time there's no one else around, no open door that anyone could walk through at any moment. I kiss him back. My whole body is saying, *Hello! Yes!* And so is his. His tongue is against mine and it is—oh my God— incredible. It's fire and fizz and fantastic. It's everything a kiss should be. It is worth everything that came before and all the loss I'll feel when these three days are over.

It's me who tugs him backward, toward the bed. And then . . . well. Let's just say we make up for lost time.

Conversations in the dark
aka
How to have a relationship in three days
aka
Living in the moment
aka
OMG OMG OMG
OMG OMG OMG
aka
Let's pretend this will never end

"We should go on a date."

"Yeah?" I've got no idea what time it is, but it feels moonlighty. Somewhere in the deep a.m. We're snuggled, all cozy.

"Yeah. Tomorrow, I'm taking you out."

"Where?"

"To the cinema. I don't care what we see; whatever's on. And then dinner. Somewhere Italian, with candles."

"That sounds amazing."

"It will be. You'll see; I'm going to be the world's best three-day boyfriend."

*

"Oh my God," Beasey groans, breaking away from our kiss. "We could have been doing this the whole time."

"Could we, though?" I say. "In an RV with five other people?"

A pause. "Okay, maybe we couldn't have been doing this the whole time."

"If we had kids," Beasey says. "We could name them Alberta and Louise."

Snuggled against him, my cheek on the firm ridge of his chest. "What about a boy?"

A pause. And then, both of us at the same time, "Edmond."

"You know what's weird is that at my secondary school, I was so miserable, but I knew exactly who I was. Like, I had my identity. I was the lonely artist. And then at college it was like I lost myself. I wasn't doing any art; I wasn't even drawing. And I wasn't lonely, on the surface of it, but also I kind of was? And now here, I've been so happy, and I'm drawing all the time, and I'm not lonely . . ." I trail off, unsure what I'm even trying to say.

"You've made friends," Beasey says, like it's obvious.

"Have I though? Or did they just kind of happen to me?"

He laughs. "That's what friendship is. Something that just happens between people."

Of course I think of Flick, the two of us writing notes to each other in the college library. Is that why it didn't work between us, why we were never *really* friends? Because I forced it instead of trusting that it would just happen?

"I guess I'm not sure who I am now. Who I'll be when I get back."

"You want me to tell you?"

I look at him. "I don't know, do I?"

He laughs again. "You're sharp and bold and independent. You take risks and chances. You let people be exactly themselves, and you don't make them feel bad about it. You're funny. You let other people *be* funny without making them work for a laugh. You're an incredibly talented illustrator. You see something in people and you bring it to life on the page. I can't tell you if you're happy, because only you know that, but I can tell you that you make other people happy. Your friends all love you for that." His smiling eyes meet mine. "Does that help?"

I kiss him on the cheek. "Yes."

Sleeping feels like a waste of time.

"Beasey?"
   "Yeah?"
   "Nothing."
   Quiet.
   "Peyton?"
   "Yeah?"
   "Me too."

"Listen," Beasey says. "I've been doing a lot of thinking and I wanted to ask you something."
   "Okay," I say.
   "Come with us."
   I look at him. I know what he means, but still I say, "What?"
   "Me and Khalil. Come with us. We can all go traveling together. You've loved all of this, haven't you? Well, it doesn't have to end, and it can get even better. Why stop at Canada?" He smiles at me, so hopeful, the corners of his eyes crinkled behind his glasses.

"I . . . Beasey, I'd love that, but I can't. I couldn't. You know that."

"Why not?"

"It would cause you way too much trouble. I'm seventeen, remember? That's been hard enough to navigate just here. I don't have any kind of a visa to go to the States—I don't even know what kind of visa I'd need—let alone wherever you're going after that. It's just not possible."

"We could make it work," Beasey says, more insistent this time. "We'll figure all that stuff out. There'll be solutions for everything you just said. And you'll be eighteen soon. Imagine your birthday in South America. We'll do the Inca Trail. Spend your birthday at Machu Picchu." He's taken my hand, squeezing it for emphasis. "And before that, we'll go to Vegas. You can draw the Sunset Strip. The Golden Gate Bridge. We'll have Christmas in Mexico."

As he talks, I can see everything he's describing in my head. Not in full Technicolor but in graphite gray, pencil sketches of our adventures. In all of them, I'm smiling, beyond happy. Beasey and I are hand in hand.

"What about Khalil?"

"What about him?"

"Beasey, come on."

"I was talking about all three of us," he says. "Traveling together."

"People don't travel in threes," I say. "For a reason."

"We could," Beasey says stubbornly. "I told you, we could make it work."

"That wouldn't be fair on Khalil," I say. "You know that. Don't do this—it's not fair."

"Do what?"

"Put it on me to say no. Point out obvious problems like the fact that your traveling companion might be a *bit* pissed off if you decide to couple off with some random girl."

"You're not a random girl."

"And stop that, too. Stop picking up on one tiny thing I say and ignore all the actual points." Is he always this frustrating?

"I just want us to be together for a bit longer," he says. "I thought that's what you wanted, too. And it's not like you want to go back home, is it? Here's a way you can travel for longer. It's not like you have anything to go back to."

The words stab. I frown. "That's not true."

"You said that yourself."

It's different when I say it. Hearing the words from Beasey makes them harsher, almost cruel. I think about Dad's emails and that first morning in Vancouver, Mum sending me the phone numbers of everyone she could think of. Dillon asking if I'd learned French yet.

"My family is at home," I say.

He's frowning at me, genuinely confused. Have I really not talked about my family at all except to complain about them? Have I made it sound like I don't love them?

"I thought . . ." he begins, then stops. I wait until he tries again, his voice uncertain. "I thought this was what you wanted."

It is what I want. Of course it is. Traveling with Beasey, the two of us seeing the world together. (Plus Khalil.) This is a way to continue this life, to make it not a detour but my actual life.

But I can't do that, can I? For one thing, this can't be my life. I know I have to go back home. Maybe not immediately, but soon. My parents have struggled to understand my choice to come to Canada enough as it is; I don't know how they'd even react if I told them I was going to start traveling properly, one country to another, with little more than a vague plan and two Scots they'd never met, one of whom I was sleeping with. (I wouldn't tell them that part, obviously, but they're not stupid, especially Mum.) Leaving Canada with Beasey would be putting off the inevitable. The longer I stay away, the harder it will be to go back, the wider the gulf between me and my parents.

And here's the other thing: if I go with him, I know what that means. It means committing to him in a way we've both actively tried to avoid. We've been able to be easy with each other because this is all temporary. Setting off with him to travel the world is different. It will mean sharing bedrooms, being the couple. It means an actual relationship, and that's something we can't have. Not now, anyway, because it could never be an equal one. Beasey is lovely—that's the best word for him; he's just lovely—and he's kind and funny and intelligent and *good*. But he's also older than me, emotionally secure compared to my constant confusion, a traveling backpacker. He is in a better place than me, and I can't use him as a shortcut to finding my own. I am grateful for him and what he's done for me, but you can't have a relationship where one is grateful for the other. I read enough books in my lonely years. I know what a healthy foundation is and isn't.

"I can't," I say. "I can't come with you."

He's quiet, sad, but not surprised. I see all of that on his face, especially when he manages a smile for me, nods, pulls me in close and kisses my forehead. When he speaks, his voice is soft. "If we'd met at a different time," he says, "I would love you so goddamn hard."

My smile is uncontrollable, spreading across my face. Who knew an "I would love you" could mean even more than an "I love you."

"One day, you'll be back in the UK," I say. "We both will be."

He rests his chin on the top of my head. I feel him nod. "Pick a Scottish uni," he says. "For your art."

I smile against his neck. "One in the Highlands, right?"

A soft chuckle. "Right."

It's Beasey who leaves first. He has to get a bus to Calgary to catch a flight to San Francisco, which is where he's meeting back up with Khalil.

"You'll be okay getting the train?" he asks me for the third time, when we're waiting for his bus.

"Still yes," I say. "Remember how I made it from Surrey to Vancouver all by myself? I can manage a bus to the train station from here." He's still looking nervous, so I say, "I'll get there really early, and I'll message you to tell you that I'm there."

"Okay," he says softly, sliding an arm around me. "If you want me to miss my bus to make sure you get there, I will."

I snuggle in close. "Don't tempt me."

Big goodbyes are always an anticlimax. There's just too much pressure on them. I'd expected we'd share a Moment, the two of us, in the last minutes before separation. Bold declarations, kisses with our lips wet with tears. But the bus approaches ten minutes after we arrive and we've mostly been standing in silence, waiting.

He puts his arms around me again and hugs me tight. Our last hug. Tears spring to my eyes, my head suddenly swimming with conversations we could have, questions I haven't asked him, things we haven't done.

His eyes are wet, but he smiles at me as he pulls back, adjusting the straps of his backpack. "Have fun in Toronto," he says.

People are getting on the bus.

"Have fun seeing the world," I say. He begins to turn, and my heart jolts with panic. I blurt, "When do you think we'll see each other again?"

Beasey stops and turns back to me, touching the side of my face with the knuckle of his index finger. "Okay if I say something cheesy?" he asks.

I nod.

"I don't know when," he says. "All I know is that we will."

He's the last one on the bus, and it's already pulling away when he throws himself into the window seat to wave. I wave back with one hand, the bus joining the traffic so unceremoniously, disappearing around a corner.

I'm alone again.

I really feel it, too, maybe even more than I did when I first arrived in Vancouver. Edmonton feels suddenly huge and I am so small and sad and British. For a second I imagine going home. Toronto seems so far away, both from here and from the house I grew up in. What's the point? What was the point of any of this?

The point was to be independent. It's not like I came all this way for a boy. I can certainly carry on without one. I pick my rucksack up from where it's been resting at my feet and hoist it onto my back, sliding my arms through the straps, wiping my eyes and cheeks dry. I'll head toward the train station now, I decide, even though it's hours until my train is due. I'll get supplies for the journey, maybe even a book. I'll sit in a coffee shop and I'll sketch the people I see. Me and my sketch pad in Canada. That was the point of all of this.

NOW

EDMONTON—TORONTO

What surprises me is how much I like traveling solo on the train to Toronto. I'd thought I'd be lonely, but I'm not. I like the time that I have to sketch and think and read. I miss Beasey, and I miss my friends, but I'm actually okay by myself. It's nice to know I really can do both.

There are delays along the way, so it takes almost a full three days instead of the scheduled two and a half, which isn't a hardship. Here, I know where I am and what I'm doing, watching Western Canada give way to the east, the sprawling, icy landscapes unrolling before me. The train has an observation car with huge windows and a domed glass roof for panoramic views and maximum gawping potential, as well as a bar and lounge to hang out in. I spend most of my time during the day and evening in there, because I like the bustle of other people nearby, even if I'm not talking to them, and my single cabin is just too quiet to bear.

The train doesn't look anything like a British train. The carriages—train cars—remind me of corrugated metal roofs with the word *Canada* and a flag for good measure emblazoned across every one. My cabin has a bed that pulls out at night, space for my rucksack, and a small, private washroom. Three meals a day are included with my package—*Thank you, Grandad*—and the food is actually good, which is a bonus. I don't exactly make friends with my fellow passengers, who are mostly considerably older than me, but I'm at least on friendly terms with them, chatting over meals and sharing greetings by name in the mornings. The *clickety-clack* of the wheels against the track is surprisingly loud at first, but I get used to it pretty quickly, though when I look back at my sketch pad for my first drawings from the train, I find a small doodle of pencil-me with her hands over her ears, scowling.

When I'm not sketching or reading, I'm researching. I start by looking up the visual arts program at the university on Vancouver Island, then move closer to home and research the Illustration BAs on offer in the UK, spending the longest on the University of Edinburgh website, daydreaming. I look up concept art degrees, creative art degrees, fine art degrees, all over the world. The world is so big and there's so much I can do—that's what I realize, there in the lounge car of a train in Canada. It's so obvious, and maybe I always knew it, but now I actually might believe it, too. I flip back through the sketch pad I've carried across three provinces, chronicling my journey. A portfolio of an unexpected adventure. It's not an A Level, but maybe it can be the start of something else.

I think about my friends, scattered over the pages, and the friends I'd had before, trying to imagine them all meeting. Would they get along? Would the Peyton my traveling friends know match the Peyton my college friends knew? Probably not. In my head, I imagine each group squinting at the other, and then me, in confusion, shaking their heads, like, *Why?* I imagine Flick shrugging and losing interest, turning back to kiss Eric.

I sigh to myself. Even in my own head, I can't keep ahold of Flick's attention. And look, I'm doing it again, distracting myself by focusing on Flick when the whole point is everyone else.

If this had all happened the other way around, if Beasey and the RV crew had been my friends first, would I ever have chosen Flick and the others after? No. My head says, *Obviously not*. Because I never really chose any of them, did I? I threw myself at them and all but begged for their friendship. It was barely even a choice for them, either.

In Canada, I'd made the choice. I'd gone back to my friends after I'd panicked and tried to run, and been myself with them, and they'd chosen me right back. Our friendship has been active and evolving, growing as we got to know each other. Even the disagreements and the bickering when the RV walls felt too close, that all counts, too. They'd been so kind and patient with me, they'd got so much right, but even when they were wrong, like when Khalil had pulled the we're-leaving-you-lol-not-really joke, they apologized and tried to make it right.

As I think, I sketch. Seva in the Sun-Ho-Van hostel, shuffling cards. Maja in her hiking boots, beaming at a lake. Stefan sitting on the bed in Tofino, chattering away. Friendship is a choice both sides make. It isn't a favor or a chore. It's not even a gift. Sometimes it's good and sometimes it's bad, but when you're in, you're in for it all. It doesn't have to be about being the same age or from the same place, you don't need to have an economics class together or let someone's boyfriend copy your notes or take whatever drugs they're taking just to make it all bearable. It can happen between two boyish Scots, a kind-hearted Russian who is not a bot or a spy, a German hiker still nursing a broken heart, two gay Swedes traveling so they can be together, and me, the runaway English teenager who'd already got so much wrong but is finally, finally starting to get it right.

NOW

TORONTO

When I finally get to Toronto, I'm so surprised by the grandness of the train station I end up spending an hour there, just wandering around, getting used to solid ground. The city itself feels dauntingly huge after the relatively small resort towns and villages we'd passed through before, even after experiencing Edmonton, and I find myself second-guessing my navigation skills and heading back into the train station to ask at the information desk for help.

"Are you sure that's where you're staying?" the friendly-but-dubious-sounding man asks me, and I think it's a weird question until I actually get to the hotel Grandad booked for me and find it's a grand, gigantic five-star majesty of a place. I stand in the foyer with my tattered rucksack and hiking boots, feeling my shoulders hunch.

"Good afternoon!" the woman behind one of the reception desks calls. "Can I help you?"

"Hi," I say, walking over, remembering Amelia at Sun-Ho-Van and her Kiwi grin, Teapot the cat in her arms. "Can I . . . um. Check in?"

She smiles at me. "Of course. What's the name on the booking?"

I give her my details and show her the letter Grandad wrote for me, confirming that I have his permission to stay there on his account. Who knew he was so fancy? He didn't seem fancy. I've never stayed in a five-star hotel before, let alone a five-star hotel in the middle of a city like Toronto.

"You're on the eighth floor," the woman says, passing me my key. "Do you need any help with your bags?"

I laugh, assuming she's joking, then realize she isn't. "Oh. No, it's fine. It's just my rucksack, so . . . thanks."

My room isn't as overwhelming as the foyer, thankfully, but it's still nicer than any hotel room I think I've ever been in. I drop my rucksack on the floor and flop down onto the bed, closing my eyes against the sheets. I'm so tired. Maybe I should just sleep for a bit.

Two minutes later, I'm up again, restless, opening the curtains to look out at the city. I'd expected it to be practically iced over, but it's not at all. It just looks huge. I plug my phone in to charge, pull the armchair so it's facing the window, and perch myself on it with my sketch pad. I know I should probably head out and explore the city, but I'm not quite up to it yet. A whole new massive city and me back on my own. No friends, no Beasey.

The room is so quiet. Empty and quiet. Yes, it's unbelievably nice, but I miss the chaotic warmth of hostel life. The color and the noise, all the people milling around each other, excitable and adventurous, wanting friends and conversation. I bet this hotel doesn't have a hotel cat.

I sigh. *Way to be grateful, Peyton.* Maybe I should just check out of here and go find the Toronto Sun-Ho if I'm not going to appreciate it here. I wonder if Grandad would get his money back if I didn't stay all the days he's booked for me.

I finally manage to get myself out of my hotel room and into the elevator, scrolling through my phone for the best food options. Somewhere I can eat alone without feeling too conspicuous; I'll have to get used to that now I'm on my own again. Maybe a Dairy Queen. The elevator doors slide open and I walk out into the foyer, glancing up to get my bearings, looking for the right exit. There's a bar to my left—actually, maybe I should just get food there? Will it be expensive?

That woman looks a bit like Mum. Weird.

Of course it'll be expensive. I can't splash out on expensive hotel food on my first night in Toronto—

Wait. Holy shit. It *is* Mum. It's Mum, sitting on a chair in the bar of the hotel. Mum, in Toronto, staring right at me. Smiling.

What the actual.

I'm frozen in place, gaping at her. She waves.

"What?" I say out loud. A businessman walking past starts in surprise, frowning at me when he realizes I'm just a teenager.

I have no other option than to walk slowly over to her, trying to figure out what to do with my face. I'm shocked, obviously, but there's the surprise of happiness, too. An old instinct is still there, buried deep inside me—the desire to run toward my mother.

"Hello, my love," Mum says when I'm close enough, standing. "Oh, hello." She reaches out and takes hold of both my hands, squeezing. She's a bit tearful.

"Hi," I say, stupidly. "What . . ."

"I thought I may as well surprise you," she says with a tearful little laugh, wiping at her eyes. "Just in case you tried to run away from me. Again."

Her face, impossibly familiar. I'm so completely spun by her being here, but also by how absolutely familiar she is, that I can barely speak through the confusion. And then she touches my face, like she used to do when I was tiny, and I start to cry.

"Darling," she says, opening her arms. I fold into them, and she hugs me.

"How can you be here?" I choke out.

"I got on a plane," she says softly, rubbing my back in small, comforting circular motions.

After we've both calmed down, I sit beside her at the table and she orders me a Coke. "Shall we get food here?" she asks me. "Have you eaten?"

I shake my head. "Not yet."

"Good," she says. "I've been looking at the menu while I was waiting for you to appear. It looks quite good."

"How did you know I'd be there?" I ask, though I can guess. "In this hotel?"

"Your grandad called us," she says. "He gave us the information about the train you were on and this hotel. Said we'd have plenty of time to get here to meet you."

Three days on a train. Wow. Well played, Grandad.

"He said he understood why I was doing this," I say. A waiter appears and sets a long glass of Coke on the table beside me, clinking with ice. "Thank you."

"He does," she says. "Far too well. But he also understands that we're your parents and you're seventeen."

"Why didn't he just put me on a plane home, then?" I ask, frustrated and a little bit betrayed. Okay, I didn't love that the family-abandoning recluse was the only one on my side, but at least he *was* on my side. Except, clearly not.

"Would you have let that happen?" she asks.

I'm silent.

"I think he was happy to be able to give you that experience," she says. "Something you won't forget. A gift."

I think about those three days with Beasey. The clickety-clack of the train sweeping through endless fields of ice and snow. The mountains.

"So you've come to take me home," I say, looking down into the bubbles in my Coke fighting with the ice. "To *make* me come home."

She doesn't reply right away, not until I look up and meet her sad, tired gaze. "I hope you'll come back with me," she says. "I'm not going to pretend that's not my hope. But I'm not going to force you, and I don't *want* to force you. I'm here because you are my daughter, and I love you, and I have *missed* you. You've been having these grand adventures so far away, and I wanted to join in. I hoped we could do some exploring together, you and me."

Is this a trick? It feels like a trick.

"I've always wanted to see Niagara Falls," she says, which makes me think of Casey and the email I never replied to. "And there's no one I'd rather see it with than you."

"What about Dillon?" I ask. "And Dad?"

Mum laughs. "You know what I mean, my love."

"Is Dad here?" I ask. "Where is he?"

Her smile fades in a way that makes my heart suddenly tense with an anxiety I don't quite understand. "He's at home," she says. "He didn't feel the same way I did about coming here. He thinks I'm indulging you, acting like I think how you've behaved is acceptable."

"And you don't?"

She's quiet, considering. "I'm disappointed at how you've conducted yourself, yes. But I also know you, and I know you wouldn't have done what you've done unless you felt like you had no other option. So while I can't condone it, I'm your mother; I want to understand it." The smile returns to her face, warm and hopeful. "And I'd like to try and do that beside you, not on the other end of a phone line. Perhaps over pancakes."

I smile back; I can't help it. "Or at Niagara Falls?"

"Yes," she says. "Right on the boat, wearing those special ponchos." When I laugh, she reaches out and takes my hand. "I've missed you."

"I've missed you too," I say.

After dinner, Mum comes to my room with me and I show her the bits and pieces I've collected since I've been traveling: postcards, ticket stubs, a Banff hoodie, a key ring.

"I've been sketching the whole time," I say. "The whole trip, like a visual diary."

"Can I see?" Mum asks.

I nod, handing my sketchpad over. She flips slowly through it, a small, unreadable smile on her face that twitches and widens as she goes. "These are fantastic, Peyton," she says. "Really. I haven't seen this kind of art from you in a long time."

"I didn't draw as much after I started college," I say. "I missed it."

"Your dad and I both loved our postcards," she says. "I know I've said this before, but you're so talented. I really admire that."

She's trying, I know that, so I smile. When I take my sketch pad back, I ask, "When did your flight get in? Are you jet-lagged?"

"Yesterday," she says. "I've mostly slept it off. If I get

a good night's sleep tonight, I'll be fine. What shall we do tomorrow?"

"When's your return flight booked?" I ask.

"Wednesday," she says.

"And you've booked me a ticket, too?"

She hesitates. "Yes." Before I can speak, she says, "But I can't force you to get on the plane. If you really, honestly don't want to come home, then I won't try to force you. Please, though, can we just have this time together? I want to hear about your adventures. I want to share some with you. I don't want to fight."

"I don't want to fight either," I say.

"Okay then," she says. "Shall we agree to, at the very least, put that on hold for now?"

I look at her, trying to figure out how much I can trust this. Finally, I let myself nod. "Sure," I say.

She smiles properly, warm and relieved. "Good," she says.

We spend the next day having the full tourist experience. We visit Casa Loma, which Mum loves because it's beautiful, and I love because it was the castle in the live-action *Beauty and the Beast*, before we ride up to the observation deck at the CN Tower. I must get my lack of fear of heights from Mum, because she's as fearlessly fascinated as I am, pressing her nose right up to the glass to look across the city and beyond, comparing the skyline to the map in her hand.

I send a photo to Beasey of me lying on my back on the Glass Floor, the city over a thousand feet below me, and he replies immediately, all caps, **GET DOWN TO SOLID GROUND IMMEDIATELY** with a selfie of his horrified face. **Wish you were here,** I tell him.

I don't! he replies, which makes me smile.

I tell Mum about Beasey—leaving out the kissing parts, and especially the sex—and the rest of my friends, explaining how well they'd looked after me, what we'd done together. I tell her how Seva is in Toronto at the moment and that I'd planned to meet up with him, and she suggests we all go for dinner together.

"I'd love to meet him," she says.

It feels like a strange but nice melding of two worlds when they meet later that evening. Mum and I walk into the bar and grill we've chosen, to find he's already at a table waiting for us, still wearing the suit he clearly wears to work. He smiles when he sees me, but it's not the same smile that I'd gotten used to.

"Hello, Mrs. King," he says to Mum, holding out his hand in greeting. That plus the suit has the effect of making it seem like he's being interviewed, this time by her.

"Hello," Mum replies in the same slightly stilted tone. "So lovely to meet you, Seva." His name sounds strange in her voice.

Honestly? It's awkward. Everything is different. Seva is more rigid here in this suit in this city, with my mother as company instead of our friends. He's awkward; his shoulders tense, his smile tight. The warmth and humor I'd seen in him from the first night we'd met, when he'd so quietly put me at ease, is stifled by . . . what? His suit? The fact that Mum is here? Being in Toronto?

It's not a bad thing, and it doesn't make me love him any less. What it does is make me realize how different people can be in different contexts, which is something of course I've always known but never seen quite so clearly before. The Seva Mum is seeing is not the Seva I know, which is not her fault or his. It makes me think of college, the Peyton I was with Flick and Travis and everyone compared to the Peyton I've been in Canada. Is one more real than the other? More me? I want to say yes, that *this* Peyton, the bold one who goes on adventures with good friends, is the real me, but it's not true, is it? They're both me. Two versions of myself of the many there'll be in my life.

Seva tells us briefly about his new job, which he says is going well, and how he is looking for somewhere to stay in the city over the six-month period of his contract.

"Toronto in winter," Mum says. "That'll be an experience! Or, I suppose, perhaps not for you? Does it remind you of home?"

I wince, but Seva barely reacts. Instead, he smiles. "Sometimes, yes, it does." I want to get up and hug him.

When we've finished, he declines dessert and says he should leave us, pulling out his wallet.

"Oh, no," Mum says immediately. "I'll be paying for this."

Seva shakes his head. "I would like to pay."

"Please," Mum says. "Let me. You've taken such good care of Peyton."

"We are friends," Seva says simply. He puts some cash on the table and slides it over to Mum. "I hope you enjoy your time in Toronto."

I put my hand on top of Mum's to stop her pushing the cash back to him, standing as I do. "I'll come out with you." When Seva has started to walk out of the restaurant, I release her hand. "Back in a sec!"

Outside the restaurant, it's cold. *Toronto cold*, I think, smiling. I breathe it in.

"Thanks for having dinner with us," I say. "I hope that wasn't too weird."

He shakes his head. "Of course not. You will return home, then? With your mother?"

"That's what she wants," I say. "I don't know, though. She hasn't even had a go at me yet, but it's coming."

"Perhaps she just wants to spend time with you," he says.

I shrug.

"Your mother," he says. "She loves you. Everything else, it does not matter so much." I'm just processing this when he says, "Now I will say goodbye." I look up at him, his familiar face softened back to his usual Seva smile, now that it is just the two of us again. "And that I will miss you."

I want to tell him how amazing he's been, how much I appreciate that and him, but he waves me off before I've even gotten two words out. "Come to England sometime," I say instead. "Okay?"

"I shall try," Seva says. "In the future, when you are a famous artist."

I laugh, shivering. "Maybe."

"You are cold," he says. "Go back inside."

"Can I have a hug first?" I ask.

He hugs me tight, like a brother. I hear him say something in Russian before he gives my back a brisk pat and then releases me.

"*Da svidaniya*," I say.

He smiles. "*Da svidaniya*."

The restaurant feels extra warm and cozy when I go back inside. Mum is sitting at the cleared table, dessert menu open. I slide back into the booth opposite her.

"Do you think the portions will be as big as the mains were?" Mum asks.

"Yes," I say. "They're huge."

"Gosh," Mum says, and I feel a tug of affection in my chest. "Shall we share one?" she asks. "This one with the brownies?"

"Sure," I say. "Let's share."

The next day, Mum has booked us both onto a day tour to Niagara Falls. She's giddy excited about it—more excited than I've seen her for years—and it makes me laugh.

"Look at you, seasoned traveler!" she replies. "I've spent the last few weeks in Surrey. It's rained eighty percent of the time. Let me enjoy my small adventure."

I put my arm through hers and squeeze as we wait to get on the coach.

Niagara Falls is everything I expected it to be. Huge— seriously, it's huge—loud, beautiful, and full of tourists. I'd been spoiled by seeing most of Jasper and Banff in the off-season, when it was relatively quiet. Here, it's jam-packed. But I don't mind, not really. Niagara Falls just inspires too much of The Awe.

"Do you remember that class project you did on Charles Blondin?" Mum asks me.

"Who?" I say.

She looks disappointed. "Charles Blondin. The tightrope walker who was the first to walk over the Falls. You did a whole project—you must have been about eight or nine. You were fascinated by him. Went through a whole phase of wanting to be a tightrope walker. Remember?"

I have a very, very vague memory of making a rope out of pairs of tights tied together, fixing it as tightly as I could from the living-room sofa to the door handle and attempting to walk across it. Was that when I broke my arm? Possibly.

"Sort of?" I say. "I can't believe you remember that."

"I can't believe you forgot," she says. "I thought it meant you were going to be a great adventurer. A daredevil. And now look at you."

"Well," I say. "At least I'm not a tightrope walker."

We're given bright yellow ponchos for our boat trip out to the Falls—Mum is thrilled—and I take multiple photos of her, me, and both of us. I've already decided that I'll re-create this moment, maybe in watercolor, and frame it for her Christmas present. I'll call it KINGS AT THE FALLS. The ponchos turn out to be very necessary, because we get soaked. Also, it's freezing.

I have the best time.

When we're back on solid ground, exhilarated and damp, we have time to explore Lundy's Lane, where I duck into a gift shop and buy a postcard of the Falls for Casey. I'm still not sure what I want to say to her, so I don't write anything, just her name and address on one side and a sketch on the other. I draw Casey as I remember her, except with a wider smile, standing on the bow of a boat, surrounded on all sides by waterfalls. I caption it CASEY SEES NIAGARA FALLS.

We get back to Toronto that evening too tired to go out to eat, so we order room service in Mum's room, which feels exciting and decadent in a way I'd never experienced before and hadn't thought she'd enjoy. But she's bright and cheerful, talking about food portion sizes, looking back over the menu and lamenting the choices she didn't make even though her burger is "just fantastic." I'm nodding along when she's saying how burgers back home won't compare, that in fact our home town in general won't compare to the "magnificence" of Toronto, until she says, so very casually, that it will be worth it to have me back at home, back to my life, back at college.

"I'm not going to go back to college," I say. She opens her mouth to speak, but I shake my head. "No, really, listen. I'm not going back. I've made that really clear."

"But, Peyton," she begins. "You can't just drop out; you have to have a plan—"

"I do have a plan," I interrupt, as calmly as I can. "Will you just listen to it? Please?" I wait for her to breathe in an impatient sigh, then nod. "Okay. I know you want me to finish my A Levels, but there's really no point in me wasting time getting qualifications I don't want and won't use. I can use that time preparing for what I actually do want. And I want to study art. Illustration, if I can. I'm going to try to apply to art courses at universities; some of them have foundation years, so it might not matter about the last two years. I'm going to put together a proper portfolio and explain the situation. If they won't take me without A Levels, then fine, I'll retake year thirteen and get the ones I need. Even if that means I have to start again and it takes ages, then fine. That's okay. I'm not worried about that. It'll take as long as it takes."

Mum is frowning. "But . . ."

"I'm going to get a job as soon as I get home," I continue. "Full time. Back at the bakery where I worked last summer, if they'll have me. Or somewhere else, if they won't. I'll work as much as I can until I know what's happening with studying stuff. I want to start earning money as soon as possible so I can start paying Dad back."

"That's not important—"

"It is," I say. "To me. And to Dad. I'm also going to volunteer."

"Volunteer?"

"Yes. I'm going to see if I can do arts-and-crafts sessions at, like, a youth center or a care home or something. I want to be doing things where I can meet lots of different people, not just people who are like me. And I want to get as much experience with art that isn't just me drawing by myself."

She's looking a little shell-shocked. "That will take up a bit of time—"

"Not really," I say. "A couple of hours a week. That's nothing. Besides, I want to fill up my time with good things. Healthy things."

Mum doesn't say anything for a while. She's clearly thinking hard, her gaze settled on the space by my right shoulder. Finally, carefully, she says, "You should be prepared that your dad might not support this."

"What do you mean? Support what? Which bit?"

"All of it. He wants you to be in education. Traditional education, earning your A Levels, so you can go on to university."

"I *can* go to university. To study what I actually want to study."

"That's not as financially secure an option, Peyton. I know you think we're worrying too much about that, but it's honestly a concern. It's our job to worry about these things. You've got your whole life to do whatever you want with your love of art and drawing, but can't you just trust us that a few years now to get a solid foundation for work is a necessary thing?"

"No," I say. "Can't you trust me that I know myself and what I want for my life better than you do?"

We look at each other. The answer is clearly no.

"You can't stop me doing any of this," I say. "You can't force me to do a degree I don't want to do."

"I know that, and I wouldn't do that," Mum says. "I want

you to be happy, I really do. But your dad, he's very set on this. If you go down this route, he won't support it. I mean financially."

"So? I'll get student loans."

"Peyton—"

"You're not going to put me off," I say. "I did everything you said my whole life, and I listened to you, and I believed you, but look where it got me. I was so unhappy at Claridge, and you knew that. And you didn't let me leave. Why didn't you let me leave?"

Mum blinks at me, guilty and confused. "I'm not sure how that's related to—"

"Of course it's related. Why do you think we're here? In Canada?" There's a long silence. "Can you please just tell me why you didn't move me to another school?" I've wanted to know for so long. Years.

Mum opens her mouth, then closes it again.

"Be honest," I say.

"It's hard to know what the honest answer is," she says. "It's so easy now to look back and say that I did the wrong thing, but that's hindsight, my darling. It's a trick; it makes things look so much easier, when at the time they were so confused."

"Just say why you didn't move me."

"Because I . . ." She closes her eyes and lets out a short breath. "I worried that you would encounter the same problems somewhere else, and that would make the damage that much worse. Long term."

For a moment, my throat closes up. She thought it was me; I was the problem. I'd get bullied wherever I went, because the problem was me. Tears sting at the backs of my eyes. I wish I hadn't asked.

"Peyton," she says, reading me. "That's not because I thought there was anything wrong with you. But I talked to a lot of people and I did a lot of research at the time. Children are cruel, and they often pick up on the kind of vulnerability that can come from being bullied in the past. What if you'd gone somewhere else and the bullies there guessed you'd been bullied before? That was my fear. Psychologically, moving schools at that age because of bullying; it can cause more damage if it doesn't work out. And often, bullying stops after a short time. I thought, on balance, that you were best staying where you were, building resilience, waiting for the storm to pass."

"It didn't pass," I say, my teeth grinding down against each other. "It was the entire time I was there. You think that didn't do damage?"

"I'm sorry," she says. "I was wrong, and I'm sorry."

"Would you do it differently if you could go back?"

"Yes," she says. "I wouldn't have sent you there in the first place. But, like I said, it's very easy to say these things with hindsight."

"Did you know about my college friends?" I ask. "Did you know that they were bad for me?"

"No," she says. "You kept yourself so distant from me. You stopped talking. But I felt like that was something you needed to do, and I wanted to respect that. Clearly, that was the wrong thing, too."

Would it have made any difference if she'd tried lecturing me about Travis and his friends? Would I have listened? No. I would have been furious if she'd said a word against any of them.

"I didn't mean for that to go so wrong," I say, stating the obvious.

"Of course not," she says. "You saw the best in them because you wanted to. I understand that. I wanted to destroy them for being so reckless with your safety, but that's motherhood. I'm allowed to feel that way."

"It wasn't all them," I say.

She frowns. "What do you mean?"

"I just . . ." I'm not even sure what I'm trying to say. "Yeah, they weren't great, but I wasn't exactly, like . . . blameless. I was all in. They didn't *make* me do anything. I made those choices myself."

Mum's watching me carefully, quiet.

"I don't want to disappoint you," I say. "I never did. But I feel like I need to understand all of this, and yeah, it would be easy to just blame them for it all, but that's not going to help me in the long run, is it? If I don't understand what went wrong, what's going to stop me making the same mistakes again?"

She still doesn't say anything, but she nods, expectant, waiting for me to answer my own question.

"I didn't try to get to know them, not really. I'm not sure I wanted to. Maybe because I knew that if I did, I wouldn't like them, and I'd have to face that, and then I wouldn't have friends again. And that's why I stopped talking to you too, I think, because you would ask me stuff about them and I wouldn't be able to answer." I shake my head. "There were so many red flags I just ignored. And I can say they're obvious now, but the thing is, I think they were obvious at the time, too? But I wanted it so badly. I *needed* it to be good. I can't blame them for me throwing myself at them, you know? I could have walked away the first time the pills came out. Or when I realized I was paying for everything. Or when I got punched."

Alarm pops on Mum's face. "You got *punched*?"

I almost want to laugh. "I've got so much to tell you."

"I had no idea things were that bad," she says. "Oh, Peyton. That night . . . getting that call." She shakes her head. "There's nothing like it. You could have died. Out there on the street. They left you. They did that."

"I know," I say. "And that was obviously bad of them. But what I'm saying is, it was a road to get there, and I chose to be on that road, and maybe the only thing that could get me off it was what happened. Maybe it needed to happen, in a way, so I finally realized what I was doing. Maybe if it *hadn't* happened, it would all still be going on. Not a big and dramatic thing like, you know, nearly dying, but like an everyday bad. Unhealthy, and me just going along with it all. In denial, I guess. Wouldn't that be worse?"

"In the long run, I suppose it would, yes," Mum says. "Did you know that one of them came round to see me?" she asks. "Casey?"

I nod.

"She seemed like she really was sorry," she says. "For what happened to you. And I had to give her credit where it was due for facing me like she did. No one else did. Certainly not that boyfriend of yours."

I roll my eyes. "Oh, him."

Mum laughs, surprising me. "I can only hope that you'll learn all the lessons you need about bad boyfriends from him, and it will help you make a better choice next time."

I think of Beasey. "I already know it will. And friends, too. Lots of lessons, right?"

She nods. "Good and bad."

I sigh. "I feel like my whole adolescence has just been . . . a mess," I say. "A messed-up mess."

"But look at you," she says. "You're almost out of it. Adulthood is so close. And you're so strong and brave and resilient. So independent." She's smiling at me, the pride on her face as surprising as it is wanted. "I wish you hadn't felt the need to run away, but my God, I'm so proud of you for how you've managed this." She lets out a small, tearful laugh. "It's a confusing mix of emotions. Being proud of something you can't condone and wish hadn't happened."

"I get that," I say. "It would be weird if you'd been, like, *Brilliant! Off you go!*"

She laughs. "That's what your brother said. *Brilliant!*" She mimics his low voice, which makes me laugh. *"Go, Peyton!"*

"Really?"

"Oh yes—your father was furious." She rolls her eyes to the ceiling. "Dillon's even talking about the two of you traveling together. I don't know how on earth I raised two such adventurous children."

"Could be worse," I say.

"It could," she says, smiling dryly. "It could be a lot worse."

When do I decide to go home with her? I'm not even sure. The decision comes in slow, not so much landing in my head as surfacing, like it had been there all along. It's so soft, in fact, that I forget to actually tell Mum, assuming she already knows. So when I say, the following day after we've stopped off at Tim Hortons for afternoon doughnuts, "Do you think they'll let me take a couple of boxes of Timbits as part of my hand luggage?" I'm surprised that she drops the city map she's holding, grabs my arm and starts to cry. Right in the middle of the street.

"Oh," I say, just as she sobs out, "Oh, Peyton," and puts

an arm around me, hugging me close to her. She releases me, wiping her eyes, laughing at herself. "Sorry," she says. "I'm just so pleased. So happy."

Maybe it's because I can't imagine being on my own again after spending this time with her, having someone I love to share it all with and knowing what a difference that makes. It's different than sharing it all with my friends, and even than sharing it with Beasey, but it still matters. Maybe it's because I miss home. My house, my bed, my clothes, my dog. Jaffa Cakes and Cadbury's chocolate. Baked beans. Walkers crisps. Ginger nut biscuits. Maybe it's because I'm tired.

Or maybe it's just time to go home.

I know I won't be going back to the life I left. Even if everything there is the same, too much in me has changed. I think that even if I went back to college—which I won't—things would still be different. Thinking about Travis and Flick doesn't make me ache with disappointment and self-hatred. I just feel kind of . . . sad. For them and me. Yes, they did a bad thing at the end, but it wasn't their fault our friendship hadn't worked. I'd wanted friends in the abstract; I hadn't seen them as real people with their own interests and wants and needs. I hadn't given them anything real of myself to respond to. Of course we had no connection.

Not that I've got any intention of going back home and reconciling with them. That time of my life is done, and I'm happy to keep it in the past.

Maybe I'll be going back to a friendless life, but even if I am, it'll only be for a short time. There'll be other people to meet and friends to make. Maybe they'll be older than me or from somewhere else. Maybe they'll be British or not. Maybe the thing we'll have in common is that we both like art, or that we've both traveled, or that we both like dogs. Who knows?

And all the while Seva, Maja, Beasey, Khalil, Lars, and Stefan will all just be a WhatsApp away. My friends, scattered all over the world, having their own adventures, making new friends everywhere they go as naturally as breathing, because that really is as easy as it is.

I don't have to be scared that I'm not good enough, not anymore. The Amber Monroes of this world—and I know I'll encounter them throughout my life—aren't the authority on my personality and who I am. I'm not worthless just because they once told me I was. I'm not friendless because they weren't my friends. I don't have to let them live rent-free in my head.

Maybe there was a time when I didn't have any friends, and it was horrible and lonely, but it was just a thing that happened, not a sign of my life. I don't have to be that person, because this is *my* life, and I am my own person, and no one has control over who I'll be but me. I have a choice, and that includes what kind of person I want to be. And I know who that is: I want to be kind. Kind like my friends have been to me, kind like Canada has been to me. I can take that gift and carry it with me. I can be a person people are glad to meet, glad to know. The kind of person they make detours for.

Our flight home is in the early evening on Wednesday, and we spend our last few hours in the city embracing the tourist life. I take Mum to a food court and introduce her to poutine, then buy us an Orange Julius apiece, messaging Beasey with a picture of me and the drink. **Did I ever tell you the story of my first Orange Julius?** He sends me heart-eyes emojis in reply.

We visit the souvenir gift shops, loading up on sweet treats and presents to take home for Dad, Dillon, and Grandma. I buy myself a small moose toy—mostly because the label declares him *YOUR CANADIAN FRIEND!*—and name him Jasper. I don't care if it's stupid; I love the idea of having a friend to take home with me.

It's not the most exciting way to end my great Canadian adventure, but I don't mind. What could compare to Tofino, the waterfalls at Wells Gray, Lake Louise? Guiding Beasey across a suspension bridge? The smell of toasted marshmallows on a freezing night outside an RV called Justin?

"How are you feeling?" Mum asks me when we're on our way to the airport.

Sad. Oddly hollow. But okay. "I'm glad you came," I say, which makes her cry, which makes me cry.

"What a pair," Mum says with a laugh, wiping her eyes.

By the time we board the plane a few hours later, I'm ready to go. Impatient, even, to get back to my old life and reboot it with everything I've gained and learned. I will come back to Canada one day, I know that. Maybe I'll even make it to Nova Scotia next time.

I take a plane selfie and send it to the RV group. I'm smiling wide, the window in the corner of the frame, my head tilted slightly toward it. **Going home!** I write.

Tschüss! Maja writes back almost immediately. **Safe travels!**

Best regards to Blighty, Khalil says. He adds an emoji of a plane and the Union Jack. **Have a good one!**

A selfie comes through: Seva, a surreptitious smile on his face, besuited, sitting at his desk. He writes something in Russian—I think it's a form of "goodbye"—and adds another plane emoji.

Another selfie, this time Lars with Stefan ducking his head into view, both of them grinning. Lars has his ski goggles on, Stefan's are pushed up over his forehead. **Vi ses!**

I wait, hoping for a message from Beasey. The cabin crew are doing their final sweep down the aisle, checking people's seat belts, closing the last overhead compartments. Mum taps my arm. "Airplane mode," she whispers.

"One sec," I say. *Beasey is typing.*

Have a good flight! A smiley face. Another Union Jack emoji.

I'm about to sink with confused disappointment, tapping my screen with my thumb to bring up settings so I can turn on airplane mode, when another notification comes through. Beasey, messaging privately. He's sent a picture. I smile as I tap on it, anticipating his sweet, selfied face.

The picture is of the two of us, our faces up close to the camera, both of us smiling wide. We're wearing woolly hats pulled down over our ears. His arm is around me. Behind us, the unimaginable ice blue of Lake Louise. I look at the picture, taking us in. I remember that moment so clearly, how happy I felt, how lucky to be there.

Whatever else happens, this happened, he's written. **And it was amazing. Have a good flight, let me know when you land. Good luck at home in your next adventure.**

I'm smiling, my eyes blurring, as I turn on airplane mode and slide it into the seat pocket in front of me. I wipe my eyes, settling back into my seat, looking out the window. *Whatever else happens, this happened,* I think. Over and over, like a mantra, as the plane taxis us away from the terminal, toward the runway.

When the engines roar and we push forward, Mum takes

my hand, like she used to do when I was very small and we were going somewhere together. I used to think it was for me, but now I'm not so sure. Maybe needing comfort and support isn't just a childhood thing. Maybe you always have those moments when you need a little boost of love. I squeeze her hand as the ground drops away. I look out the window, watching Toronto shrink beneath us until it's a patchwork of city in a giant expanse of ice and snow. I turn back to Mum and smile.

"Off we go," I say.

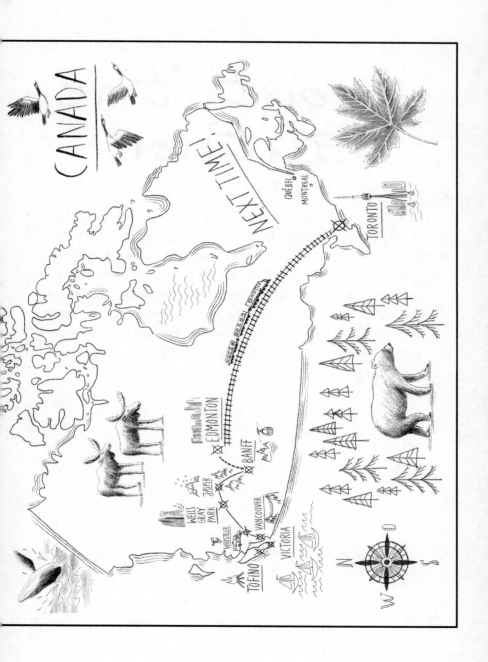

about the author

Sara Barnard is the author of *Fragile Like Us*; *A Quiet Kind of Thunder*; *Goodbye, Perfect*; and *Destination Anywhere*. She lives in Brighton, England, with her husband and their grumpy cat. She studied American literature with creative writing at university and never stopped reading YA. She has lived in Canada, inter-railed through Europe, and once spent the night in an ice hotel. She thinks sad books are good for the soul and happy books lift the heart. She hopes to write lots of books that do both.